Sharon is a writer and painter with thirty years' experience in the arts. She established London's innovative gallery Aspects, was a founding figure of the New Designers Exhibition, Festival Coordinator for the inaugural London Design Festival and Director of The Sorrell Foundation.

She was an external lecturer at the University of the Arts London for 20 years and has curated over one hundred exhibitions, including exhibitions for the Royal College of Art, the Victoria and Albert Museum, Somerset House and the Arnolfini.

Her lectures to architectural practices discuss the benefits of interdisciplinary creativity and, in particular, the effects of colour on our lives.

Forthcoming titles by Sharon Plant include *Caravaggio, the Cardinal and the Courtesan, Grow Old Along with Me* and *Poetic Stories.*

To the wonderful Ian Ellis Wood,
who laughed and cried
in equal measure.

Sharon Plant

THE LIFE OF RILEY

AUSTIN MACAULEY PUBLISHERS™

LONDON · CAMBRIDGE · NEW YORK · SHARJAH

A CIP catalogue record for this title is available from the British Library.

ISBN 9781528902816 (Paperback)
ISBN 9781528902823 (E-Book)

www.austinmacauley.com

First Published (2018)
Austin Macauley Publishers Ltd
25 Canada Square
Canary Wharf
London
E14 5LQ

The Journey to Aunt Lizzie

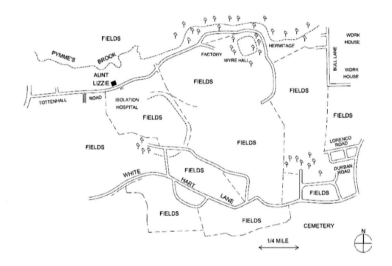

The Riley Family Homes

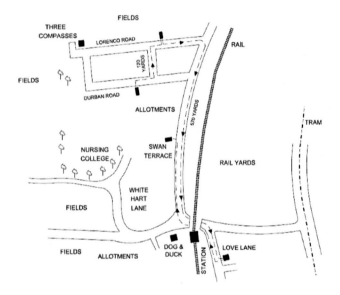

Nichols Square

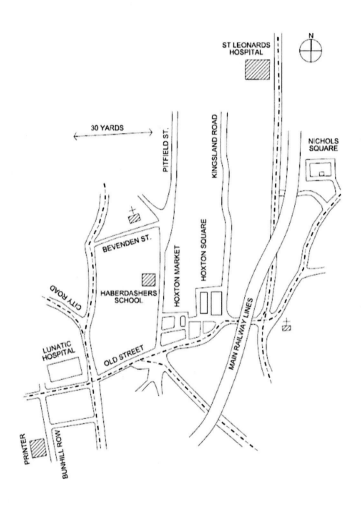

Chapter 1

To Describe It As A Happy Childhood
Would Be Stretching It

We skid along the bleak corridor of Durban Road, I think we must be late for tea. She tells me to hurry up but I am afraid. She seems very cross; I want to take her hand but I daren't. I wonder if we're going to make it; more's the point, I wonder if we're going to make it in time.

It is 1908 and I am six years old. We live in the very last house and Mum is in a mad flurry to reach it before whatever is about to happen, happens. I scramble to catch hold of the handle bar of the pram, my feet sliding on the paving stones, my legs whipped by the flapping wings of her coat.

Mum, Mary Riley, doesn't go out to work; she says she is too busy looking after us three, and even if she wanted to no one would have her because she's married. She is short, and a bit skinny, and our dad says when she was young, before us kids, she was reckoned a bit of a catch. He sticks his chest out when he tells us this, and I can do a good copy of his chest when I have something special to say. Mum's quiet, not like Dad; she has long wavy hair that she sits and brushes for hours, her thoughts in a place where we're not welcome. *We*, is my older brother William, who we call Billy, me, then my younger brother Charles, we call him Charlie. My name is Raymond, they call me Ray.

Our dad works in the pencil factory packing the pencils into boxes and sometimes testing the chemicals in the lead. He reckons it's a stupid job, any fool could do it blindfold he tells Mum, but it puts bread on the table and that's all she's interested in, bread on the table. He says the boss of Kyles Pencils is as stupid as his job, though the boss is talking of sending Dad to night school, to further him in the trade, and this has become a prospect of some pride and much boasting on dad's part.

'For a night school man such as myself,' he says, standing in front of the unlit fire, his thumbs tucked behind non-existent braces, 'I believe it would be right to move the evening meal to a later hour.'

I wonder about this and look uneasily across at Mum. She doesn't like to be put out at the best of times and an hour later would be mightily difficult to arrange, of that I am sure. We are sat in a row, squashed together on an old sofa, three pairs of eyes staring up at him, each listening for Mum's response.

'The evening meal?' she says. We keep our eyes fixed steadfastly on Dad's thumbs.

'That's right, Ma.'

More rocking backward and forward on the balls of his stockinged feet; a proud moment spoiled only a little by a yellowed toenail poking through the tip of one sock.

'What evening meal's that then?'

'The family meal.'

'The air pie and windy pudden', you mean? That evening meal?'

Our evening meal, as he likes to call it, is a slice of bread with something on it, if we're lucky. I peer cautiously at Mum and am relieved to see that for once, she is smiling. I grin at Dad. This is nice; all of us together in the room, smiling.

On this particular evening in 1908 we fly along the skiddy road so that Mum can catch sight of Dad before he leaves the house. In this she succeeds, more's the pity. There is trouble in the air and she can smell it. When we reach our door she sniffs small sniffs, to detect the exact cause of the trouble, then she declares, *I'll kill him*. She is going to knock his block off and this is something I do not want to see: I run straight back out onto the street to play.

The rain has miraculously stopped and a late evening sun is making the road steamy. My best friend Joe and I are playing swamp, sliding our feet through a greasy mud and wading the air with our arms crying *crocodile to the right, alligator to the left*; the smell of warm earth and musty wool oozing up our nostrils. Joe and I play swamp a lot. I am the master of the expedition and what I say is what Joe does; this is how it is with me and Joe.

At a critical moment of charging and yelling, during which I am required to kill Joe twice, and bomb his raft with clods of sticky leaves to ensure he submits to my mightier power, I am stopped by the appearance of Mum carrying our Charlie. I am three years and four months older than Charlie and I am allowed outside where he is not. My face changes from surprise to horror when I see that Mum is crying. She waves for me to come, which I aim to do fast as fury so as Joe doesn't have time to put his nose in where it's not needed.

'What's wrong?' I ask, glaring at Joe, who has run to stand at my shoulder with his thumb stuck in his mouth, taking up his position to stare frog-eyed at Mum. Mum reckons that thumb is the only clean part on Joe's body and it irritates her whenever she sees him.

'Nothing. Go indoors, Ray.'

'We're not done yet, Mum. Joe's raft is about to…'

'Go indoors to your father.'

'But it's only five o'clock.'

'Father will get your tea.'

'Why? Where are you going?'

'To Grandma's.'

She means to her mother that lives in Jacksons Road. Something has happened, and forgetting Joe is stood beside me, I start to wail.

'I want to come.'

'You can't come, Ray. Go in.'

'Why is Charlie going? Let me come.'

I am three years and four months older than Charlie and as such I should be allowed to come. Mum pushes me away angrily.

'Go indoors, Raymond.'

She calls me Raymond when I make her cross.

'Don't make such a fuss.'

I watch her walk down Durban Road and out of sight. Crying heavily now myself, blub and spit mixing with salty tears, I run indoors to find dad. Joe remains on the doorstep sucking, and looking after Mum.

'Dad! Dad?' I tear through the house leaving muddy footprints on the bare floorboards. He isn't in our rooms, we live on the first floor, but muffled voices are coming from downstairs where Mrs Wheeler lives.

Mrs Wheeler's rooms smell of cabbage and cats' wee. Whenever I have to go there I want to retch, and today I do this noisily, so much so that Dad, who is consoling Mrs Wheeler with cuddles, frowns at me and flicks his hand at me to go away.

What's wrong with Mrs Wheeler then? It's not as if it's *her* mum has just walked off down the road.

Backing out sulkily, I sit down on the bottom step of the stairs and push my head hard between the rods of the banister until I am sure I have imprinted their knobs and dents on both sides of my face. I run my hands satisfyingly up and down the newly sculpted flesh.

Someone blows their nose, Mrs Wheeler I suppose, and Dad comes out holding her hand. They push past me up to our rooms and I follow a few steps behind.

Dad is showing Mrs Wheeler where everything is in our larder. He points to Mum's saucepan and the dented kettle, which I look at too, to see if it is any different from yesterday. Then he shows her where Mum tucks the matches to keep them out of Charlie's way. He reaches down the washing tongs and stands tapping them against the palm of his hand. I think they might have forgotten I am here.

'And this, Mrs Wheeler,' I say helpfully, 'this is where my mum's hair brush and comb are always kept and they're not to be moved or there'll be hell to pay. She keeps them just here, and she uses them whenever she passes this mirror as she says it doesn't wobble her face so much as the window does, which she only uses when the mirror is all steamed up on wash day.'

Mrs Wheeler and my father stare at me but nobody speaks.

Having introduced Mrs Wheeler to the most important of Mum's utensils I turn on my heels and head back out to the swamp.

Mum's departure is my first big memory and it doesn't feel good. I tuck it deep inside me and cover it with other thoughts that aren't quite so scary; then I pretend it isn't there, and in a way that I don't understand, Mrs Wheeler becomes my new mum.

She cooks for us in the evenings and occasionally she flicks the dishcloth at Bill in what I presume she thinks is a motherly way, though our mum has never done this to us. Bill ignores her entirely, almost to the point of being rude; I worry he is going to get his comeuppance from Dad but Dad says nothing.

It's true that I'm missing Mum and Charlie, but I sure do like this new arrangement with just me and Bill in our room. Bill has always been the oldest but now *I* am the baby; it feels special to be the baby, though I'm sad that Mum isn't here to enjoy it.

Mum also misses my first day at St Bernard's Infant School, which is an even bigger disappointment as I am to go to St Bernard's until I join Bill in big school and I am sure she would have wanted to be there, to mark the occasion in some way, to tuck a clean handkerchief, if she could find one, up the sleeve of my jumper. As it is, Dad pokes a box of six pencils into my pocket that I know he has swiped from Mr Kyle's pencil factory, pats me once on the head and shuts the front door.

I amble up Durban Road feeling good and grown up to be taking myself off to school, and I am walking nice and tall until I see a few other kids coming along holding their mums' hands. A hard lump builds in my throat and I have to break into a run to force it back down into my stomach.

Bill is four years and ten months older than me so he knows everything. It was him that told me I was never to go to the toilet when I got to big school, I was to hold it till I got home because at big school there is a hand that reaches up and pulls your todger off if you have told a lie that day. As I am a royal liar I am scared stiff of big school and as Bill is an even bigger royal liar, he is my hero.

'All right, Bill?' I ask, as he slams in from school, kicking his boots off into the corner of the room. 'Do you need to use the toilet? I've put some newspaper in for you.'

Bill is the best.

Glancing down at his trousers to check if there are any telltale signs of misadventure in the bumpy region, I cry out in horror. 'Aw Bill, what have you done to your knees?'

Mrs Wheeler looks over from the stove; Dad lowers his newspaper.

'It was nothing; I tripped.'

'And your eye?'

'Banged my head on the wall.'

'Your jumper's all torn. Mum'll be...' I check myself and glance across at Dad.

'Shurrup,' says Bill, pushing past. Bill hates any mention of Mum.

Mrs Wheeler returns to stirring the pot; Dad lifts the newspaper.

I need so much to ask about Mum but there is an unexplained rule of silence and I know she is a forbidden subject. I would be told it had nothing to do with me, it was between the grown-ups. It seems to me as if she has been gone forever, though Bill says it's no more than two weeks, he says I'm to go outside and find something to do to cheer me up, and to stop asking dim questions.

So I am made up when Dad asks if I would like to go with him to see her; I think my face will split from the smiling. I run around the house doing all the necessaries as if I am setting out on a long journey. I gob buckets of spit into my hands and smarm my hair down just how Mum likes it. Bill and I only have one pair of underpants, which we are supposed to keep for best, but I can't find mine. Bill's are under the bed, lying stiff amongst balls of fluff; I flick them hard against a chair-back and climb in.

Running to the oven I pull up a chair to mum's mirror to inspect myself. I grin. She can't bear to see tears, snivelling she calls it, so I grin even harder, scrunching up my eyes to show how real a grin it is. By the time we set off to Grandma's I really look the business; my face aches so much I have to bite the inside of my bottom lip to keep the edges of my mouth up near my ears.

Bill's stiff pants chafe my legs so badly I have to walk with wide steps, which I pretend I do to avoid the puddles. The prickly jumper that I have dug from the bottom of a pile of sour smelling laundry is so scratchy I keep pulling it away from my wrists. With my lips pinned tight shut and grinning widely I look like the barmy boy from Bedlam but I don't care tuppence; I am going to see Mum, with her long wavy hair and her cross face that I miss so much. She is going to be so pleased to see me, all spruced up and shiny. I can't get there fast enough.

As we turn into Jacksons Road I see Grandma Edna stood on her step, which goes straight onto the road the same as ours does, her arms are folded across her wide and lively busters and she is wearing her flowery pinny. Dad stops at the sight of her, so I drop his hand and run, throwing myself at her, bouncing off her liveliness and making her laugh to catch her breath. Dad wanders up, taking off his cap to wind it round and round his hand.

'Hello, Edna.'

'Hello, John.'

They stare awkwardly at each other for a while.

'Shall I come in then?'

I look at them both.

Too polite.

Too slow.

Where's Mum?

Squeezing past Grandma's wide legs, which are stood as if she's guarding the doorway, blocking my way, I run to the sitting room to Mum and Grandpa who are seated on either side of a low wooden table.

'Here's our lad,' says Grandpa. 'Come to see his little brother.' Charlie is reaching out for me from the armchair. In my excitement I throw myself at Charlie and hug him till he squeals. Then I turn and throw myself at Mum who sits stiffly in an upright dining chair. She doesn't kiss me; Mum never kisses me.

'Well!' I say, all fluster and expectation, 'What's for tea?'

Grandpa laughs and ruffles my hair. He takes my hand and leads me out to the scullery where he explains there is going to be some grown-up talk but that I can spend the time playing in the garden.

This is okay by me.

Grandma's garden is small, an odd triangular patch of land left over from the surrounding houses. It has thin and windy paths weaving between the rose bushes, and I can run round them until I am giddy, and then I can throw water over my face from her garden tap. Sometimes the water floods my nose so that it runs out of my eyes and my ears, and I choke and splutter, and when I'm nearly drowned Grandpa gives me a wallop on the back of my head which spurts the water back out like the jet from the drinking fountain.

I don't know what's going on in the sitting room. I don't know what they're saying. They don't shout. No one seems to cry, their voices are low and mumbly, especially Grandpa's which rumbles quietly whenever I poke my ear inside the back door to check they are still there and then, best moment of all, Mum comes out to me and says, *Come on Ray, we're going home.*

Ray she calls me.

My mouth drops open and I turn on her my grinniest grin, but she has already gone back into the dark of the scullery.

After that, things at home are just fine and dandy. Mrs Wheeler goes back downstairs to her cats and Mum cleans our two rooms with a powerful smelling liquid that she says will get rid of the filth.

Charlie and I look around for the filth but we can't see any, she has done a really good job.

But the filth nags at Mum; she says it is too much to cope with, we have to move.

Chapter 2

Saturday's Child Works Hard For Its Living

Mum has told Dad to gather all our things, of which there are not many, and wheel them round the corner to Lorenco Road where to give him his due, he has found a flat. Living in a flat is something special after living in rooms, something really special.

'It's a palace, Dad!'

'At six shillings and sixpence a week rent, yes lad, it's a home fit for a king.'

I whistle at Charlie to show my amazement; fancy us being grand enough to pay six shillings and sixpence a week to live in a flat.

'Two bedrooms, a kitchen, an outside lavatory shared with only one other family. Pretty soon I'll be able to show Joe how grand we are. I'll be moving into long trousers, like Bill, won't I Dad? Now that we live in a flat.'

'Well, hold your horses, I'm not sure about that, Ray.'

'Bill was in long trousers at my age.'

'Go and ask your mother, lad.'

'She'll say no.' She always says no. 'You ask her for me.'

'If she says no, she says no.'

'Joe will be so jealous when I get long trousers and I live in a flat and all.'

'I'm sure Joe will cope.'

'Not Joe. Joe's terrific jealous. He'll do this.'

I pull my bottom lip down as far as I can and crease my forehead into thick folds.

Dad frowns and scratches behind his ear.

We don't live at the end of a street any more, now we live in a flat in a building in the middle of another long road stretching away to another far horizon. On the horizon of this road is a pub called The Compasses and it is here that Dad has really moved to. At the end of each day, the hooter burps to announce freedom from the pencil factory and the men trail out, their heads bent low against the wind.

Dad doesn't go to night school for long, he says it's not all it's cracked up to be, in fact, he could teach that teacher a thing or two about pencils that would make his eyes water. Instead, Dad goes straight to the pub.

Dad is what they call a nasty drunk.

I watch other drunks, rolling out of The Compasses in pairs, cuddling and belching in a way that seems to be very funny to them, but never Dad, he gets mean and spiteful. Many mornings Bill and I stand at the table at breakfast time, sharing a slice of bread and dripping before school, trying hard not to look at Mum's swollen lip or the puffy mauve graze above her eye.

Sorry as I am for her, and I am sometimes very sorry, I have other things on my mind. I have graduated to junior school and these are trying times; a young man of nearly nine years has to keep alert. Sadly, however alert I keep myself, I am always in trouble. I'm not potty about trouble, especially as there already seems to be plenty of it indoors. I keep my head down and concentrate on the dripping.

In the same week that I move to junior school, Charlie starts in the infants and it is my job every day to take Charlie to school, which is quite a distance from where I have to get to.

I have to show him to his teacher who puts a mark in her book, then take him round to the playground to wait for the bell. He is always blubbing but I don't mind. He looks cute cuddling up to me; all the little kids gather round to see what's wrong. I like that.

'Nothing wrong here,' I announce in a gruff young-man-that-already-goes-to-junior-school kind of voice. 'Just a bit of the collywobbles.'

Charlie clings tighter, his head buried deep inside my coat. He doesn't want to look at anyone. A nosy girl that is about his height stands as near as she can to offer advice. 'It's because our teacher smells,' she says, nodding her head wisely, like girls do.

She's right though, his teacher is not nice and she does smell, but what can I do.

'Be brave, little soldier,' I say. 'The week's almost done. It's Friday, there'll be jam for tea.' Charlie looks at me miserably, a thick rill of green snot soaking down into my jumper.

'And maybe Bill will be home.'

Dad's mum, Grandma Bessie, lives in Wood Street, which is some distance away in Walthamstow and she doesn't visit us much,

19

but my brother Bill, who is now thirteen, has taken to visiting Grandma Bess and staying for months at a time, going to school with Dad's youngest brother who is called Arthur and who is almost the same age as our Bill. We don't see so much of Bill these days.

Charlie stands bolt upright, his eyebrows twisted to their regular question mark: can his big brother Ray be telling the truth, will Bill really be home for tea?

'You know how he loves jam,' I say in explanation, anything to help Charlie through the day.

By the time I reach my school I am late, of course. Huge clumps of bright woolly clouds just made for cloud gazing have been hung along the route to distract me: a fat and furry bee too heavy to lift its backside out of a flower; a lumpy old man with frothy hair playing a fiddle. As I amble across the playground looking up at what must surely be a huge white floating caterpillar, I can be sure some thin lipped, sour faced teacher will be watching me out of the staffroom window, itching to use his newly serviced switch. By break-time he will have found a reason to.

Standing out of line in the milk queue, polishing my boots on the back of my long socks, poking Joe, I hear:

'Riley!'

'Yes, sir.' I jump to poker-rigid attention.

'Go and stand outside my room.'

'What for, sir.'

'Don't talk back, boy, just do as you're told.'

'What did I do, sir? I'd truly like to know.'

'Are you trying to be clever, son?'

'What do you mean, sir?'

'Are you being insolent, Riley?'

'No, sir.'

'Do you call those boots clean, Riley.'

I look down at Bill's scuffed cast-outs. I have packed newspaper into one of them to cover a hole and am pleased with their dryness but wish they shone a little more like they used to when Bill first wore them.

'We don't have any blacking, sir.'

'Pardon?'

'I said, we don't have any blacking at home, sir.'

'Sorry, I still didn't hear you, Riley. You'll have to speak up.'

My face reddens. 'We don't have any blacking at home, sir!' I shout, as loud as I can. 'We live in a flat! My dad pays six shillings and sixpence a week for our flat, which is more money than we ever paid for rooms! Sir!'

I get six of the best for my smartness. And six more for noise.

Despite the fact that we can now afford to pay for a flat, money is always short, and it never runs to pocket money. Any money we get has to be earned.

I sometimes run an errand for a neighbour, which might bring in a farthing, but paid jobs don't come often. More frequently we're sent on an errand and our payment is a clip round the ear when we come back empty handed, and sometimes the same if we come back with our hands full. Payment of any other kind would be nice.

At lunchtime a gang of us boys stand sheltering under the bicycle shed to talk about this problem. One boy called Denny is doing really well. He is taller than most of us and pretty looking with dark curly hair that somehow means he gets away with more from the grown-ups.

'Sundays I goes down the church,' says Denny, 'and get a whole penny for pumping the organ. That's easy money. Then on Tuesdays and Fridays I carry Mrs Hatt's water from the outside tap up to her top floor so's she can give old man Hatt a bath. And on Saturdays I help down the market, runnin' for 'em. Doing the odd jobs.'

We shuffle our feet about, kicking at loose stones.

Lucky sod.

I catch Joe's eye thinking the same.

Lucky sod.

We are tickled pink when we hear that the older boys have taken their revenge on pretty boy Denny, and chased him from the church until they've caught him, and stuffed his head down Mrs Beadman's outside toilet. Denny says he isn't bothered, but I can tell it riles him, it has stopped him crowing that's for sure.

I am on the lookout now though: where to earn the much needed pocket money? I've been watching Jess, the girl next door, heading out with a bucket, floor cloth and scrubbing brush and one morning I stop her.

'Where you off to then?'

'Going door to door,' she says, rightly startled, as I am nine by this time, and though she must be about my age she is little and scrawny and not used to being spoken to by grown-up boys like me.

'Where d'ya go then?'

'Along Wood Green High Road. Sometimes into the side streets.'

'What's the bucket for?'

She looks at me as if I'm barmy. 'To hold the water.'

'Oh, right.'

Jess pushes past, all business-like, like girls get when they're on a mission and I watch her walk off down the street, her feet clipping along the stones, one sock dangling around her ankle where her garter had given up its elastic.

Well, two can play at that game, I think. Plenty of doors to go door-to-door with as far as I can see, plenty of work to go round and not upset the big boys like Denny did. I walk inside and find Mum's bucket and floor cloth and off I go, in search of doors.

I stroll around the streets until I find myself a nice road with fat glossy doors. The houses are bigger than in Lorenco Road and there are trees in the front gardens and paths to the front doors, which are painted a thick shiny black and stood under a small roof. That's a grand idea, I think. You could step outside your own front door and check what the weather was like without getting pissed on like you do in our house, which opens straight onto the pavement.

This is something else that I'm learning now that I am nine-years-old and out making my way in the world, I am learning to use some of the grown-up swear words, though I'm careful to keep them in my head when I'm at home so's Mum doesn't know I use them.

I stop outside the first door of my chosen road. It isn't until I'm stood under one of the small roofs that I begin to wonder what on earth I'm supposed to do with the bucket. I start to feel nervous and I'm just about to turn on my heels when I hear the locks being thrown back and the door creaking open.

A tall thin lady stands in the doorway and after looking me up and down, she takes the bucket out of my hand and tells me to wait there, which I do, not wanting to leave without Mum's bucket as she would have a blue fit to hear that I'd gone to a posh house and given her bucket away. As if they didn't have enough as it is, she would say, and there's your mum working her fingers to the bone to make ends meet!

Perhaps the lady thinks I've come to sell the bucket. I ponder this. That would be okay. She could give me a bob, I could buy Mum a new thre'penny bucket and I'd be coppers in.

The tall thin lady returns to the porch and plonks the pail onto her tiles, water slopping over the edge into my shoe.

'That'll be a penny and don't go getting cheeky and asking for tuppence.'

I stare at her. 'What d'ya mean? I've got to buy the water?'

She sighs, and looks at me again as if she's considering my mental stability.

'You scrub my door step, lad, until you can see your face in it and I pay you a penny for your trouble.' She clicks her tongue against the top of her mouth the way Mum does when her mirror steams up, then she shuts the door.

I am half way through the first step and beginning to wonder if I can live without the pocket money as I still can't see my reflection in the tiles, when two girls come toward the gate; the older one I know vaguely from school. She nudges her friend.

'Hello, Ray. What you doing?'

What is it about girls that they can talk about the sodding obvious as if it has some mysterious meaning? I look up.

'Ah, hi. I'm just earning my way. You know, making a few readies.' I've heard Bill talk about readies. I have no bloody idea what they are but they are definitely good to have.

The one I know nudges her friend again. 'Where's your bag?'

Bag? What bag? Did Jess have a bag? I don't remember seeing any bag. I can feel myself getting hot.

The girls giggle from behind their grubby fingers. I hate girls.

'If you have a bag you might be given some pieces; crusts of bread or broken biscuits, you might even get a bone with some meat left on it.' They look at each other, nodding knowingly like old hands. I stare blankly back at them.

'Have fun, Ray!' they scream. 'Don't work too hard!' And they run off down the road howling with laughter.

I wonder if they are making it up, but the following Saturday I take a brown bag that Mum has squashed flat into the sideboard drawer and I hold it out when I hold out my bucket. The lady of the house cracks the code and when she hands over my penny, she gives me a bag of stale cakes.

Uh-huh, I think, as I sit swinging my legs on her garden wall, crumbling the cake into my mouth; thanks girls.

Henceforth, every Saturday morning at eight o'clock sharp, I begin my round and I don't return home until three in the afternoon. Mum is waiting for me, and my money, and the bag. She gives me tuppence back for myself and that is my pocket money. I think a few of my special words. But now that I've felt the jingle jangle in my pocket, chinking up and down and running through my fingers as I walk, I've got the itch for more.

Picking up a bag of crackling from Cann's Fish and Chip Shop on the way home from school, I see the handwritten sign for a babysitter. Gobbing into my palms and smearing my hair flat with a combination of spit and cooking oil, I go to the counter holding my back straight and my legs stiff to keep me standing tall.

'Hey, Mrs Cann. I just seen your sign for a sitter to look after Dolly some evenings. You know, I could do that.'

Mrs Cann wipes her hands down her apron and looks at me doubtfully.

'I'm good with children. I'm always looking after our Charlie and he's turning out just grand. He's a bit on the quiet side but I get him drawing all sorts of things, he's a great drawer, and you can tell what everything's meant to be.'

Mrs Cann glances across at her husband who eyes me sideways and snorts.

'And it's on my way home from school so I could be here at your busiest times, right through the early evening rush.'

'I don't know, Raymond,' says Mrs Cann, smiling between me and her husband, who has dismissed me and turned to deal with his next customer. A queue is starting to build up.

'I'm good at feeding as well. Mum's always asking me to spread the drippin' for Charlie as I know you can't leave a child with a knife. I could do that for Dolly.'

'Hey, anyone serving 'ere?'

'Hold on a minute will you, Raymond?'

'I can wipe bums as well, Mrs Cann.'

'Hold on a minute, Raymond love.'

'Cod, chips and peas twice, luv, heavy on the salt.'

'What sort of hours could you do, Raymond?'

'Any nights, Mrs. While she were asleep, I would just be sitting, quiet, like this.' I stand very quiet, looking at the ceiling, which is spattered with dead flies and hard peas that have been shot up there by the big boys.

'Or if she was wakeful I could play with her, like this.' I jiggle my hands around bouncing an imaginary toy along the counter.

Mrs Cann checks to see her husband isn't listening; I can see she is softening. She wraps the man's order in yesterday's newspaper and passes him his change.

'OK, Raymond. Start tomorrow. I'll need you for a couple of hours each school night, get here by four if you can, and I'll pay thruppence a week. How's that?'

'That's mighty good of you, Mrs Cann. I'll be here sharp tomorrow night. I'll bring one of Charlie's pencils as a way of introducing myself to Dolly. Kids like that sort of thing. See ya!'

I am full of it I am; I now have me two jobs. I sure am getting the hang of this pocket money malarkey.

I decide it isn't really necessary to tell Mum about the new job but I saunter home, taking my time to concoct a story for my lateness. When I reach the flat I realise it won't be heard; as I open the door there is uproar. Charlie is crying so mum clips me round the ear.

'Where've you been?' she shouts, but she doesn't expect an answer.

Apparently, we are on the move, again. Mum hasn't paid the rent money *because Dad has poured it into The Compasses*; the landlord has given us notice to quit and Mum is in a lather.

She's gonna kill Dad.

She's gonna string him up and hang him out to dry.

She's gonna shove his pint pot where the sun doesn't shine, wherever that might be because the sun shines everywhere as far as I can see, apart from in the coal hole. We have to be out before the end of the week or the bailiffs are coming to take the furniture away, apart from the beds that is, they never take the beds.

I have stopped to watch bailiffs going into houses on my round, settling myself comfortably on a garden wall with my bag of bits, taking in the scene as it unfolds. The husbands stand awkwardly in the doorways raking their hair, looking bewildered, while the women wail almighty blood curdling wails at the removal of every insignificant heirloom.

I am pretty impressed by the bailiffs; they don't falter in their step or bat an eyelid, they just march straight on down to their van and at the end of it, doff their cap at the man of the house and sometimes they say, *Sorry Gov*.

I can hear myself saying 'Sorry Gov!' to the poor sod whose worldly goods I have just carted off to my van. 'Sorry Gov!' I would say, and mean it to.

The dads look done in, what with having nothing to sit on and the wailing and all. They go and lie down on their beds, which I know are still in there.

At our house I stand in the doorway to take in the commotion. You would think we owned valuables the way Mum is directing the proceedings, ordering the neighbours around the room, telling them what's got to be carried to where and how careful they're to be with it. The neighbours are letting us put our chairs, three, and a stool, and our table, into their back garden until Dad can find another place for us to live.

Needless to say, Dad is nowhere to be seen.

But Dad is the proverbial conjurer; by the end of the week he has pulled our next home out of the hat and we are installed in another two rooms in Love Lane, tucked in behind the station. It isn't so bad. It isn't a flat but I can see the trains passing from the back window and I can still get to my school, and I don't have to give up my step cleaning round, or Dolly, who continues to need a sitter most nights of the week.

I am just starting to spread my legs under the table when my nine-year-old life takes an unexpected and entirely unacceptable downturn.

'Right then, Ray,' says Mum. I've arranged for you to go away.'
Away?
Seaside away?
Poorhouse away?
To join Bill at Grandma's away?
'You'll be going to live with your Great Aunt Lizzie.'
'Who?'
'She's not really your great aunt, she's a distant cousin of Grandma Edna's but that's too complicated for you, so you're to think of her as your aunt.'
'Why?'
'She's well to do, got a big house and she needs a companion.'
'What for?'
'Because she's old.'
'But I don't like old people.'
'You'll like this one.'
'Can't she get a companion her own age?'
'None of your lip, Raymond.'
'Why didn't you ask me if I wanted to go?'
'Because you would have said no.'
'Too bloody right I would have.'

Before I know what has hit me I am on the floor, she is that quick I haven't seen her hand in time to move before it catches me across the side of my face and sends my chair toppling. Tears of pain and rage prick my eyes and then worse, spill over onto my cheeks leading to the second clip on the other side. As I've said, Mum can't abide snivelling.

So that is that. They are giving me away. I am too expensive to feed and too unimportant to clothe; they are giving me away to some old biddy I don't know from Eve.

Mum smartens me up as best she can and then instead of taking me herself to meet this Great Aunt Lizzie, she takes me to Grandma Edna's where she tells me that grandma will be escorting me the rest of the journey. Mum, it seems, has to go home to get on with things.

Things?

Things?

The Great Aunt who is not even a proper relative with a kinship that can be remembered by a boy, lives at a distance so far flung my own mother cannot negotiate it, and on top of that she has *things* to get on with!

I stare at her.

I have given my mum the best bacon ends from my bag of bits! I have guided Charlie through all sorts of misdemeanours on the instruction of keeping him out of her hair. I have used my talents as a doorstep scrubber to polish our step in Love Lane until you can see your face in it. If there is more a boy can do for his mother to want to keep him, I, for one, do not know what it is.

I don't want to leave her and I tell her so.

'I don't want to leave you!'

'Be a good boy now, Ray.'

'I don't want to go, Mum.'

'Mind you behave yourself.'

'Why can't I stay with you? I won't eat much. I only really need my bag of bits.'

Grandma Edna takes hold of my hand.

'I could get another job, easy. I know a boy that pumps the bellows at the church; I reckon I could do it with him. His name's Denny Pell, you know Mrs Pell Mum, works in the newsagents.'

'Come on now, Raymond,' says Grandma, 'or we'll never get there. It's a long walk to Palmers Green.'

She holds my hand tight and I trail out of the house sobbing.

She is right. It is a bloody, bloody, bloody long walk to Palmers Green.

Chapter 3

Maudlin' They Call Me,
If They've A Mind To Call Me At All

The Great Aunt Lizzie lives in a magnificent house in Tottenhall Road, Palmers Green; posher than any of the houses round where we live and she doesn't want for a scrubber as her doorstep shines like a new penny.

In between the sobbing and the gagging, which I am doing plenty of, I sneak a look around the entrance hall. Grandma and I are stood in an Aladdin's cave where I swear all that glisters is pure gold. Large clusters of lights seem to be dripping from the ceiling. A jewelled clock ticks noisily on a side-table, demanding that I pay it the attention it deserves. Well not me. I've been dragged here kicking and screaming and I'm not about to be impressed by a bit of sparkle. It might not even be real.

Of course, when I tell Joe what I've seen, it'll be real then.

The Great Aunt Lizzie glides away in front of us like she's got skates glued to the ends of her legs. She waggles a floppy wrist at me and I follow obediently into the sitting room, my eyes peeking up at Grandma who is managing a little gliding of her own.

If I was impressed in the hallway, my eyes pop out of their sockets at the sight of the sitting room. I have never seen so much furniture in one small space. There are side cabinets stacked with busily decorated jugs and plates, a tall Grandfather clock, glass fronted dressers full of sparkling goblets, fat china urns, and more armchairs squatting about this room than God made bums to sit on them. A fire-grate is stacked so high with wood and coal it's about to burst its belly. Heavy material is hanging in great swags at the tall windows, like I'd sometimes seen in the windows of the houses where I'd scrubbed the doorsteps. Joe and I had imagined making battle uniforms out of some, me in the bright red and green clobber, Joe in something plainer, as befits a foot soldier.

I cuff my nose along my jumper and wonder what Charlie is doing, if he is missing me already, if Mum is telling him I'll be home for the holidays. The thought prompts a fresh spurt, which promises to spill out of my lower lid. Grandma sees I am welling up for another burst of snot and tears, and she gives me a sharp jab in the back with her knuckle.

'No more of that now, Raymond, or Lizzie'll think you're not grateful.'

I hang my head lower and pretend to be deciphering the patterns on the fancy rug, the shapes swashing backward and forward in a blurry salt lake.

'You're in a good home now.'

Tiny squares of orange and black come in and out of focus in a frenzied dance.

'You'll have nice clothes to wear and you'll be looked after good and proper.'

Though she is silent, or maybe because she does not witter away as Grandma does, I can tell the Great Aunt Lizzie is a cut above Grandma, which makes me rather sad.

Grandma had explained, as she had tugged and pushed me first along the streets and then across fields to the posh house, that marriage to a man of business had brought great wealth to her second cousin twice removed, though not a lot of love. Grandma thought love didn't make a pig's ear of a difference and that you could live quite happily without it if you could do it in comfort.

I thought about our rooms in Love Lane; neither money nor love seemed to be in great supply, it must all happen when I'm out in the yard, playing with Joe, all that love stuff that you hear about.

Orange and black zigzags swim about the rug in furious darting movements like the minnows Joe and I had watched in the slow streams spilling across the marshes, until the day Joe fell in, scared the bejesus out of himself and got a whack for wetting his clothes. I smile, despite myself, at Joe's forlorn face as he pulled himself out of the water, tangles of river weed dripping from his eyelashes.

The Great Aunt's cool, thin hand scoops up my own and says, surprisingly nicely:

'I expect you'd like something to eat wouldn't you, Raymond. Come along now, let's go and see what we can find.'

Miserable and jarred off, I am always hungry. My stomach groans like there's no tomorrow, enough to drive my mum to her wit's end.

'Raymond, if you can't control that stomach of yours, you'd best take it where it'll stop bothering me.' Joe and I go and lie on a bank to turn the rumbles into conversation.

'What was that then?' he'd ask after a particularly loud gurgle from my stomach.

Joe was an expert on nothing.

'That was, *Tower Bridge is a long bleedin' way from here.*'

'You don't say? I didn't hear nothing like that.'

'Ar, what d'you know, Joe, you're daft as a brush.'

'I reckon you might be right there, Ray, but least my belly don't rumble.'

I look at Joe to see if he's taking the mickey. He's concentrating on a long blade of grass. Daft sod is Joe.

'Let's go and see what we can find,' says the Aunt, bringing me back to Tottenhall Road.

What we can find is beyond my imaginings even for King Arthur's banqueting table. She leads me into what Grandma jokingly refers to as the ballroom. I can tell she's teasing but there's no doubt Grandma loves the room as if it were her own. At one end of it, double doors open onto a long garden thick with blue and white flowers, some of which have seeped into the house and planted themselves in vases around the walls, wafting a headachy perfume. The wooden floor is polished to a high glass in readiness for a dance.

A long table running the length of the room has been spread with a glaringly white cloth on which doorsteps of sparkling white bread and homemade strawberry jam are piled.

I intend to say I am not hungry, in protest at this skulduggery, the Great Aunt apparently colluding with my own mother to press gang me into service, but my stomach makes it clear that if I don't eat soon I will faint and have to be rushed to the nearest hospital for blood transfusion and food injections where they will pump mushy bread and jam directly into my blood or I will die.

Okay, just this once; after this I'm on hunger strike until they come and fetch me home. I throw a look of scorn at Grandma's retreating back and fall to devouring the sweet white bread and syrupy jam. Grandma returns with what she says is an ice cream soda, something I have never tasted before; the sticky sweet smell as I draw it to my lips makes water spurt into my mouth. Charlie would love to taste this.

If I was impressed with the dining room, I am astonished by the bedroom and I have long since given up trying to hide it; my chin drops so low onto my chest the aunt has to scoop it back into place.

This is to be my room, smaller than the other rooms, and overlooking the street as opposed to the garden, but massively compensated for by the huge bed, which has matching sheets and pillowcases, and a thick woolly blanket that it must have taken a farm load of sheep to knit. I have never seen a case on a pillow before. Or for that matter a pillow. I think of Charlie alone in the single bed at home, with only his jacket to keep him warm.

'Is this room all for me?' I ask, sounding like Orphan Arnold. 'Are there other boys in other rooms?' I begin to wonder if companion means something else in grown-up terms. Perhaps I am to sweep the chimney and fill the coalscuttle; I regret eating so much of the bread and placing myself in the aunt's debt.

Grandma is busying herself with a feather duster on the landing. 'What are you thinking of, Raymond. Of course not. You are to be your aunt's sole companion. You should feel honoured.'

I feel reluctant.

'What does a companion do?'

'Why he…well, I expect your Great Aunt will explain that to you all in her own good time,' says Grandma evasively.

This is worrying. Neither my mother nor my grandma will explain what I am to do. It must be bad.

Great Aunt Lizzie continues the tour, taking me through two large spare rooms to her own bedroom, which is larger than the whole house on Love Lane. Here she stops, a little shyly, as if she's showing me a secret. I can't see the secret myself, it's a large room; a large room, pretty though it might be, is still only a large room.

I look at her properly for the first time and she blushes. I smile at her. I know the power of a good smile; her lips curl up at the edges to reveal a row of tiny, pearl white teeth.

Then she leads me to a room I've not seen before, an indoor bathroom, with an inside toilet and an extra washbasin. She twiddles the taps to show me how they work as if I couldn't have worked that out for myself, then she heads back downstairs, throws open the door to the final outrageously large room with carpet over all of the floor and a gallery of pictures around the walls.

In the middle of this room is a big round table, on top of which sits a black book. This looks worrying; I can feel the tension rising. Grandma, who has been trailing the route behind us, catches my eye and raises one eyebrow. She doesn't know what it means either but we are both of the opinion that we have reached a testing point.

I circumnavigate the walls stopping at each frame, the longest wall presenting a line of dark oil paintings, the shorter window wall showing photographs of the aunt in younger days. I stop to identify her stood beside monuments and armless statues and become lost in the search for the young aunt amongst a small group, when I am reminded of my whereabouts by the sound of grandma clearing her throat. As casually as I can, I wander to the middle of the room where I nonchalantly drag a finger around the rim of the table, working my way toward the book.

I am good at my letters and have no problem with the words. Written in a large, gold embossed, olden style script is 'The Bible'; my heart skips a beat. Am I to be sacrificed? Joe and I have slaughtered enough insects in our time to know the joys of death.

The aunt has drawn a chair into the middle of the room and tells me to climb onto it, where she begins to measure me from head to foot for heaven knows what. My coffin? My heart beats fast. Where has Grandma gone?

The aunt is muttering to herself.

A disgrace: tape measure around head.

A scandal: tape measure around chest.

A discredit to the family: tape measure to the crotch. I am starting to sweat.

'Grandma!' I shout.

'No shouting, Raymond. What do you want?' asks the Aunt.

'Nothing,' I say. 'I just wondered if Grandma was still here.' What would Bill do if he were faced with the threat of death?

'She's still here. She'll be here until three o'clock every Monday; that's when she finishes.'

'Right.'

Finishes.

Finishes what?

Stirring the cauldron?

Sharpening the knives?

'I'm going out now, Raymond, I'll be back shortly. Your grandma is in the kitchen. She'll give you some milk if you ask politely.' Then she is gone.

I head straight for the safety of the kitchen where grandma is loading a large range with a pastry pie fit for Old King Cole. The ceiling is hung with enough copper to empty a mine. Placing my face close to the convex bowl of a mixing dish, I see my eyes pop out like fish. I pull a stool close to the baking table, my tongue exploring a hole in a tooth where a strawberry pip has lodged itself.

'How did she get to be so rich, Grandma?' I ask, staring in fly-like fascination at my many reflections in the gleaming cookware.

'Never you mind,' she says. Then, apparently ruminating on her distant relative's wealth and the second-hand pleasure it brings, she adds, 'Industry and parsimony, in equal portion, I should reckon.'

I consider this to be a particularly invaluable piece of information, but Grandma is too busy to be interrupted, so I content myself with drawing patterns in the flour dust left on the baking table by the pie's preparation.

When the Great Aunt returns over an hour later, she has a large parcel that she places with a flourish on the newly scrubbed kitchen table.

'For you,' she announces with obvious pleasure. 'Let's have those clothes off you.'

'For me?'

Remove my clothes? I think in alarm, but I'm distracted by the parcel. I've never had a parcel before. It'll be the brushes, for the chimney. I'm to mount the chimney straight away, and in the altogether, so as not to spoil my clothes. I am none too happy with this companion lark.

'New trousers,' she says, unravelling a pile of items from the package. Long trousers, I note.

'New shirts, a jacket, two warm jumpers.'

It's spring. Mum says we don't need jumpers in spring.

'Some shorts to play in. A hat. A coat.'

'All new? For me?'

I am tearing my clothes off as fast as can be.

'A new pair of shoes, black, and three pairs of socks.'

I push my dirty feet inside them. The aunt looks away in what might be distaste.

'Pants and singlets are in this bag. You can put them on fresh tomorrow, after you've had a bath.'

'What are these?' I ask, holding up a pair of hairy red and blue tartan shoes.

'They are your slippers; for wearing around the house.'

Shoes for wearing around the house. Now there's an idea. Shoes for wearing outside and shoes for wearing inside. What will they think of next?

I should feel grateful. I have never in my life had a single piece of new clothing. I go to the tall mirror in the entrance hall to try on happy, but it won't come. The clothes feel lovely. The house smells fresh, every surface is clean, thanks to my own grandma it seems. The kitchen where Grandma will be every Monday sends out wonderful aromas, but something isn't right.

My aunt asks Grandma to run me a bath before she leaves and grandma proudly shows me the towels and the new bar of soap, then she shuts the bathroom door and is gone.

I stand to consider the sizzling water. It looks deep. Too deep. I might drown. I am too afraid to get in, so I slosh the water around noisily and sing a bathing song that I've heard Bill sing sometimes, then I sit on the toilet for ten minutes to pass the time, swirling my fingers in the water and drawing on the misty windows. I dribble a bit of water onto my face and rub it into the towel, which I notice turns brown; I twist the towel so that the brown is tucked inside, then I leave the bathroom.

I don't know where to go. I always know where to go in my own house, there's either the main room or the bedroom. If there's a fight going on in the bedroom, I can always go back to the main room but there's usually company in one of them; Charlie sprawled on the bed tearing up paper, Mum cooking or washing in the kitchen, Dad sleeping on his arms at the kitchen table. Am I supposed to go and be a companion?

I creep down the stairs to find the Aunt sitting close to a roaring fire, a pair of spectacles balanced on her nose, reading a newspaper. I am so surprised to see her reading and the fire looking so cheerful, I shuffle forward into the room, enticed by its welcome.

'Hello, Raymond. How was your bath?' She looks at my face and frowns. 'I've made a list of the jobs I'll expect you to do every day.'

Ah. Here it comes.

'You're to light the fire each morning.'

I'm on for that; Mum won't let me anywhere near the matches at home even though I've had a lot of practice out in the alley with Joe. Here's a chance to prove the man I am.

'And fill the skuttle every morning and again in the evening when you come in from school.'

No problem there.

'At the weekends there will be a big box of wood to chop to last us for the week.'

An axe?

I get to play with an axe?

'And you're to polish the cutlery once a week.'

Can do can do. Do I really get to play with an axe?

Can she honestly be saying that?

She's not such a bad old stick.

'You'll get up at seven thirty each morning and you will be in bed by eight each evening.'

'What!' I say, appalled.

'You mean pardon, Raymond.'

'I go to bed whenever I please at home, Great Aunt Lizzie.' Aunt Lizzie seems delighted that I have used her name.

I smile a good smile to add weight to my words, using the space of her flustered silence to add further argument to my cause.

'Mum finds it useful to keep me up late as I can be such a help, around the rooms, with things.'

'Well, we shall see. Perhaps eight is a little early.'

My smile turns to a manic grimace, a fearful hysteria overwhelms me and I cartwheel across the rug. She is malleable; I can win sometimes. The Aunt looks nonplussed at my tumbling, her hand presses to her throat in sympathy with her furniture, possibly wondering if she has made the right decision.

A week goes by and the Aunt and I conduct an elaborate dance to learn the patterns of each other's lives. I can't say I dislike her, she's a little rigid but not unpleasant, but I'm lonely and I worry that if I talk to her about home it will seem rude. I lie between the crisp white sheets and look out at the stars: Hello Charlie, are you looking at the stars too, can you see the three stars in a row? That's the belt of a great giant and he's watching over us to make sure no one does us no harm.

Grandma arrives the following Monday morning to walk me to my new school, as it's no longer possible for me to walk all the way to the old one every day. My new shoes clip smartly along the road for the twenty-minute walk, Grandma shuffles slowly at my side. When we reach the school gates she disappears and it is only then that I realise we haven't spoken. No, *How've you been? Your mum's missing you. Charlie has torn his knee. How is the great aunt to whom you are only very distantly related treating you? Would you like to come home now?*

I look up and down the road for a few minutes; perhaps she has popped into the corner shop? The school bell clangs and I know she isn't coming back; I walk through the big swinging doors, where once again I am on my own.

At the end of the day I wait at the school gate until I know for certain Grandma isn't coming and then I turn to make my way slowly back to Tottenhall Road.

The Aunt is furious.

'Where have you been?'

'I waited for Grandma, but she didn't come.' I try manic, and bowl past her into the entrance hall, using the rug to skid on the waxed floor tiles but she is not to be amused.

'The school is a ten minute walk away, Raymond. In future you will be home ten minutes after school ends.'

Ten minutes. Grandma and I had taken at least twenty. I shall have to run all the way, and then I'll be late. I scowl into the room and I think some of the special words that I keep privately tucked in my head.

This time-keeping shenanigan is not the only thing I don't like. I am a prisoner. I am never allowed out onto the street to play and I am forbidden on pain of death to set foot in the garden. The wood chopping is conducted in a small, bricked area from which, as soon as it is done, I must return indoors. I can't go out and no one can visit. Despite the glories of the axe, there is little mileage in wood chopping if I am not at liberty to describe my exploits to the likes of Joe.

'There's plenty for us to be doing indoors, Raymond,' says the Aunt, ignoring my sullen glare. And she means it.

Mum lets me wander the streets, playing with Joe until hunger forces me indoors but the aunt has other plans. She plans to encourage me in my schooling, which she does with great zeal.

She buys me writing books, pens and pencils, a pair of compasses, crayons and a huge drawing pad; I am so delighted with them that for a while we are both warmed by my enthusiasm. Anything I make at school, little wooden boxes, clay bowls and the like, she buys them; something Mum would never do. She even begins to knit me a pullover and insists I sit with her to watch the stitches develop.

Knit one. Pearl one.

Now my turn.

Pearl one. Knit one.

What a sad sack I am, like two old ladies, only now I understand the word companion. It means, to make someone be the same as you, despite their obvious lack of inclination or ability.

On three evenings a week she teaches me to knit; thank God I live too far away for Joe to knock on the door. On the other three evenings we do school work.

Sunday is special.

On Sunday we do hymns.

Chapter 4

God Was On A Roll When He Came Up With The Notion Of Boredom

How many boys of ten do you know who fall back wagging their legs in the air at the thought of doing hymns?

None.

How many laws have been introduced to put an end to this wicked past time?

None.

Every Sunday morning I am given the hymnbook and told to learn a hymn by lunchtime. That's okay, I think. I know loads of hymns from the school assemblies. I'll *learn* the ones I know. How sad the Aunt would be to know that her attempts at religious instruction are being used to explore my skills at conmanship. These are skills that boy and man might need at any given moment and I thank my aunt for her guidance. However, while I might admire these skills in others, such as Pretty Boy and his gang, I am myself sadly lacking in the attributes of the conman and I soon run out of hymns I know. I experience a rapid fall from grace as the aunt becomes more and more exasperated by my unexpected and inexplicable memory loss.

In an effort to apologise for her crossness over my bible studies, Great Aunt Lizzie buys a wooden jigsaw puzzle that I am to finish as she reads aloud to me. She seems particularly fond of someone called Dickens, reading long sentences about some old fella who doesn't like Christmas, and quite frankly, what with all that was happening to him, I was not in the least bit surprised. But if it were not for the tantalising promise of each new piece of jigsaw puzzle, that it might by some mysterious piece of fortune slot snugly into that unlikely shaped hole, I could well fall into a sickness and fade away with boredom.

Like a cooped bird I long for the weekends to end, so that I can get out of the house into the fresh air, away from the heavy Sabbath smog of the sitting room.

On Monday mornings I walk slowly, as I have been told to do, down the road away from the Aunt's house; she watches from behind the curtains.

Once out of sight, I run and kick-jump off the trees, I leap for low hanging boughs, I call to stray dogs and whistle at birds. I look as happy as the sand boy and I wonder what Mum would say if she could see me.

She would say to herself; well there, he's forgotten us already. He has a new life and it suits him fine.

But it isn't so. I want to see Mum so much I picture her waiting for me, just around the bend, and when I turn it, I see the wings of her coat disappearing around the next corner and I chase after her. By the time Christmas arrives I have still not caught up with Mum.

I tell myself she's busy; Charlie keeps her busy, and Dad, and I expect she's busy with Bill as he must be home by now. And the filth, there's always some filth to deal with, she said so.

'Are you looking forward to Christmas, Raymond?'

The Aunt and I are decorating a magnificent pine tree that she has set in a tub in the hall. I suck the smell up my nostrils in gusty lungfuls.

The parlour and the dining room are decked with holly boughs, just like in the song only now I can see what the singing is about. The boughs are tied with red and white bows, and we have painted walnuts, which I have never seen before, with gold lacquer, and tied them onto the boughs with ribbon.

The house smells of other things too: oranges for a start, I was so surprised to see one I squeezed its waxy looking skin, and spice, and there are brightly wrapped sweets in glass bowls on the dresser, and she has wound up a gramophone to play a Christmas tune as we work. It is my job to wind the box.

'Yes. Very much.'

'What would you like for Christmas?'

'I would like to go home.'

The Aunt stops in the middle of tying a ribbon. She speaks very softly and I know I've hurt her feelings. 'I meant what present would you like. You know it isn't possible to go home, Raymond.'

'Yes, I know, but I don't want a present, I would like to go home.'

38

'Your mother and father have asked if I can look after you now.'

'I would like to go home, just for Christmas day, to see my brothers.'

She looks at me unhappily. I am a disappointment to her but I can't help myself. I persist.

'I will come straight back, but I would like to go home, please.'

My aunt has been giving me a thre'penny bit every Saturday as pocket money, but as she supplies everything I could possibly want I have been saving these little nuggets in a sock and hiding them under my pillow. When I last counted I had three shillings and nine pence; I plan to spend this money on presents for my family.

I can already picture the grand homecoming, with me arriving like Saint Nicholas, bringing good tidings and joy in the form of presents for all forms of men. I tell my aunt about my savings hoping she will congratulate me on my diligence.

'That is too much to spend on presents, Raymond. You must only spend half of that sum and save the rest for important things.'

I do a little tap dance.

I win. I win.

'I will ask your grandpa to take you to the shops,' she says, reaching high to tie one last bauble to hide the regret I hear in her voice. I swirl around and launch myself across the room. The chair leg catches on the carpet runner and Great Aunt Lizzie dashes forward to cushion its fall.

'Bravo!' I cry, taking hold of my aunt's arm and spinning her up the centre of the carpet to the thrum of the music. Aunt Lizzie laughs, corrects her position and holding me at a ladylike distance, waltzes me around the room.

'Lighter on your feet, Raymond.'

'Like this?' I glance down to confirm I am on tip-toe.

'Head up, Raymond.'

I lift my chin and stand on her foot. 'Sorry.'

'Listen for the beat.'

I can hear the beat, 1-2-3, 1-2-3, skipping gently beneath the tune.

'And a twirl at the end of the table.'

I negotiate a second chair and a side table with some difficulty and am surprised to find I am facing the correct direction.

'Excellent Raymond, gold rosette for effort!'

Great Aunt Lizzie takes a gold ribbon from the holly bough and pins it on my jumper. I stand up tall with delight.

Sitting at the window watching the feathery softness of the snowfall, I am like bottled gas waiting to explode, a bubbling pot ready to splutter, spill and flood the floor, spoiling the orange and black oriental scene below. I have been sat here since seven this morning watching for Grandpa, wonderful old Grandpa, with his gently plodding voice and his firm, warm handshake. Grandpa is taking me to the shops.

I have no idea what I will buy. The thre'penny pieces clonk heavily against each other as I drip them through my hands.

Mum should have a new coat, with buttons down to the bottom to stop the sides flapping open and letting in the cold; she'll be needing that in this sort of weather. I slide the coins safely back into my pocket.

'Don't draw on the window, Raymond.'

And Bill needs a new pair of boots I'll be betting. Billy boy, striding out the door in that determined way he does, his big shoulders hunched up high to meet the brim of his cap. And Charlie will be old enough now to ride a bike.

'Raymond, stop it. You'll smear the windows.'

And Dad? A new pipe. One of those special pipes that Great Aunt Lizzie calls a meerschaum. Dad always has a pipe on the go. He'll feel good with a long white stemmed…

'Raymond!'

And then I see him, turning the corner, a black smudge against the white background, getting closer and closer until he is scratching and trailing his way through the thick snow on the front path.

'He's here!' I cry, pushing away from the window so fiercely I send the chair flying.

'Grandpa!' I shout, flinging open the front door and running down the steps to throw myself onto his chest.

'Well, well, what have we here? A tall, handsome stranger has accosted me to wail at me for no obvious reason. Help! Someone!'

'Grandpa it's me, Raymond Riley. You remember me don't you, Grandpa?' I am filled with horror. I have been gone so long he doesn't know me.

'Raymond? Raymond Riley? I don't think…'

'Yes, Ray, Raymond Riley, son of John and Mary Riley, as lives down by the railway in Love Lane.'

I can see his face finally recognising me, holding me at arm's length to inspect his find.

'*Oh… that* Ray Riley, well bless my cotton socks. Look how he's grown,' says my grandpa to an invisible friend.

I stand up tall as he takes my hand in his great paw.

'And meatier too. With rosy cheeks and sparkly eyes. My, my. How's the world been treating you, little man?' He folds an ape-like arm around me and leads me back toward the house.

'Life's okay, Grandpa, it's okay,' I say, pushing my voice down a few notes to approximate the new little man in me. I am to spend the day with my grandpa and I am eager to be the man he sees in me.

The Aunt is none too impressed with my purchases, which I empty out of bags and boxes all over the dining room table. Grandpa stands to watch, his chest bubbling into tiny chuckles as I present each purchase for inspection.

A pretty new apron for Mum, the slender pipe for Dad, a harmonica for Bill, a boat, a fire engine and some mice made of sugar, one pink, one white, for Charlie, and paper and string to tie them in.

A waste of money, she declares.

Grandpa laughs.

I don't care. It is Christmas tomorrow and I am going home.

I fret all night, working myself into a sweat: if I fall asleep I won't wake up in time, I shall be so tired with all the worry I shall sleep right through Christmas day, or worse, the Aunt will change her mind. My eyes shoot open at the thought. Would she stop me, at the last minute? Send a message to Grandma saying not to come and fetch me? I fall asleep screwing the sheets into a blue funk of twisted knots.

On the dot of seven thirty I sit bolt upright, immediately aware of an urgency. I race to the bathroom, throw a flick of water at my face, pull on my best clothes and gather my parcels into a bag. It has been arranged that Grandma will come for me. I am pacing the hallway when she arrives at eight o'clock to take me home. I grab my coat, ready to leave immediately but the Aunt stops me.

Panic.

She's going to change her mind. I won't be able to go. She's going to say she thought it was better to invite Grandma to stay here for Christmas dinner.

'Raymond. Before you leave, go into the parlour. You will find your Christmas present from me on the table. Don't be too long as your grandma is waiting to go.'

Relieved and irritated by the delay, I rush into the parlour where standing on the table is the largest toy box I have ever seen and pictured on the lid is a magnificent train set. My eyes spread like saucers. I tear the lid off the box: there is a station, two trains, carriages of different colours, lengths of straight and curved track and pictures to show you how they slot together. I am thrilled; I feel bad – I haven't bought a present for my aunt. Little feathery trees are lined beside a tiny stationmaster and his passengers, all dressed in bowler hats and carrying tiny briefcases. I put down the box and rustle around inside my bag of presents until I come across one of the two sugar mice.

Sorry, Charlie.

'Thank you, Aunt Lizzie,' I say. 'It's wonderful. And this is for you.' I cross my fingers behind my back: let it be the white one. Let it be the white one with one eye fallen off and a bent whisker.

'You shouldn't have, Raymond,' she says frowning, peeling away the Christmas paper to reveal the white mouse. 'It's a waste of money but I shall eat it all the same.' Then she does something ghastly, she kisses me on the head.

'Let's go!' I announce, grabbing my bag of packages and hurrying Grandma towards the door. 'We've a long way to go so best get started.'

The Great Aunt Lizzie is stood on her step, waving. I know this but I don't look. Grandma wishes her a Merry Christmas but I push my face down in the collar of my jacket and pin my eyes to my toes. If I don't look I'll get away. If I don't look at her, I'll break the spell and I'll be free to return home.

God has thrown a blanket of snow a foot deep across the fields and streets between Great Aunt Lizzie's house and home. Grandma grumbles that the snow is getting into her bones but I am too excited, and well-shod, to care.

'I can see it,' I shout, bounding back like a puppy to check that Grandma is still moving forward. 'Just across the next field, I can see the railway line and make out Love Lane. Climb on my back, Grandma.'

'Get away with you, you lunatic. I'll flatten you to a cow pat.'

The house looks perfect; like the Christmas cards on Great Aunt Lizzie's mantelshelf. It stands in a row of houses alongside the railway line, the grubbiness whitewashed clean by the snow.

'I'll run on ahead Grandma, to warn them we're here.'

I break into a trot, which accelerates to a sprint as I get closer and closer to home. Hot and excited, my heart pounds as I race across the last two fields, packages banging against my legs, my arms pumping to increase my speed. In Love Lane I slow to a trot and then drop with a clump on the doorstep, banging the door with my fist.

'Hello! Hello, everyone! It's me. Ray Riley. Open up.'

I check the packages have survived; I can't wait to see their faces. I can hear footsteps coming toward me down the hall and then, Mum opens the door. I am so excited, my heart stops banging and for a second I have to steady myself against the entrance wall.

'Oh, it's you Ray. What's that you've got there?' She is pointing at the presents.

The house by the railway is unchanged, apart from that it has shrunk, the rooms have imploded. Two beds still stand on bare floor-boards in the front room with a table and wash basin beside them, and the back room is still the kitchen, with no furniture other than the wooden table, the three chairs and the stool.

Mum and Grandma sit down immediately at the table to talk, leaving me to watch from the doorway, a dismal scene. Charlie is lying awkwardly on the floor in front of a fire, one skinny leg protruding to a grubbily bandaged foot. He is drawing with the stubby end of a pencil on an already full piece of paper. I glance furtively to the corner for the crutches.

'Hi, Charlie. Remember me? What have you been up to then?'

'I know you,' he says, not looking up, 'you're my brother and you live with the rich lady now and you don't take me to school no more.'

'But you're grown big enough to take yourself to school now. Just look at you. How is school?'

'Okay.'

'Are you learning your letters?'

'The teacher don't smell no more.'

Charlie himself smells a little high; I guess he no longer detects her odour above his own.

'What have you done to your foot?'

'Knocked the teapot over. Dad took me to the hospital. Got a boiled sweet.'

'Well that's all right then, eh? A boiled sweet! I've brought you some Christmas presents, do you want to see?'

Charlie's eyes widen, belief beggared.

'You got presents for me, Ray? Just for me?'

'They're nothing much.' I say, pushing the small pile towards him, watching him tear at the wrapping paper, feeling rotten. If I'd

43

thought they'd get this much of a fanfare I'd of spent the rest of my savings on him.

'Have you got loads of things, Ray? At the rich lady's?'

'No.'

'Do you have sweets and cakes, Ray, with the rich lady?'

'No.'

'Do you have a dog?'

'Definitely not. It's just the same as here. Grown-ups don't like dogs in the house.'

'That's what Mum says. Dogs mess up.'

Charlie throws himself onto the bare floor to push the fire engine along the grooves.

Grandma leaves; she'll come back for me in the evening.

It is desolate here; I don't wonder at Grandma's going. For a start there's no music. Even though I haven't paid much attention to the music the Aunt plays, it tinkles around in the background keeping me company. There are no nice smells; the Aunt's house smells of pine and blossoms, depending on what room you are in. But mostly, there is no colour; I had forgotten how grey home is.

Mum sits in a sickly slump, the apron still folded on her lap, staring unseeing at Charlie who pushes the fire engine around the floor. I can't smell any cooking. A jug of what looks like cold tea is sat on the floor beside her chair.

'I've a present for Bill, too. Is he coming home?'

'Why would he do that?' she says, not lifting her eyes.

'To see us all, of course, to see his family, for Christmas.'

'You better take a seat if you plan on waiting for him.'

'And one for dad… I'll leave it here for him.'

I know where Dad is. And I have worked out that the jug beside Mum's chair is the reason she isn't with him, she has obviously taken to bringing her ale requirements home.

And there we sit. I get down on the floor and push the engine back and forward with Charlie long enough for the fire to go out. By the time Grandma arrives to take me back, I'm cold, hungry and ready to leave.

The Aunt asks if I've enjoyed myself. What can I say? I have to tell her the truth. I haven't enjoyed myself at all. Her eyes crinkle sadly; she pats me on the arm.

Chapter 5

The False Homecoming

Thankfully, the Christmas holidays end and I return to school. During the next two years with my aunt, I neither visit my family nor do we receive any of the family as callers. I miss Mum every day with a thumping pain that never ends.

Isn't it odd?

Here am I, thrown out of the house like yesterday's slops. Don't you think someone would feel some remorse? Doesn't anyone clap their hand on their forehead and say to themselves in a dumbfounded voice; *Whey hey, now just hold on a minute here, this is our lad, being brought up half way across the other side of the world and us not giving a thought to whether he sinks or swims? Let's get ourselves in gear here. Let's fetch the nipper back home to where he belongs, with his kith and kin.*

You'd think so wouldn't you?

Well not so bloody likely.

There is nothing so raw as the thought that they simply don't care. There's no describing what this can do to a lad, but for starters it can make a magnificent liar out of him. No way will I be sitting down to talk with Joe about bygone days to be reminded that even my own mum didn't like me enough to want to keep me. No way! Joe would have a field day on that one.

It is 1914 and everyone is buzzing with excitement; we're going to fight the Germans and we're going to win; it won't be long before it's over.

The school is asking for money to help the Red Cross so Great Aunt Lizzie sends me in with a penny every Monday morning, while in the evenings she teaches me to knit socks and balaclavas for the soldiers in France.

I am a bloody knitter, but I keep such evaluations to myself and she is pleased with my efforts. I take our offerings to the school hall along with the other kids.

Standing in the hall doorway I watch as the clothes are bundled into huge paper parcels: we are sending our patriotic loyalty for king and country to our men in France. We are all doing our bit. We are pulling together. Great Aunt Lizzie believes we are doing ourselves proud.

Then, one Saturday morning, the usual studies with my aunt are interrupted by a visit from her son. I have already met him several times and as before I am sent to another room, out of the way, with an instruction to *get on with something*. Great Aunt Lizzie closes the door firmly and again, as before, I press my ear to the doorjamb. The familiar conversation begins.

Lawrence Delaney needs money. His mother has money. The money left him by his father has not stretched as far as he'd hoped.

Gambling, she snaps.

Bad investment advice, loan sharks, he argues.

She *hummfs* and *pshshs* at her son, who I can hear pacing up and down the room.

He has had the misfortune to encounter usurer, pawnbroker, extortioner, tickshop-keeper and none has treated him with anything but disdain, and being of a trusting nature he has stood by and watched, helpless, as his inheritance has trickled from his pocket.

The Great Aunt is unsympathetic. I recognise the impatience in her voice but he is eager to press his point. And desperate.

I have jobs to do and if he makes her angry she will be grumpy with me when she discovers after his departure that I have sat idle through the day. I creep out by another door into the kitchen to clean the cutlery.

Where can all that money have gone? His father had parcelled out the benefits of his financial wisdom and *pff*, the world's unquenchable thirst for loot had pillaged this poor man's pocket with the grasping hands of a pirate.

I am in the process of laying out the knives, forks and spoons into tarnished piles, pondering the treacherous world of grown-ups, when it hits me: I don't give a damn about this poor man and his lost inheritance, and what's more, I must go home. I *must* go home now, get out of this house and back to Mum and Dad and my brothers. I desperately need to see Mum and they need me.

I leave everything just as it is, slide past the argument in the parlour and creep up the stairs to my room. I dress quickly in my best clothes, roll my everyday wear into a bundle, push as many of my books as I can carry into my school satchel, slide the train set out from under the bed and with my bundle under my arm, slither back downstairs, back past the arguing room and out the front door. I daren't pull it shut for fear of discovery. And I run.

I run down the steps, out of the gate and I don't stop until I reach the main road, where I falter. I'm not sure which way to turn. If I could find the pencil factory I could tell Dad that I have run away from Great Aunt Lizzie and beg him to take me home, but the only route I know takes me past Grandma's and if she catches me she will march me straight back to the Aunt. I have no choice. It is my only chance of getting home, so off I go.

When I get to Jacksons Road I pause, clasp my satchel tight, squeeze the bundle under my arm, and run as fast as I can past her house. It is a warm day and neighbours are out on their doorsteps. Some of them see me but I don't stop, I just keep running. Morning Mrs, I say in my head. Good day, mate, I say. But only as I run.

After Grandma's I slow up a little and begin to enjoy the sunshine.

This is brave.

This is me doing what feels good for me for the first time and enjoying it. My fear begins to subside as the roads become ever more familiar. Crossing a big field I recognise the Weir Hall and from there I go on to Silver Street, following Bull Lane across another field until I reach White Hart Lane, where I begin to feel safe, I'm almost home.

Eventually, I come out of a field at the top of Lorenco Road in which lies The Compasses Pub.

Nearly there.

I begin to skip.

Nearly there.

Past the pub, down the lane, along the long road, down another lane, past the station and there is the door. I am the escaped convict arriving at the safe house. Relief washes through me; I have reached Love Lane, I have come home. I take in the moment then go slowly to the door and knock. The anticipation is killing me; they're going to be so surprised.

The door opens and a stranger looks out. I glance up and down the street to check I'm in the right place. My heart begins to beat fast and my hands go clammy. I can't think what to say.

'What do you want?'

This is surely every child's nightmare. I have arrived home and no one knows me and I know no one. Everyone has up sticks and moved away. There must be some mistake. I feel myself going giddy and reach for the wall to steady my legs. I am sabotaged.

'Yes?'

'I'm looking for Mr and Mrs Riley.'

'They're long gone, love.'

I am having difficulty breathing. 'Gone!' My mind, in a blind alley, is having trouble understanding this information. I am falling through space, a twirling unremembered mass, my name on the tip of everyone's tongue.

Raymond?
Raymond?

Could they place me?

Not quite; I was beyond recall.

While I had been committing hymns to memory, my family had been pushing me to the dusty recesses of their minds, placing me in limbo, a faint voice from the past, which if they tried extra specially hard, they could forget altogether.

Well I am back to haunt them, the ungrateful sods.

'What name was it again, dear?'

I look at the voice in the doorway. 'Riley.'

'Try Swan Terrace, love. The lady was talking about rooms over that way, but I don't know if that's where she ended up.'

'Thanks, Mrs,' I say, beaming gratefully up at her for solving the mystery of the forgetful parents.

There has always been something unnaturally optimistic about me. Anyone with any self-respect, arriving home to find them all gone, would have hoist his bags onto his ladybird back and headed off somewhere where he was wanted. Somewhere, for instance, like a wealthy great aunt's who, though not overly affectionate, did almost everything in her power to feed, clothe, warm and support a foundling such as I. But do I do that? Do I hell. I trail up the road and turn into Swan Terrace.

Swan Terrace is a sad state of affairs, just four houses standing on their own, stuck together like an amputated arm waving out helplessly into the blue yonder.

The door of the third house is stood open and I know from instinct that this is the one but I hesitate, not wanting to march myself off another precipice.

'Mum?' I call, two or three times. I'm a desperate specimen. 'Mum!'

A woman appears from the first door in the passage.

'Who you looking for?'

'The Rileys?'

'She's in the two back, if she's not in The Dog.' And she disappears.

So, we have come full circle. Two rooms. I climb the stairs, taking care not to brush against the filthy walls, and look in at the first door. There is Mum, washing in a bowl, getting ready for Dad's return from his Saturday morning's work. She senses me watching and turns slowly.

'Well, what are you doing here? Come for another visit?'

'I'm home to stay, Mum.'

'You are?' She throws me a puzzled look, then tucks her chin in tight to her neck. 'Like hell you are.'

'I don't want to live with Aunt Lizzie anymore.'

'Well you can't stay here, if that's what you're thinking?'

'But I want to come home, Mum.'

'There's no room. We're already falling over each other, what with Billy being here again.'

Bill's home! No one had told me. 'I don't mind cramped.' I look around. 'I can hear what everyone's saying. It will be cosy.'

'Cosy my eye! You get straight back to her this instant. What on earth will she say at you running off like this. She'll be worried sick.'

'She'll understand. I'm lonely, Mum. I miss everyone. I want to be here with you all, I want to see my brothers.'

I can see she's getting agitated. She moves to the dining table and picks up her brush.

'There's no room, Raymond.'

I look about the living room. 'I could sleep in the corner.'

'There's no room,' she cries.

If I wasn't so distraught I'd have recognised the inn keeper somewhere in this speech.

'I'll sleep in the yard.'

'You'll get straight back to where you belong.'

'I belong here.'

'You wait till your father hears about this. He'll be livid. You wait till I tell him what an ungrateful little sniveller you are.'

She's right. Dad will be mad as hell. I'll have to get to him before she does. I drop my bags and run from the house towards The Dog and Duck. I run straight past the entrance as I can see him striding towards me coming down the road, full with the anticipation of his jingling pockets, happy to hit the hops. Now is a good time and I run full pelt into him, hugging him hard.

'What's this we have here?' He holds me back at arm's length, pretending not to know me. 'Not our Raymond?'

Though I now recognise this as a form of greeting it still doesn't wash.

'Lord but you're grown. What you doing down this neck of the woods, lad? Have you got the day off?' He chuckles. He's in a good mood.

'I'm come home, Dad.'

'Have you now?'

'For good.'

'How's that then?'

'She's nice and all that, the Aunt, but I want to come home now, to be here, with you all.'

'She treats you fair and square?'

'Yes Dad, she's good, but I want to come home.'

'And she feeds you well?'

'Yes Dad, we have cooked breakfast on Sundays.'

'Cooked breakfast eh?'

'But I want to be with you.'

He looks at me, thoughtful. 'Well on your head be it, lad.'

He tosses his arm around my shoulder and we wander down the street to his happy place. I leave him at the pub door and walk slowly home to sit on the doorstep.

I can't have been gone from the Aunt's for more than two hours but Grandma knows of it. I sit on the step, drawing lines in the dust with a twig, and watch as she strides towards me, mad as a bull. At the doorstep she stops, crosses her arms across her ampleness and glares.

'What's your problem, Raymond Riley?'

I can see Dad walking home from the other direction.

'Have you gone stark staring bonkers?'

Mum hears the commotion and joins Grandma on the step at the same time as Dad arrives at the door.

'We take the trouble to set you up for life and you throw it back in our faces.'

Mum stands with her hands on her hips, nodding at the accusation, waiting for Dad to speak.

'You don't get many breaks in life, Raymond Riley, things aren't handed to you on a plate, and when they are, you don't throw them away. Now you get back there before she changes her mind about you.'

'No. I'm staying here.'

Mum screeches, raises her hand to me but Dad grabs it.

'I think we've washed enough of our dirties on this doorstep, don't you Mary? We'll be going inside now, mother,' he says to Grandma, 'no need for you to stay.'

Grandma's mouth hangs open. I'm sorry for that, but it is her or me.

And he closes the door.

He's forgotten me: I'm still sat outside on the doorstep but *yes*, I shout inside, punching the air, *yes, yes, yes*, Dad is on my side, Dad has made it possible, I'm come home, the prodigal son.

I'm a born sucker for the scriptures.

Chapter 6

Billy Won't Be Coming Home No More

I am twelve-years-old and have two more years of schooling to get through; this is a much greater priority to me than the war, which rages on, and for which we are suffering many hardships.

The women and Billy are bringing in the money from the munitions factories and boy, are they happy to be out there, earning the readies. But things don't seem to match up to me. Either the Rileys are on their uppers and the shops are full, or we're awash with coupons and the shops are empty.

I stand in front of the grocery store looking at three sad slabs of butter propped jauntily against a lonely bag of flour. We're being blockaded by the Germans; they're planning to starve us out, like we'd walk to the coast, our hands held high above our heads shouting, okay, you win. That'll be two pound of pork sausages, please, and make it snappy.

Mum orders me to join any queue on the rumour of a delivery of some vital foodstuff: potatoes, sugar, tea, you name it. I stand there for hours, inching expectantly around street corners only to find the shop is in the next country and I am at the end of a human snake, each scale of which is stood with an empty shopping bag over an arm and varicose veins in both legs. The supplies have usually run out by the time I reach the front of the queue. I come up trumps in the line for a jar of jam, only to be overwhelmingly disappointed to find it is made from turnips.

'You'll never taste the difference,' says Dad. 'Get it down you and be grateful. There's young lads in battle would die for a slice of bread and turnip.'

That, I'm sure there is, but this ain't one of them.

Billy is still living with us; it's great to have him around. He calls me sergeant, he's great Billy is. He's earning a fortune in the powder mill but he's eighteen now and we're on tenterhooks for his call up papers, which arrive all too soon.

William Riley is told to report to the King's Royal Rifles for training. Joe and I think this is the best.

'So, where's he gone then.'

'Dunno. Top secret that is. He's gotta be there for six weeks.'

'Is he learning how to kill the Germans, then?'

'Course he is you silly bugger. What d'you think he's doing, taking tea with the king?'

'Does he like killing, then?'

I think about this. 'Course he does.' I take aim with the long stick I'm carrying for this very purpose.

'Do they practise on real Germans?'

I look at Joe. 'Sure do.'

'What, they actually kill them?'

'Dead as door knockers.'

'Do they take a long time to die?'

'Lingering deaths, some of them. Billy says it's grisly.'

Joe screws up his face. 'And he doesn't mind?'

'Nope. He's tough, like all us Rileys, made of stern stuff.' I blast my stick at an innocent blackbird who takes flight in terror.

'Missed,' says Joe.

I think a withering comment but I don't say anything; Joe can be bloody annoying sometimes.

Now here's the thing about Joe, he's a serious sort of chap with a grimness that when pushed verges on the downright dismal, and that can be draining on the patience, at least it can be draining on mine. But then again he's great for falling in.

Anything requiring a bit of support, some objectionable following and he's there, bringing up the rear. I like that about Joe. If I say to him, get your butt down there quick, that's just what he'll do, no questions asked. Unless it's one of those times when his mum's playing up and he's having a sulk. Today's sulk, as he's obviously having a major one, probably has something to do with the pudding basin haircut his old lady has just given him, not to mention the scissor nick to his right ear.

'Nice haircut,' I say.

'Shut your gob,' he answers, his right hand cupped over his right ear.

I grin. He grins back. We both win.

Bill finishes his training and goes into the army. He is given seven days leave and then he is shipped to France, where he manages nicely for three months before being shot in the hand, nothing major, but enough to stop the flow of letters for a few weeks. I think, with him being wounded and all, he'll come home to convalesce, but then a letter arrives to say he's been resting at his base and that soon he will be returning to the line. By that they mean The Front Line.

Joe and I have a Front Line. We use old Mrs Clay's washing line, from either side of which we lob clods of earth at each other. It is my idea to call these clods of earth *sods*, which is, I explain to Joe who listens in disbelief, exactly what they are, so we shout the news out loud knowing no one will mind.

'Take that sod.'

'No, you take that sod.'

'Here's another sod.'

'Another sod in the eye.'

'Sod.'

'Sod.'

Mrs Clay complains to my father and we have to find another Front Line.

Once back on the line, Bill's letters come less regular and when they do arrive they don't say much, just how he would like to be home. Well I know exactly how he feels; there's no better place. You can live in a hencoop and it would still be the best place to be if it was home.

Then his letters stop.

It is my job to write our letters. Mum and Dad stand over me telling me what to say, watching the curling shapes spreading across the page, making me read them back two or three times to check if I've written it as they've said it. I write to The War Office to see if Bill's regiment has moved elsewhere, or if perhaps his hand is bad again. The War Office has nothing to tell us so I write to the Red Cross, who write back telling us to write to The War Office.

Dad is getting steamed.

Then a letter arrives containing little things belonging to Bill, a small sepia photograph of Dad, stood in a waistcoat in the doorway of Love Lane, another brown photograph of Mum holding Charlie, the lacy edges curling, stood in Grandma's garden, smiling and waving Charlie's hand at the camera.

His medals and harmonica arrive after the war is over.

Our Billy has been killed in battle near St Quentins, France.

Dad weeps and wails, his beautiful boy, his firstborn. Thank god for the drink, he cries, I can forget in the drink. But he doesn't. He stumbles home from the pub howling like a pent up dog, complaining that his throat is a heavy ball of burning lead, pulling pain into his stomach.

Mum sits alone at the table, not crying, not speaking, just staring at the window; I have no idea what is going on in her head. The walls close in on us, soaking up our loss until they can hold no more, the hurt clinging to the plaster like a festering wound for everyone to see.

Charlie and I groan and whimper, our swollen eyes brimming, our hearts aching. He was nineteen-years-old. I am so sad, I know I will cry forever; I give him all the tears I have because he will never come home again.

Chapter 7

Money, Money, Money, Money, Money

I am fourteen-years-old the day I leave school; it is 1916, the war trundles on.

Joe and I have decided to go into munitions; we've been offered jobs at Eleys Sporting Cartridges in Edmonton, which has adapted nicely, funnily enough, from its peacetime occupation. Our job is to inspect bullets.

Once a bullet always a bullet, if you ask me. For nine and a half hours every weekday and five and a half hours every Saturday Joe and I inspect bullets, for which we receive 12/6 a week. Mum takes ten bob, leaving half a crown for me.

Eleys is a massive factory, chock full of machines screaming their tasks at the ceilings, which bounce the clatter back to the walls and eardrums of everyone below, most of whom are blaring conversations at each other to make themselves heard above the noise. The old-handers, those who have converted from pre-war sporting activities, have compiled a private language of lip-reading and signing, instantly excluding us new recruits, who resort to shouting into each other's ears at close range, our hands cupped around our speech to guide it into the waiting receptacle.

When we leave the factory at five o'clock our ears are humming with a sweet deafness that coddles us through the evening, a woolly warmth protecting us from the distant thuds of the night guns that echo across the Channel.

At first, I throw myself into the job like a maniac; it is rhythmically monotonous and I am happy to be lost in the repetitive motions of select, look, turn, poke and replace. Then one day I think, enough's enough. I'm off to find the Gov'nor.

'Mr Bacon, I want a different job, a machine job.'

Joe has watched me get up from the bench and stares as if I've lost my wits.

Mr Bacon slices his thick fingers through his oily black hair. He cocks his head in a pretence at straining to catch my words.

'Riley, you're too young for the machines,' he mouths, spraying a sizeable glob of saliva in my face. 'You must be sixteen to operate.'

'I want more money, Mr Bacon,' I scream back above the din, nuzzling my face into his Morgan's Pomade.

I catch sight of Joe's mouth dropping wide and I have a flash of Great Aunt Lizzie's hand scooping it back into place. 'I want to be on piecework, earning the bonuses.'

Mr Bacon looks at me, then at his watch. He's not going to give it to me straight away, I can see he's considering something but I've to wait for it. He hooks his index finger to indicate I should follow and I grab my things. Raising my eyebrows at Joe, I give chase into the next shop.

'Miss Wren, the forelady, will see you in a minute.'

When Miss Wren, the forelady, emerges from behind her office door, every part of my body stands to attention.

'Mr Bacon sent me,' I say, stupidly, trying hard not to let my tongue loll out down the length of my chin.

'Mr Bacon?' she queries, apparently at a loss to know whom such a personage might be. I point in the general direction of the machine shop.

'Ah! I've been asking for some help in wadding. Come with me. Your name is?'

'Riley, Miss. Ray Riley,' I say, levering my tongue back into my mouth and performing a sort of salute at the same time.

'You'll be packing the wad into the cartridge cases and after a week you can move on to piecework, if you measure up. You usually work in pairs but my spare worker is sick. I had asked for two more workers. There's no one else available in the machine shop?'

'Oh yes Miss, young lad named Joe, very conscientious, like me, very hard working, never late, he'd be your best bet, by my reckoning.'

Miss Wren looks at me uncertainly and disappears into the machine shop, returning minutes later with Joe, his face a picture of wonder, his tongue likewise an unprecedented protuberance from his lips. I waggle my eyebrows at him. We follow Miss Wren.

'There are the trays,' she points. Both of us stare at her dainty little hand, each finger tipped with blood red nail varnish.

'When the wads are in the cartridges, you pack them in the trays, one of you working the bench, the other bringing the trays from the machine shop.'

Then she leaves, Joe and I staring after her, Venus de Milo reunited with her arms, gone to claw her way back onto her pedestal. I'd seen her before in one of Great Aunt Lizzie's books.

Snapping our heads back into position we fall to work, racing backward and forward, me dashing to get the trays while Joe attacks the wadding, filling the trays with the cases as fast as any pieceworker on the line. We are both smiling. I look up and catch Joe's eye. His thumb goes up; 'I owe you,' he mouths.

Too bloody right you do, my son.

Joe and I settle into a comfortable pattern. I knock at his mum's on the way to the factory, walking quickly so as to maintain our record for early arrivals; workers are docked a quarter hour pay for lateness and we have no intention of losing the readies for a few minutes speed.

We work fanatically until the morning break, then like mad men until the lunch hour. In these breaks we rest against a wall behind the factory, taking in the sun, Joe reading a newspaper, me too. There are many days I would prefer a book, one of Aunt Lizzie's gold embossed volumes, but the boys would rib me, taunt la-di-da to see me stood around with some posh malarkey.

Others at the factory cross the road to the cafe for a hot meal; Joe and I buy a ha'penny cup of tea to have with the cheese sandwich we bring with us each morning, choosing to have our hot meal when we get home. At least, that is what Joe does. I usually arrive back to an empty house. Mum and Dad can be seen through the large plate window, silently propping up their heads in the public bar of The Dog and Duck, cheek by jowl with other old sots of the street, devotees of Bacchus, all.

Dinner is a long time coming, sometimes it doesn't come at all. Worse are the nights that are foodless and hostile, alcohol inflamed nights when Dad is vicious and I end up receiving a back hander for daring to suggest that *food* might be a good thing after a long day's work.

Joe and I stay in the packing shop until the war ends in November '18, but what now?

The bullet market crashes and Joe and I receive our cards.

I feel sorry for Joe, he's not particularly street wise and I reckon I'm about his only mate. He looks so doleful, stood on the pavement outside his house reading his card through watery eyes.

'Don't take on so, Joe. There's plenty of others just like us, in the same boat. Thousands are out of work.'

'That's supposed to cheer me up is it, Ray?'

'No, I don't mean that, I just mean you've gotta be a bit philosophical about these things. We've had it good for the past fourteen months, there's no saying we haven't.'

'Mum's sick, Ray.'

'I know that Joe, but look at it this way, at least while your ma's indoors poorly, she's not down the pub spending what you've worked for all week, is she now? Look on it that way, on the bright side.'

But Joe can't do it.

'You take everything so much to heart, Joe. You gotta lighten up or you'll be the death of you.' I laugh at that. 'Get to feel comfortable about yourself and stop worrying all the time.'

'I know, but with Pop gone, I'm all Mum has and if I don't put food on the table, who will?'

Jeez he can be a sniveller can Joe.

'Ah Joe, it's no different for no one else. My mum's been laid off same as us so she's got nothing coming in. Nor are they dashing about selling pencils either, I can tell you, so that's Dad out of work. Even Charlie, who only just got himself sorted out down at the printers, has been laid off. We're a whole family on the dole.'

Joe's eyes widen in horror. I'll say this for Joe, he can be seriously sympathetic when called.

'For Pete's sake Joe, it's not the end of the world.'

Dad draws eighteen shillings a week on the dole, my brother Charlie gets squit as he isn't old enough to pay stamps, and owing to some mistake, I sign on for three days and when I turn up on the Friday to collect, I am told there is nought for me, due to a query on my card.

'Query,' I bark at the pay clerk, a little less philosophically than might have been expected.

'What sort of bloody query?'

'The sort that says there's no money here for you.' The pay clerk is tucked comfortably behind a glass panel with a smug look on his face.

'Very bloody clever. What am I supposed to eat? Scotch mist.'

'There's plenty of others in the same boat.'

'That's no good to me is it mate. *I* can't feel *their* stomachs curdling.'

I stare fiercely through the glass barrier. 'Well I hope you're pleased with yourself, you self-righteous…'

'Next, please.' The line rustles and fidgets behind me.

'And you don't even know what the query is?'

'We are not here to answer questions, we are here to pay out legitimate claims.'

'Well there's none more legitimate than me! Tell him Joe! We worked long hours, the same hours actually, at Eleys and what's due to this one here,' I indicate Joe with my thumb, 'is exactly what's due to me.'

'Not according to your card, sir. Next please.'

I am bursting with indignation, frustration and philosophy.

The wicked irony of it is, apart from Dad's dole, the only money we've got coming into the house comes courtesy of Bill. Mum is drawing ten pound ten bob on his behalf on her pension book and there he is, two foot under, if he's lucky.

Life is pain and then you die, that's the sum of my philosophy.

But I persist.

I join the queue every week with Joe, only to be told each Friday of the unsolvable query. If I think the arguments in the dole queue are something, they are nothing compared to what I get when I arrive home Friday evenings with no money.

'Go back and get it,' he snarls.

'I've tried,' I plead. 'I've done everything I can to collect the money. I've been back to Eleys to ask them to reissue my card. The labour are not interested.'

'Get back down that exchange and get that money, you lazy ike.'

'Aw Dad, don't say that. I've asked what the query is, no one knows,' I whine, knowing this will infuriate him even more.

'Don't think we're going to keep and feed you when you're not bringing in any money.'

'Where do you expect me to go?' I wail.

'Good riddance, you're no son of mine.'

I am definitely a son of his, the oldest son of the household, I am man enough to work every day God sends and with overtime and I am fool enough to believe he cares.

It's true, I didn't fight for king and country, but I get the distinct impression he'd be as happy mourning the loss of two sons as one.

I am sixteen-years-old and I feel as wounded as if I was six. I like to imagine Dad is plagued with a horrible remorse after each tirade, that he licks his wounds and plans to lick mine, that he inflicts a punishment on himself far greater than any I might consider. I like to think that we keep our own accounts, but I doubt this is true.

Get a job or marching orders.

I wander grimy backstreets with a gaggle of post-war, post-work, spectres. We stop, my new found army and myself, as a single body, to read the *closed* and *no vacancies* placards outside factories, outside offices, to continue as a pack, weaving through known and virgin territories. Slowly, individuals peel away, disillusioned by the hunt, until one day I am an army of one and I find myself at the back of the meat market.

A sign is being pinned on the door of a cafe: *Vegetable Chef Wanted*. I'm a lucky bugger I am. That's me. I head straight for the door. *Chting!*

'Yes?'

'Come about the job.' I look around at the spindly wooden tables, a crumpled ashtray on each.

'Can you peel?'

'Sure can.'

'Scrub?'

'No problem.'

'Wash?'

'In my sleep.'

'Starting today?'

'Yesterday.'

'In you go.'

What a talker.

What a hole.

Thank God I am no vegetable chef, my disappointment would be overwhelming. I think about the gleaming piles of cutlery on Great Aunt Lizzie's kitchen table. I place my face near a greasy saucepan with no hope of seeing my reflection.

That's a laugh, I say to myself as I do this, and I do, I laugh, pleased to have a job. Pleased to be able to say to Dad, I'm bringing in the money, you're not; put that in your pipe.

My new boss pushes his bulk through to the kitchen.

'Here's the orders, lad. Prepare the vegetables for the lunches. You're to take nine breakfast trays out to the market men. When that's done, come back and scrub the boards, return and collect the trays, all nine mind, wash the lot up, finish the scrubbing, both rooms and the flight, and when that's finished, the lunches can go.

'Each tray holds four lunches with cutlery, salt and pepper and four cups of tea. Collect the empties, bring them back and wash the lot ready for tomorrow.'

Vegetable chef was stretching it a bit.

'You start at four-thirty sharp, working right through, no breaks, to twelve-thirty, Monday to Friday, Saturdays you finish eleven o'clock – there's no lunches down the market on a Saturday.'

'How much?'

'£1 a week.'

He stares at me, daring me to comment, his fist forming a meat cleaver in my imagination.

'Sounds good.' Lucky bugger indeed.

So here I am at 4.30am, staring sightless out of the night black window, up to my elbows in potato peelings, freezing my joints to cripple's claws in the icy water, helped no doubt by the thin blood inherited from my father's side according to Mum, wondering if Joe and the other lads are feeling the pinch of post-war Britain, which in my opinion is more of a crush than a pinch.

Crushed is what we are. We won the war didn't we, or maybe I missed something. Whatever the problem is, the sweet taste of victory is not happening in my backyard; *bitter is best* is the slogan on our manor. If it wasn't for Billy I could forget the war altogether, but I remember Billy every day. I don't cry anymore, leastwise not in the daytime, but when it's dark outside, like it is now, the tears roll down my cheeks and the hard lump in my throat grows large enough to choke me.

'What's up wi' you?'

The boss brushes past my back, a cigarette hanging from his bottom lip, glued on by spit.

'It's the onions.'

He looks me up and down, knowing he hasn't had onions for weeks, and walks away, saying nothing. I'm a good worker, strong, fast and silent. And I'm as desperate for my pound note as he is for his pound of flesh.

On the fourth Monday I drag myself out of bed at four o'clock and grope towards the washbasin in the pitch black where I stand shivering, fumbling for a candle stump.

I'm still a bit displaced in the new surroundings. I'd come home a fortnight ago to find the household on the move once again: houses in London are thin on the ground and we have been lucky enough to get two large attic rooms in a draughty tenement in Wood Green.

Feeling along a shelf for a candle, my hand slides across a small package, to which it returns with interest. Since we received the letter with the news about Billy, Mum and Dad have virtually ignored the post. Not that we get much, what with knowing so few people that can write, and the fact that we are virtually gypsies, the post has the devil's own job finding us and when it does, it is left unopened or worse, it gets taken down the carsey unread. I light a candle bit.

Dear Raymond Riley, I read.

Eleys Sporting Cartridges has had the good fortune to go into partnership with Nobels of Waltham Abbey, Fine Sporting Equipment for Gentlemen of Leisure. The expanded company requires a new workforce and the Directors are seeking the services of people with a knowledge of the trade. We would be pleased if you would report for work on Monday 15th.

Yours truly
Alan Eley.

Well bless my soul, I think. I am the lucky bugger after all, the sort of chap who, when everyone else is stepping in dog's mess, spots a glimmer and dives for a lucky penny.

Monday 15th?

'Today!'

I throw water on my face, hold my ear against the other door to confirm Mum's snoring, then rake her sacred brush through my hair. It's an ungodly hour but I'm keen not to lose my chance. Who cares if I'm there early. I don't want them offering my job to some other schmuck because they can't see me at the front of the line. This one's got my name on it. And off I set.

With the gas lights doused at midnight the streets are still in shadow but I know them well enough and I'm not bothered by the dark. I strut my way through street and field, my hands deep in my pockets, my stride loping and manly, as becomes a lad as has been sought for a job. When I reach the tram stop in Lordship Lane I sit myself on the low wall to wait for the 6.15, which will take me to Bruce Grove Station where I can change for the tram to Waltham Cross, after which I can walk the twenty minutes to Waltham Abbey for the seven thirty start.

I arrive at the factory gate just as they are calling the names.

'Bob Richards?'

'Over here.'

'Come through, son… Raymond Riley?'

'Here.' He beckons me through the gates.

'Tom Watts?'

'Yes.'

'Ethel Thomas?'

'That's me,' squeaks a lemony voice.

'Joe Johnson?'

'Yup!'

Well I never!

'Right, that's the lot. Sorry lads and lasses, I'm afraid that's all I need for the present, you can all go home. Perhaps there'll be something next Monday.'

The crowd looks at him with the exaggerated eyes of the hungry. He looks right sorry for them, does the Gov'nor. I do too, I hope.

I'm in. I'm in.

I eye Ethel Thomas as we walk across the courtyard behind the boss.

I'm in.

'Twenty eight shillings a week,' he is saying. 'Seven-thirty to five-thirty weekdays, seven-thirty to twelve Saturdays.' I'm doing my sums. Fifteen bob to Mum for keep, leaves me thirteen bob for fares, clothes, food and women. Not exactly going to take them by storm but beggars aren't choosy.

We are given overalls and I watch fascinated as Ethel does something nifty with a scarf, securing her endlessly unruly wires up inside a turban. We follow the Gov'nor onto the shop floor and the memorable wall of sound hits me. The boss moves into signing mode and indicates the different benches we are each to work on. I am a little disappointed not to be placed with Ethel, who seems aware of my lingering and gives me a sly waggle of her fingers as she departs. I grin. I am shown to my bench and fall easily into the routine.

I have been checking bore gauges for a few hours when I look up to see someone that I sense has been staring at me for a while.

Dennis Pell!

He gives a slight nod and I rearrange my face to a puzzled, quizzical look. Slowly, I let him see the penny drop. Ah, Dennis Pell, my face reads, Pretty Boy, at work in the factory. Well good for him. I nod. He receives my nod and passes it on down the line. I follow his lead to another bicycle shed face. My, my, they're coming out of the woodwork, it's a shed convention.

Dennis, cool and relaxed in a way that only the handsome fully master, saunters across the grass to me in the lunch break.

'So, how's it going, Sunbeam?' he says, puffing on the end of a slim white cigarette, which I note is not hand rolled. 'I heard you'd gone up in the world.'

I look up at Pretty Boy seeking a tone of grievance but finding none. 'That'll be the rich relative you'll have heard of I expect. Yeah, you could say I've been out and about a bit, but Mum needed me back home so I cut short my rub with the gentry. It's nice to know the money's there though, wouldn't you say, Dennis?'

I watch Pretty Boy ascertain the likelihood of this information. Was it likely that this toe rag who could just about clean a doorstep would be related to readies? He doubts it, and his doubt keeps him happy.

'What have you been up to then?' I ask

'Oh, this 'n that. I've bin engaged twice,' Pretty Boy draws a long drag on his cigarette to let this information register, 'but it didn't suit me.'

'Twice!' My eyebrows have shot up to play with my fringe.

'Yeah. Nice girls, nice girls. Sisters actually. But not really my type.'

'What did you get engaged to them for then?' His news has put me at a disadvantage. I think of returning to the rich relative story but realise he has already dismissed it as improbable.

'Ah, you know girls, they love a bit of security, even with a bloke they are fairly certain thinks almost nothing of them.'

'And why two sisters.'

'Well, that was kindness really, on my part. I didn't think it was fair that one of them should be able to boast over the other, I'm not interested in that tit for tat stuff that girls go in for, so I reckoned it would even the score, and then I could move on.'

'You're a fast worker, Dennis, I'll give you that.'

'Practise makes perfect, son, practise makes perfect. You seeing anyone?'

'No, not at the moment.'

I say this a bit too quickly, wondering if I can count Miss Wren of Eleys Sporting Cartridges who once brushed past me in the corridor, scraping two pointed projections along the side of my arm in a manner that nearly made me faint.

'No one in particular that is.'

'Well you should think about it, Sunbeam. It does wonders for you. If you fancy it, me and the boys'll be heading for the dance hall on Saturday, you can tag along if you like.'

'That's decent of you, Dennis. I'll think about it.'

'Denny, if you don't mind Sunbeam, Dennis is what their mothers call me.'

''Course… Mine's Ray, though I expect you remember that.'

'Sure do, Sunbeam. Outside The Palais at eight.'

'I'll bring Joe, if that's okay.'

Pretty Boy shrugs a non-committal shoulder, which I take to mean bring what you like, it's no skin off my nose.

'We'll be there, no problem. Joe's not much of a dancer though, will that make a difference do you think?'

Sorry Joe

'We're not going there to dance are we, Ray.'

He laughs, cuffs me a light punch on the arm and wanders back to the factory door. Break is over. I can hardly contain myself until the hooter so's I can tell Joe. This is it, we're on the road. That's two bigguns you owe me, Joe Boy.

Chapter 8

My Two Left Feet

Saturday night arrives and Joe and I are in a dash to catch the tram for The Palais.

'What do you think of the suit, Ray.'

'Not bad, not bad at all. Your dad's is it?'

'That it is. It was his wedding suit. But he put on weight once he married and he hardly wore a stitch out on this one.'

'It certainly looks in good condition, Joe.'

'Are Dennis and Fred bringing girls or coming on their own?'

'I didn't ask. On their own I think.'

We reach the tram station just in time to jump on our ride. There is a lively crowd on board, dressed to the nines in readiness for whatever Saturday night might bring.

'Mum and I have been practising you know, reminding ourselves of the steps.'

'What do you mean?' I gawp at Joe. This is a bolt from the blue. 'Are you saying you can dance?' I thought his mum was sick.

'Sure can. Mum and Dad were champions and she's walked me round on her toes since I was knee high to a china man. Along with teaching me the piano, they primed me for the dancing cups.'

'What about the modern stuff, you'll probably not know about that.'

'Sure do. Mum went dancing every week, up until she took poorly.'

This is bad news.

'Still, we're not really going for the dancing, are we Joe,' I say with significance, desperately trying to remember my spin around the table with Great Aunt Lizzie. Head up. Straight back. High on the toes.

'You might not be Ray, but I certainly am. Girls are suckers for a good twirl. Mum has told me all about it.'

Oh good grief. What am I going to do? Caught with my pants down by this unexpected turn of events.

The Palais is satisfyingly dark when we arrive; we stop just inside the entrance to let our eyes acclimatise to the smoky shadows. Circular tables swim into focus around the edges of the dancehall, each with a faint orange lamplight glow. Girls are sat in pairs at the front tables, their handbags balanced on their knees, their hands cupped over their mouths whispering to their neighbours. The boys are lined along the back wall, smoking, and attempting to look as if they couldn't care less. The girls know this is not so.

Occasionally a boy breaks rank and moves in to ask a girl onto the floor. She glances slyly at her friend who she asks to watch her bag before rising to take his arm.

On the stage at the far end of the hall a twelve-piece band is floating its way through a soft waltz, the stage is swathed by glittering green curtains speckled with stars. I turn to Joe and see he is grinning, his shoulders swaying slowly with the rhythms. Rolling my eyes I nudge Joe in the direction of the bar.

'Did you see that Ethel Thomas as we came in?'

'I could just about make out my own feet, never mind Ethel Thomas,' says Joe, taking a sip of his pint.

'She's sat over there, with a mate.'

'What're we waiting for then?'

I've a pint in my hand, a swagger in my hips and I'm better looking than my mate. What can possibly go wrong?

'Hello there,' I call out, before Joe can catch up. I check them over. The mate is really something. Sadly, Ethel has spotted us crossing the dance floor and jumped up to grab my arm.

'You going to introduce us then?'

'Of course, this is Susan, boys, Susan this is Ray Riley and Joe Johnson, we work together at the factory.' Ethel breaks into a squeal of laughter as if this piece of information is in some way compromising.

Susan smiles a perfectly even smile and shakes both our hands. Ethel's arm tightens its lock.

Joe knows what his best move will be. 'Would you like to dance, Susan,' he says, offering a gentlemanly elbow.

'Oh do, Sue, you know you've been dying to, she's a fabulous dancer, Joe. Me and Ray are fine, sat just here. Give us your bag.'

Susan hesitates, then giving a slight shrug, she turns to Joe who guides her onto the dance floor and I have to say this for him, he's a man of his word. Ethel and I watch transfixed as he whirls her around the floor, his arm gently supporting the small of her back, his feet nimbly manoeuvring the turns, Susan's smile growing wide with pleasure as the other couples move out of their path to allow them through in silent acknowledgement of their greater skill.

'Would you like a drink, Ethel,' I say, in need of libation to lift my spirits.

'That'd be nice Ray, mine's a rum and black and Susan's is a snowball.'

I don't remember asking if Susan wanted a drink.

'Coming right up,' I say, bouncing out of the seat and virtually trotting to the bar.

Calm down Ray, I tell myself. Ethel is fun. And she certainly beats propping up the wall with the other flowers. I buy Joe a second pint, just to show there's no hard feelings. On the way back across the dance floor, drink seeping into the cuffs of my shirt, Pretty Boy catches my eye and gives me a thumbs down.

Sod off, I think. I don't see Cleopatra hanging on your arm.

Three or four dances pass before Susan and Joe re-join us at the table.

'You were terrific,' squeals Ethel, jumping to her feet to give her friend a kiss. 'Everyone was watching you.'

Susan blushes, interestingly so does Joe.

'She's right,' he says. 'You're a superb dancer.'

'You're not so bad yourself.' Then she smiles that unnecessarily brilliant smile at him and Ethel and I sit gawping like a pair of gooseberries.

Is it really as easy as that? A few spins on the dance floor and you're there, in love?

'We need to go to powder our noses,' announces Ethel, taking Susan's hand, as interested as I am in this turn of events.

'Don't go away boys or we'll be very disappointed, won't we Susan.' Susan smiles. She seems to have got that off to a tee.

'Does she speak?' I say to Joe, unable to shake off feeling narked with him.

'She doesn't need to, did you see her dancing?'

'Christ, you're a sucker, Joe Johnson.'

'Happy sucker I think you mean,' says Joe, grinning widely. So I grin myself, pleased to see him so chuffed. 'What do you think they're saying?' he wonders.

'Girl stuff. You know, Ethel'll be saying mine's a cracker, what do you think of yours? And Susan'll say he's all right, shame about the suit, that sort of thing.'

Joe's smile widens. There's no getting to him. He's up there somewhere near the moon and I haven't got what it takes to bring him down.

The girls come back, duly powdered, and we sit in silence for a while, watching the dancers shuffling around the floor. The band strikes up a tango and Joe and Susan rise simultaneously, a roomful of eyes turning to watch them as they take their positions for the dance. Ethel and I are plunged back into our own togetherness, which by no stretch of the imagination is being regarded with envy by anyone. I am conscious of one voyeur but I shall deal with him later.

We pick up where we left off.

'Dad is door to door just like you've been, though he's not on his hands and knees, he's on the brushes, with the Kleeneze.'

'Who needs brushes?'

'Well, round our way, where there's a bit more money, they have them for all sorts: shoes, clothes, hair, furniture, a brush for every job, that's one of his lines. He's really good at it, they say he's got the gift of the gab.' More squealing.

'They say I take after him.'

Great.

Pretty Boy catches my eye and waves. He's heading this way. I fiddle with the buttons of my jacket, stretching out my legs to look casual.

'How come you're not up there, like Joe, skipping the light fantastic?' Ethel asks.

'Dancing's not really for me,' I say, looking across as Joe conducts the fanciest bit of footwork this dance floor has seen tonight. 'I taught Joe all he knows, then gave it up, it's not good for the health.'

Ethel snorts loudly into her rum and black just as Pretty Boy reaches our table.

'Hello there, lovebirds. You seem to be getting along nice and cosy.'

Ethel, bless her, looks delighted.

'Where's your lady friend this evening, Denny?' she asks.

First name terms, I note, feeling an unreasonable flash of resentment.

'She and her sister are washing their hair.'

'On a Saturday night?'

'You know the ladies, there's no telling what they'll do next. Which leaves me foot loose and fancy free and if you don't mind,

Ray, I'd like to give this young lady the benefit of my company on the dance floor. If that's okay with you, of course.'

He stands and holds his hand out to Ethel. Ethel, unsure, turns her face to me. What a predicament. If I say it's okay, I'll look as if I don't care. If I say it's not okay I'll look possessive and overbearing, or worse, I'll look as if I do care. Thank you Pretty Boy.

'I think it would be polite to let the lady decide for herself,' I say, passing the buck.

'Ooh Ray, how sweet, two handsome fellers fighting over me,' Ethel shrieks, and I wonder if she is capable of conducting herself in any lower decibel. 'You know I don't like to be a disappointment to anyone, so I'll go for a spin with Denny, as he's a friend of yours Ray, but I'll be straight back. Don't you worry now, I won't be gone long. Look after the bags, Ray.'

'Thank you, Ray,' says Pretty Boy, giving me a wink and a second thumbs down.

Ethel and Susan and Joe and I become regular patrons of The Palais. Joe and Susan are quick to rise to celebrity status, prompting applause when they stand to take their first dance any Saturday night, local heroes both. I clap along with the other onlookers, nudging any newcomers into support, nodding my approval as any good manager does. We have been walking out for about six months, having a laugh, enjoying ourselves, but this evening Ethel is in a mood and I am on my guard.

The band is doing a nice Duke Ellington number. Ethel has returned to one of her favourite subjects, the lucrative business of selling brushes. I'm fairly sure I know where this is going.

Her dad earns a lot of money, they have a nice house, her mum and dad are happy, etc., living well on brush income. In the middle of Ethel's explanation of the difference between bristle and horse hair I realise, I do not give a fig.

Looking towards the entrance doors I float the spectre of Great Aunt Lizzie across the hall, allow her an *excuse-me* on Joe and Susan, and watch as they glide around The Palais, her dainty footsteps in perfect time with Joe's.

'Ray! Are you listening?'

'Of course, bristle or horsehair. My mother is a bristle lady.'

I had not meant to offer up this nugget, she has tricked it out of me. I pinch the flesh of my palm in annoyance. Ethel sits higher in the chair, clutching her bag towards her stomach.

'So, you have a mother then do you, Ray? That's nice. I was beginning to wonder, you being so secretive and wary. I said to Susan, you're a bit of a dark horse.'

Man of mystery, that's me.

'You'll have to invite me to tea to meet this mother,' she suggests, tentatively, aware she is overstepping the mark. Susan has confided to Ethel that she's sure Joe is about to pop the question; Joe has confided the same to me. I can tell that Ethel is eager for progress of a similar kind.

'Mmmmm,' I say vaguely, having no intention of taking any girl back to our rooms, which are too disgusting, to meet my parents who are too unpredictable to contemplate introducing.

'Would you like to dance?' I say, rashly.

'Ray Riley! I didn't know you could! What a night of surprises.' She is manoeuvring herself nearer to that greatest surprise of all.

I shrug, hoping I'm achieving the look of nonchalance I used to watch for on Billy. 'This doesn't seem too difficult to me,' I say, following her lead. 'You know, I had dancing lessons once.'

'Blimey, you're spilling the beans tonight, Ray. First I discover there's a mother, now you're hinting at a life among the middle classes. Dancing lessons indeed.'

We shuffle around the floor, me squelching down into the crowd where I can hide my inadequacies, Ethel standing tall on her heels, delighted to be on show. I pull away and look at her face. She's a good sort really, she's had to sit there for six months wearing her best stepping out clothes, watching the other girls show off their frocks and she hasn't griped once. I could do worse. Would a life with Ethel be so very difficult? She's got a ready smile, turns anything into a joke and what she lacks in the looks department, she could probably make up for elsewhere. Go for it, Ray. What's the problem?

I continue in my head, using the music to hide my mental arguments.

The fatal flaw Bill, is this niggling distrust of my capabilities. Look at the mess Mum and Dad have made of it.

That's no mess. They've adapted together, they understand each other.

The drink is not an understanding it's a stupor, and an ugly one.

That's them Ray, not you.

Who's to say I'm not tarred with the same?

So you like a drink, so what?

Supposing I don't take refuge in the drink? What would I do then when it turned bad?

Assuming it turns bad, of course.

Bill, I'll not be selling bristles. I'm not cut out for the door to door.

You were once.

Well not anymore

It's your call, Ray. Just remember, it can get lonely.

'I'll take you home now Ethel, if you're ready?'

'I'll get my bag, just hold on while I say goodbye to Susan.' She smiles at me. I can tell she thinks this is it.

She's not going to be happy with me one little bit.

Chapter 9

A Place To Draw Breath

In a furious temper, Ethel swings a large white bag over her head and slices it through the air, the buckle scraping my skin to a satisfying tear of flesh.

'You're a disgrace Ray Riley. You've no right to lead a girl up the garden path in this way. One minute you're inviting me home to meet your mother, the next I'm told you think it's best we don't see each other no more. Well that suits me just fine, as it happens, fine and dandy.'

For a second time she swings wildly with the bag, this time clunking it down on the back of my neck.

'John Scarp in Supplies has been asking after me for months and I'll be only too pleased to let him know I've finally got rid of you. I told Susan I was fed up to the teeth with you. You're dull, you can't dance, you never take me anywhere nice, you're tight fisted, and there's Joe buying her stockings and a pretty floral scarf with long feathery fringes that we'd both seen in Maisies, and which I told you about the very next day, and you can just about be bothered to get up off your backside to fetch me another drink. Anyhow, I told Susan I was finishing with you tonight and that's what I'm doing. Don't come calling after me anymore, Ray Riley, I've found me a new beau with manners, and a sense of fun, and a wallet that opens.'

Ethel glares at me one last time, contemplating a third strike, before strutting off down Wood Green High Road, the heels of her shoes tip tapping along the pavement, her bottom springing from side to side in indignation.

I stare after her in amazement, my fingers creeping to the back of my neck where a trickle of blood is oozing into my shirt. Correct me if I'm wrong here but hadn't I taken her dancing every week, gone ice skating at Alexandra Palace whenever she'd wanted, taken rides out on the tram where I bought her ice-creams and winter bottoms, helped her climb stiles in pencil tight skirts, when she really should have been wearing slacks, and piggy-backed her with some difficulty whenever the ground got too muddy? Hadn't I?

It's true, I didn't buy her the scarf but only because Joe got there first and we couldn't find a similar one for me to buy. We'd looked at a little handbag but Joe thought Ethel liked the large sort, we'd panicked and left saying we'd have to think about it, but we never could think about it enough to make up our minds.

Just as I'm learning to avoid antagonism at home, I land myself with a female hell bent on my ruin. I don't need a reputation for playing dirty, and I don't deserve one, but Ethel will make damn sure I get one, she'll take her losses badly.

Joe tells me I have to lie low, the women in the factory are on the warpath, I am the factory cad, Pretty Boy Denny Pell contributing cheerfully to their cause, an irony not missed on Joe and I, to whom I have repeated the story of his sisterly betrothals.

The days at the factory are gloomy without the friendly banter of the girls, who in inverse proportion to their hatred of me have turned up their charm on Joe, presumably so that I can witness my loss.

After another grim day of low lying, I slink home from work to find a visitor sitting at the kitchen table, her handbag clutched to her bosom, a handkerchief pushed against her nose as if to defend herself from infestations in the air. Grandma Bess has arrived on an unannounced, uninvited visit to her son who, she is pointing out, has not taken the trouble to visit her in nearly two years. Grandma Bess is annoyed, justifiably so it seems to me.

'You'd of thought that just once in two years he could of dropped in, but obviously not, he's far too busy to spare me any time, or his father, or his younger brother for that matter. I'm not expecting him to stay long, just long enough to let me know how he is. For all I know, he could be dead.'

'He's not dead.'

'Well he could be dead for all I know, Mary, gone up in smoke or knocked down by a tram, for all I know. And here I am, sixty-years-old, having to ride three trolleys to get from Walthamstow to see him. What does he think I am, a young woman? I'm not, I'm sixty, sixty-one next birthday, a mother needs to know her children are alive and well. It's only natural.'

'He's not dead, Bessie.'

'And it's disrespectful. A mother looks after her children until the tide turns and then they look after her back. You see it everywhere, apart from here that is, where you've got an inconsiderate son who doesn't think to let his mother know whether he lives or dies, and a wife who knows what it's like to be a mother and should be reminding her husband to get in touch. Men find it difficult to remember these things; that's what a wife is for.'

'He's not dead, Bessie.'

Mum continues to receive Grandma's barrage. Gran looks much older than I remember, gnarled and wrinkly, her skin squashed into crumbly folds that are both crusty and soft at the same time. I compare her to my other Grandma, whose decline I have been party to, witnessed every Saturday when I've been sent to Jacksons Road to do her chores, a decline that insinuated itself so gradually into daily life that I was blind to its happening.

I can see the rheumy wetness around the old lady's eyes, her fat knees bulging beneath her skirts, her broad hips spreading themselves away from the buttock bones to droop over the edges of the chair. The only occasion on which the two grans had met was Mum and Dad's wedding. Each had stood hooked proprietarily to their own child, staring solidly at the camera. It hadn't been their idea of a good match; he could have done better, as could she.

With hindsight, they had turned out to be a perfectly matched couple. What began on the wedding day, the toasting of the bride and groom, had unwittingly heralded the slow slide into the now permanent anaesthesia of alcoholic oblivion.

Gran is reprimanding Mum on the mess around the sink, the slops bucket needs emptying. Her jowls, falling in swathes to curtain the sides of her face, bobble up and down as she talks.

Having stood in the doorway watching, I move to place my bag on the table and nod a hello to gran; she changes tack to grill Mum about our rooms, pausing imperceptibly to nod back. Has her son thought of applying for better accommodation?

No, Mum thinks he probably hasn't.

Has he got a job now that there's more work around?

No again, he hasn't.

Grandma Bess grows red in the face. I cross the room to fetch her a glass of water.

Mum is also getting agitated. I can see her mind has wandered to where Dad is, to the addled inmates of the bar, amongst whom she neither has to speak nor defend herself.

Running through Mum's head will be the tirade she throws at him whenever she is under pressure: he should be here to sort this situation; he should solve this problem, he should get a job, he should pay the rent, he should deal with his own mother.

Mum jumps up, stopping Gran in mid flow; she is going out to see if she can find him.

'You wait there Bessie, I won't be long, I'll run and meet him as he comes along the road from work, hurry him up, he'll be so surprised and so pleased to see you. Ray will keep you company.'

I know exactly what this means. It is seven o'clock. She is going to fetch Dad from the pub, and she will bring him home when it closes, sometime after midnight.

Grandma Bess doesn't know this, yet.

'So, how've you been keeping, Ray? You're looking fine. Eleys treating you well?' I slip in a nod. 'My Arthur's still at home you know. Such a good lad. You should come across and see him sometime. He'd like that. He used to love having your Billy come to stay, such a shame, such a pity, we often talk about him.' She sighs and looks distractedly at the wall.

'How's Charlie getting along? I hear he managed to get back into the printworks, sounds like he's going to be a grafter. Look how tall you've grown; you've got your dad's strong jawbone, I'll warrant you that. Are you foreman yet at Eleys? I hear they're on the lookout for management, you'd be just the sort of chap they'd push up the ladder, if you've a mind for it. You were lucky to get in there, fell on your feet, as usual. Always were the lucky one, weren't you Ray. Why don't you come on Saturday and you can stay the night, and Sunday night as well if you've a mind to? You can go to work from our place.'

I calculate the journey from Walthamstow to Waltham Abbey, it is quite a hike but it could be worth it, home is miserable and I'd be pleased to get away, a few days would do me good. I reckon the journeying might be worth the effort.

'I'll come across this weekend then, Gran.'

'Your mum and dad won't mind?'

'Why would they?'

She gives me a long look. In her mind, a family that doesn't care if their children are there or not has a deep and unpleasant flaw, but she lets this pass.

'No need to bring anything. You're about Arthur's size if you need to borrow.'

She runs on, delighted at the prospect of a visitor, determined not to let me slip through her fingers. Grandma Bess and I sit and wait.

After an hour or so she wonders aloud where Mum and Dad can be, will they be home before she has to go to feed Arthur? She starts to fidget. I fetch her another glass of water. I would like to offer her some tea but I know we haven't any in the house.

'This isn't good enough, Ray. In fact, it's a disgrace.' She has guessed where they are. 'Why do you put up with it?'

I shrug. 'What else can I do? They're okay, Gran, we muddle along.'

'Have you had any tea?'

'I ate at work.'

'Everyone eats at work, Ray. Then they eat again when they get home.'

'I'm not that hungry.'

She stands up quickly; she has made up her mind. 'I have to be going now, to get Arthur and your grandad's tea. You're to promise me you'll come and visit, don't change your mind.'

She snatches at her handbag and rustles out of the room, surprisingly sprightly despite her weight. I stand at the top of the stairs listening to the tutting that wafts up the stairwell as she makes her way out onto the street.

Walthamstow it is then, every other weekend for the Saturday night, trying hard not to make ripples at home, slipping into the new pattern as imperceptibly as possible.

But I enjoy it so much, my visits begin to stretch to include Friday and Sunday, and then I am spending every weekend there, having such a good time, talking with Arthur about everything and especially about Billy.

My happiness alone is enough to prompt the inevitable row at home, but what really sets her off is that I let slip that I am giving Gran four shillings for each weekend. Mum doesn't think this is necessary. She thinks I should go to visit and let Grandma keep me, after all, we're family. We don't charge them every time they come to visit us, and besides, all my money is needed at home. There are some obvious flaws in this argument but Mum works herself up into a lather all the same.

'How dare she take money out of our purse, she's no right to take what doesn't belong to her.'

A door creaks open along the corridor for a neighbour's ear to enjoy our squabble, more juice for the landlord when he next calls for overdue rent.

'She hasn't worked hard for it, she isn't struggling to put food on the table. You tell her you can't pay the money to her anymore, it's needed here.'

'I wouldn't feel right not offering her anything, Mum.'

'It's enough you have to pay all the fares to get there. That's money could be spent in this household.'

'Not for food though, Mum.' I lose my calm and say things I should keep to myself. 'There's never any money left over for food. We couldn't even offer Grandma a slice of dry bread when she came. It was shameful.'

She blinks at me, a little surprised. I am now almost a foot taller than Mum, a fact I don't suppose she has noticed before this evening. 'Don't get lippy, Raymond,' she says, steadying herself lightly against the wall.

'Nor for cleaning stuff. There's no money to keep the rooms clean. The place is a mess and it stinks. Visitors, and there are noticeably few of them, hold their noses against the stench.'

'You wait till your father gets in,' she says, her words catching on each other, her tongue becoming tangled with her teeth.

'Wait for what, so's we can watch him falling over with the drink as well?'

She'd like to stop this line of conversation. 'You're only going over there so's you can get out whoring.'

I am appalled that she should say this. 'I'd be touched if I thought you cared.' Now she's got me mad. 'I go to Walthamstow for a warm bath, a hot meal and a clean bed, for a couple of nights a week. And it's nice to talk to people who can stand upright. Is this how you drove Billy away? I should have paid more mind to Billy, he could see what I had coming to me.'

Mum stares at the wall. 'Going over there so's you can give away my money to others as don't need it.'

'Grandma Bess has got every right to the money. She does something useful with it. She feeds me for a start, and she buys me things.'

'What sort of things is she buying you? Where are these things?' She pushes herself away from the wall to grab hold of me but unable to direct her actions to any effect, she sinks into a chair at the kitchen table.

Charlie wanders into the room. He's been working an evening shift at the printworks; his arms have been dyed a deep indigo that without hot water and soap he is unable to shift. He crosses the inked appendages and leans back against the wall, watching impassively, his brows furrowing. I cast him a nervous glance, I don't like him to see her like this.

'Well I don't bring them here do I, Mum,' I say, softening my voice for Charlie's sake. 'They'd be straight in the pawn if I did.'

'What sort of talk is it then that's so special? Talk about me, I suppose. Very cosy. About how I'm not good enough for her precious son. About how he should have married the girl that lived next door, that knew how to sew and cook, and was so popular with all the grown-ups.'

'She never mentions you, Mum.'

This isn't true.

She thinks her son is a waster and her daughter-in-law no better; she is thoroughly ashamed of them both. She thinks I should move out permanently and leave them to their own devices. She thinks this is no way to live and I should go and live with her and Grandad where she could put a proper roof over my head. What's to stop me?

You'll be sorry, one day I'll move out for good!
Fine. Go.

That's what's to stop me. The thought of hearing from her own lips that she doesn't care, of seeing the emptiness in her eyes, which I make believe isn't there.

Grandad has heard all about our home from Grandma; she doesn't spare any details, but he's a kindly old man who won't rock the boat, won't dwell on what he can't change; he makes up for it by treating me special when I'm there, giving me good thoughts to take home. He says everyone needs a bit of loving.

That's what I need to do, I need to find that bit of loving, that pair of eyes that don't welcome me for my pay packet only to chide me for its lightness. Someone to sing:

Won't you come home, Ray Riley?
Won't you come home?
You've been away too long.

Like Grandad sings when he knows I'm listening.

He potters around the tiny house, taking Grandma's arm as she passes with his dinner tray, spinning her in a pirouette before twirling away to explore a jacket pocket for a bright white handkerchief. I am shy and delighted by their intimacy, grateful for the contrast with home, thankful that they welcome me by letting me see their pleasure.

No, I won't bring home gifts or stories from Walthamstow as I know Mum will discredit them and it will spoil my refuge.

Chapter 10

For Love Of Arthur

Last weekend I went with Grandad to help him haul heavy wood home from the wood-yard; gales had played mighty havoc with Grandma's fence and Grandad had promised to fix it.

This week I've another job to do: I'm to go with Gran to the market, to help her carry her bags home. What with the arthritis in her joints and the rickets in her legs, it's a struggle on her own.

The string bags, filled with potatoes, cooking apples, flour and butter are cutting across my palms, stopping the circulation at my fingertips, which have gone white. Gran weaves from stall to stall and I follow in her wake.

It isn't quite the thing for a lad running on twenty to be out shopping with his gran, but this isn't my turf and I'm not likely to bump into anyone I know. In any case, it's what happens in normal families, I see it plenty of times, I even nod at other sons and grandsons who have been forced into similar labour. We shrug our fake discontent. *But what's a lad to do?* we signal to each other. *It could be worse.*

I pretend I am one of them. I pretend I too am one of the walking wounded, long suffering in the expectations of my elders. Whereas in fact, my pretence is a front, a cover up behind which I hide the fact that that is precisely what I am, I am one of the walking wounded. I don't suffer any impressive amputation or hold my arm in a pitiful sling, but I can see my wound clear as daylight in my head, where no one knows about it, sitting right here, blazoned on the inside of my skull just for me to consider. Homeless, is what it says, I am a displaced person, a rejected piece of flotsam. It would be a golden pleasure to know someone sought my company, just for me.

Wounded soldier that I am, I will not let them win; no one is interested in a soldier who is only a little brave, and someone is going to be very interested in me.

I pull myself up straight, tuck my shoulder blades into my back and stride after gran, gulping in the smell of the bakery, occasionally dropping the bags to smooth my hand over the rolls of embroidery fabrics, turning the bobbins and buttons alongside her as she hunts for just the right shade of blue for her curtains.

Gran has made me a shirt, the first new piece of cloth I have worn since Great Aunt Lizzie's; the smell of the cotton, its fresh stiffness, makes me stand tall again as I had for my aunt.

Negotiating my way between other browsers I slip in close to gran, sniffing fondly at the combined scents of her Lily of the Valley soap and the chalky rose of her face powder. Exhaling a long breath, I clear a sharp pain in my shoulder, my clenched muscles relaxing to lose their grip, like a snake shedding its former skin.

She looks up and smiles. 'What about this shade, Ray.'

'Looks good to me, Gran,' I say, winking at the young girl serving, who winks back.

The market is bubbling with fruitful transactions and commodities desired. Trolleys clatter over cobbles, which growl happily, vendors call out the delights of their produce in an attempt to arrest the attention of us, the passers-by, the would-be punters. Gran hooks her arm around mine and leaning on me, steers me forward.

She stops at one of the vegetable stalls to poke the cabbages. 'I've to do something special for this weekend.' She is squeezing her way through a pile of dark green foliage, opening the leaves to check for what she loudly calls livestock. The stallholder frowns. 'Arthur's bringing home his girl to meet us.'

I grin an apology at the stallholder.

'I reckon they'll be good enough Mrs, even for Arthur's girl,' he says.

'This one please,' says Gran, ignoring him.

'We're to get out a table cloth.' Gran digs her elbow sharply into my ribs making me stumble with my load. She giggles.

Arthur, six years older than me and really my uncle, being Dad's youngest brother, though I've never seen him that way and he's made no fuss of me calling him by his first name, is going to have difficulty finding a girl good enough for his mother.

Arthur is a seriously good looking bloke, and this is his problem. Gran assumes every girl that gets him has tricked her way into his affections, Arthur being such an easy going, gentle type of guy.

He is tall, like Dad, and he stands straight and high, his slender waist topped by a triangular torso, wide shoulders tapering down to the slim hips. Whenever I'm walking along with him the girls turn and stare at us; we pretend not to notice, at least I'm pretending, there is a possibility that Arthur doesn't actually notice, he never mentions them.

He's not over talkative, which suits me nicely as I get enough of that from Joe, whose promotion to under foreman at the factory has brought with it an easy confidence and a lot more chat. But Arthur's silence is never oppressive, he simply observes, considers and files away, an easy silence that occasionally rumbles up into a quiet laugh as something tickles his eyesight, giving rise to a mini eruption of mirth. He's infectious. My eyes glance in the direction of his to work out the cause of his amusement. He'll smile at me, point to ensure I've caught his drift, throw his arm across my shoulder and wander along thus embraced for a few paces, until a new distraction throws him off on another train of thought.

'Ella, her name is. And Arthur says he hopes I'll like her very much.'

'Sounds serious, Gran.'

She presses her lips tightly together and nods.

Chapter 11

You Have To Be In A Good Place
For Good Things To Happen

I have been sitting on the back step shucking peas into an enamel colander. Gran has busied herself quietly all morning, deep in thought. It is twelve o'clock. The potatoes are roasted to a crispy amber; the cabbage, washed clean of the livestock, has been boiling for nearly an hour; the linen is thick and creamy on the table, Grandad has cut a few London Flag stems from his garden and placed them in a vase at the centre. Gran goes upstairs to change into a high-necked blouse.

When she returns, we take our places in the tiny hallway, standing to attention, squashed in our efforts to be both formal and welcoming.

The gate hinge creaks and Arthur's key scratches at the latch, we jostle around in a nervous flurry, I don't know who is more excited, me or Grandad.

Arthur flings open the door. Grandad dives to shake Ella's hand as Arthur tries clumsily to remove her coat.

We all speak at once.

'So lovely to meet you at last, my dear.'

'Won't you come through.'

'Mine's Ray, I'm the nephew that's more of a cousin, pleased to meet you.'

Arthur leads her to a seat next to him at the dining table; Gran slips away to the kitchen.

'Well now, Ella, tell us all about yourself. Are you warm enough, dear? Would you prefer to sit over here by the fire? There's so little of you, you can't have any fat keeping you warm. Does she ever eat, Arthur?'

'I'm fine, thank you, Mr Riley. The Flags are a lovely colour,' she says, peering round the tall floral display.

'We grow them ourselves, don't we love,' he calls through to the kitchen, where pans are being dropped loudly into the sink. 'Providing you put them in the sunshine up against a warm wall they do just fine. Arthur can cut you some to take home if you like.' Arthur starts to answer as Gran appears with the serving dish.

'That smells splendid, doesn't it Arthur?' Arthur looks at Ella but I am guessing his mind stays firmly on his mother.

She's a pretty little thing, her dark hair curling loosely around her face, black eyes nestling lazily beneath the precise sweep of her eyebrows. I can see why Arthur is love-struck. Gran's back stiffens as she takes her seat; she can see also.

'It's nothing much, just an ordinary chicken.'

'The potatoes look perfect, better than my mum's ever do, don't they Arthur?'

Arthur laughs nervously.

'They're not quite my usual standard but they'll do.'

'You have very high standards then, love,' says Grandad, easing into the conversation in an effort to smooth his wife's nerves. 'Be so kind as to pass me the carving knife, Arthur.'

Grandad hacks away at the bird to distribute wedges of chicken onto gran's best china.

'Are you a breast or a leg man, Ray?' he smirks.

'That'll be enough, thank you,' says Grandma, tartly.

'Very high standards indeed,' he continues, his lips quivering at the edges.

'I like to think so,' says Gran.

Arthur studies the tablecloth, believing she intends this as a thinly veiled comment to mean that Ella is not quite the full florin; his knee is bouncing up and down making the table vibrate. Ella smiles around at everyone, blissfully ignorant of the jury's verdict.

Against Gran's better judgement, Ella becomes a regular visitor, usually for Sunday dinner or sometimes tea, depending on her and Arthur's plans. We play cards and dominoes through the cold winter weekends but as spring returns, they venture back out to the countryside for their walks. One Sunday Ella asks me to go out with them.

'No thanks, Ella, two's company and all that.'

'Nonsense. It's a lovely day, come on. We're taking the tram out to Chingford Mount, we'll have a picnic.'

I look at Arthur.

'Mum'll be pleased to see the back of us all, won't you Mum?' he says.

Gran nods, her eyes not lifting from the knitting pattern.

'I'll grab my jacket.'

I dash around, pulling off yesterday's shirt, puffing my breath into my hands to check its acceptability and throwing cold water under my arms. Gran keeps the fire burning the year round and the room is a sweatbox. I run a comb under the water and glide it through my hair. Not bad, I think, studying the results, casual but slick. My chiselled face looks back, excited. It's good of them to invite me, fresh air and fields, oxygen in my lungs, exactly what I need to clear the winter smog.

The three of us head for the tram, Ella hooking her arms through both of ours, our footfalls settling into an easy, loping rhythm. Ella talks, we listen, occasionally Arthur mumbles.

Arthur's jumper must be hot, is it hot? she wonders. The breeze whipping at her skirt is fresh, *Perhaps she should have worn a thicker one, do we think she'll be cold?* Her shoes are new, *Do we like them?* Arthur's change is jangling in his pocket, *Doesn't that annoy him?*

We are not meant or allowed space to respond, she is perfectly happy in her own private conversation.

I steal a glance across at Arthur; his spare arm swings loosely at his side, a mop of soft curls fluff in the wind, a small smile flickers on his face. That is where I need to be, in that place that feels safe, where you are not always on the alert, anticipating trouble. Arthur's there, Joe's there, lucky sods.

I leave Aunt Lizzie's to return to the bosom of my family, when the bosom of the family doesn't want me. Well, I'm not going to let them pull me down; I'll just have to find a bosom that does.

Arthur looks across and catches my eye. He grins, as people sometimes do when simultaneous ideas cross their minds.

No tram can carry us to the top of The Mount, it is too steep, so we travel as far as The Albert Pub where we get out to continue on foot. Ella buys a cake in one of the few remaining shops before the fields overrun the houses, stopping to stretch her feet outside her shoes. Looking up, she contemplates the steepness of the hill.

'Lily!' she calls suddenly, to a young woman coming out of the shop. 'Lily Cartwright? It's me, Ella Foster.'

Lily Cartwright's long auburn hair is caught by the breeze to flutter like a flag in the sunshine, it reminds me of mermaid's hair being tickled by sea currents. When she turns her face to Ella's call, I stifle a gasp, which Ella kindly smothers with a laugh. This is not any old mermaid, this is the Queen of the Mermaids, with skin, untainted by make-up, a cold creamy richness as befits a creature of the deep, its whiteness tinged blue in accordance with her royal blood. Across her nose a few faint freckles are sprinkled, like gold dust on alabaster, the merest hint that she is human after all. Her mouth, a coral bloom, is graceful and welcoming. Her ears, dainty and shell-like, prepare themselves to hear the pleas of her subjects.

Trying hard not to look obvious and failing abysmally, my eyes flick over the rest of the mermaid and are indecently excited by what they see: curvaceous without being buxom, feminine without being frail. I return to the face, its deep green eyes have long straight lashes. A challenging, almost defiant face; I believe I can rise to the challenge, I know I must.

'How are you?' Ella is saying. 'You remember Arthur, of course. And this is his cousin, Ray.'

I pounce forward, thrusting myself in front of Arthur, taking her small hand in mine to force my palm against her own.

'You're looking well, considering,' says Ella, carefully. 'Gran said you've been nursing your mum. How is she? Keeping you fit, by the look of it.' Glancing up the steepness of The Mount, Ella comes to a decision. 'Do you want to join us for a picnic up there. I could do with some female company.'

Yes.

Say yes.

Yes would be really good.

'No, I can't, I'm afraid.'

'Arh, come on Lily. I don't want to be the only one they moan at for being slow. Come on,' Ella urges. 'We've got a cake and some ginger beer. You've got, what've you got in your bag?' Ella peeps in. 'Biscuits! Ideal. Come on, it'll be fun.'

Real fun.

More fun than you can possibly imagine.

So much fun you'll be knocked for six and the Gods will be astonished at your interest in us mere mortals.

Ella is speaking to me. 'Lily's nan and your gran are old school friends, they go way back.'

I nod enthusiastically.

Think of a witty retort, any witty retort.

An inane grin is all I can muster, reminiscent of that barmy boy from Bedlam.

'I really can't. I'm on my way to my uncle's for tea, in Diana Road. The biscuits are for him. I come across when Mum isn't too poorly, for a change of scenery really. They're expecting me.'

'Well, what are you doing after tea? You could come out with us for the evening, couldn't she Arthur?'

Please, please, please!

We could live at the bottom of the sea.

Sea is fine, wet but I'd get used to it.

What's wet, between friends.

I look across at Arthur to see if he's okay about having us tag along. Speak now Arthur or forever hold your peace. Arthur is distracted by a loose thread unravelling from a button on his jacket. For Pete's sake.

'That would be fine,' I blurt. 'As you can see, Arthur has more pressing things to attend to.'

Arthur has no objections; he is in love with Ella, what difference does it make to him if someone else is around, he might even enjoy showing off his love to a new audience.

Lily is wavering. 'Where will you be going?'

'We'll walk out somewhere, by Connaught Waters maybe, it's pretty out there.'

The mermaid hesitates, still unsure. 'Well, I don't know the place, but I'll come if you like. I won't be able to stay too long though, Dad will worry.'

Yes, yes, yes!

I burst into a sweat, the nearest thing I can do to a public yelp without looking a complete idiot.

'We could call round for you at six,' I say, eager to clinch the assignation.

She turns to look at me for the first time, she knows the deal; I feel a flush of terror burning the back of my neck.

'I'll meet you on the corner at five thirty,' she corrects.

'Okay.'

As she walks away in the direction of Diana Road, I launch myself off the ground to punch the summer air.

A bosom, a bosom, at last, a bosom.

I am more nervous than I dare show Arthur, and Grandad would only tease. Gran irons the shirt she made for me and sweeps down my jacket with the clothes brush. I sneak a glance at it to see if it is a Kleeneze brush; it is.

Every time I think I'm ready, I feel the sweat trickling in my arm pits and I have to take my clothes off again to sloosh, pat myself dry and lie on the bed, my arms flung wide, listening to the thud, thud, thud of my heart. Eventually there's no putting it off any longer.

'Are you coming, Casanova?' calls Ella from the bottom of the stairs.

'Be right down.'

I try for laid-back and careless but Ella sees through me in an instant.

'My, aren't you looking sweet,' she grins, and seeing me flush, explodes into a laugh. 'Oh, come on Ray, let's get you there before you pass out.'

The evening starts well. We catch a tram out to Connaught Waters, a nicely crowded tram requiring us to squash up close on the seats.

Sitting gingerly at first, trying not to brush too close, I soon give way to the trams swaying and loll heavily in her direction. She smells sweet, soapy flowers, reminding me of Great Aunt Lizzie.

I pretend to listen as Ella points out features of the journey: places where she's been caught short and had to spend a penny, metal grills where she has tripped, lost her heel and been rescued by a passing Galahad, doorways in which she has sheltered from downpours, so torrential she hasn't been able to see as far as the other side of the street, never mind get home in time for her curfew. 'Where've you been, the back end of beyond?' her dad had moaned. Three sets of eyes follow her guided tour, smiling indulgently, grateful for her banter, saving any of us from having to invent our own wit or intrigue.

The sun has streaked the sky pink by the time we arrive at the lake. Arthur and Ella walk on ahead, arm in arm, giggling, stopping occasionally to wonder at Arthur's stone throwing. Lily and I follow behind, talking about the lake, how deep it might be, whether it holds fish, whales, mermaids? How dense the forest is, whether the night draws out fox, badger, small deer? Easy talk, nothing clever.

She has a light, gentle laugh, a trickling, gurgling sound, like water disturbing loose pebbles in a stream. A laugh that lurks, bides its time, springs up unexpectedly and not to any pattern. It makes me work hard to establish an approach that pleases, probing for common ground, running indiscernible checks on her history, trying as casually as possible to assess the likelihood of my fantasy becoming a reality, and all the while, chasing that elusive ripple of laughter.

The ground around the lake is hummocky and in the dusk we repeatedly topple onto each other until finally she puts her arm through mine to steady us. Arthur looks back at one point to see how we are, he has become my guardian. He smiles and waves.

The sky has turned to a navy blue night when Lily becomes agitated. 'I've three trams to catch to get home from here; I've usually left my uncle's by seven. Mum and Dad will be worried if I'm not in by eleven.'

'I can see you home, if you'd like.'

'Well, if it's not too much trouble, thank you.'

It is not too much trouble at all but the evening trams are slow in coming and Lily is unsettled by the lateness of the hour, her previous lightness becomes tinged with regret and concern. Although I notice this, I am punch drunk with excitement, my nerves balanced somewhere between pain and delight. I'm not thinking very clearly when I ask, 'Is it much further?'

'You did ask to take me home, I didn't ask you to. You can go back if you like. I'm quite used to looking after myself, I really don't mind.'

'No, it's not that. I was just wondering how far, that's all.'

'But honestly, I don't mind if you go. It is a long way for you to come and I don't want to put you out.'

'No, I want to stay, to see you home safely.'

All that hard work thrown away on a misthought sentence.

'I'd like us to meet again, next Saturday maybe, what d'you think?'

'Well I don't know. I'm needed so much at home at the moment. And I'll still live the same distance away.'

'That's not a problem. I was only up visiting my Gran today, I'm not often out that way myself. It'll be easier to get to you from my place, but it wouldn't be a problem even if it wasn't.'

She seems to soften a little. 'Well, if you don't mind, if you're sure,' she says, a little too distractedly for my liking.

This isn't the enthusiasm I was hoping for.

'Shall I pick you up at seven? We could go dancing?'

'That would be nice. It's a long time since I've been to the dance hall, almost a year in fact. I doubt I'll know the latest steps, you'll have to guide me.' She smiles, as if she has finally granted herself permission to enjoy the idea. 'I'll meet you on Kenninghall Road.'

She appears to want to keep me at a distance; whatever arrangement is suggested she alters it, just a little. I try not to mind this, but I certainly notice.

The week until we next meet takes a month to live through, it's like waiting for Mum to smile: I wait for it with every nerve in my body.

Get a grip Raymond Riley I chide, you're in danger of blowing a gasket. Will she be the same? Did she topple toward me intentionally as we walked? Does she like me? And the big question, how much does she like me?

I'm frustrated that I didn't manage to pull off a happy ending last weekend but she was tired, I tell myself, strained by our first meeting. In an effort to make time move more quickly I imagine alternative finales, ones in which I sweep her off her feet, ones in which she falls on me in a distracted swoon.

Thus absorbed, I drop materials at work, misconnect parts on the assembly line and mislay tools. Twice I forget to eat my lunch. I am checking the clock for the hundredth time that minute when the boss comes to give me a warning to pull my socks up.

Joe, who has seen him heading my way, wanders past to pat me on the shoulder.

'Nice is she?'

'Joe, she's heavenly.'

When Saturday finally arrives I am ready early, my mood swinging wildly between bravado and terror. Supposing she doesn't turn up. Should I go to her house to find her? She might need help. Her mother could have taken a turn for the worse. Will she be there? She might leave me waiting, some girls do.

As I turn the corner I see her, looking casually into a shop window, dressed in a pale green tailored suit, the seams of her stockings drawn straight up the back of her slim calves, neat little shoes laced across the tiniest insteps. Her dark red hair is caught up in a complicated arrangement of net and pins.

'Hello, Lily, good to see you, you're looking nice.' I don't know what to do. I can't kiss her, though I want to. I hold out my hand to offer a handshake.

'Hello.' She appears surprised, as if I have startled her out of reverie. 'I was miles away. Do you still want to go dancing, only I'm not sure I've got the energy, it's been such a difficult week. But don't let it stop you, I can always go another time?'

That's thrown me. Now I'm confused. Is this a brush off? I lose my nerve.

'Would you prefer to call for Arthur and Ella, to go out with them again?' I ask.

'I'm easy.'

In my opinion, which I don't voice, she is anything but.

We catch the tram across to grans but Arthur and Ella have already gone out. Things are not going to plan.

'Let's see if we can find them, perhaps they've gone to The Albert.'

This is my big mistake, starting the process of trailing from pub to pub on the hunt for Arthur and Ella, who it really doesn't matter if we find or not. I can tell she isn't enjoying this but having begun the trail I can't find a way to end it.

'They could be over in The Green Man? What do you think?'

'I'd like to go home Ray, if it's all the same with you.' My heart sinks. I've blown it.

We are more comfortable with each other when we settle on the tram. Relieved not to be aimlessly walking the streets, we talk easily as we had at the lake, about school days, our work, and housing shortages. I discover she enjoys skating.

'We could go skating if you like.'

I take her as far as her doorstep where she hesitates, reluctant to invite me in. I wonder if I can pull off a good ending this time, though my bruised courage is in need of help. I daren't ask her if she's enjoyed herself as I know she hasn't. And I'd like to explain that a pub crawl didn't suit me either, but I'm none too keen to expose myself to questions on that score, not yet anyway.

'Thank you for bringing me home,' she begins. 'It's been really nice meeting you Ray, and at any other time, in other circumstances, I'd be delighted to see you again but I don't think…'

I fall on her, anything to stop that sentence. My fingers snag in the fine mesh of her snood. Trying to ignore it, I place my lips firmly on hers but miss the target, slipping off the glossy crimson wax to smear away across her cheek causing a nasty red gash. Tugging at my fingers the hair net gives way, releasing a metal waterfall of hairpins. We both look to the floor and as our heads go down, our foreheads clunk together.

This is so going well, I think.

She bursts out laughing.

'Shall we try that again?' I suggest, I am beginning to master ludicrous.

Lily smiles a disarmingly warm smile. 'Some other time perhaps, when I've got my breath back, and my armour on.'

'What about next Saturday then?'

Fingers crossed, I watch as her thoughts move from farce, to consideration, to oh why not.

'Okay. I'll meet you at the tram stop at seven.'

'I'll call for you at six-thirty,' I say.

I'm getting the hang of this. I can be a determined bugger when I want to be and right now I want to be, now that I know this is the bosom I plan to stake.

Chapter 12

She Came To Slay My Dragons

There is no waiting for Saturday. By Tuesday morning I've made up my mind; by Wednesday evening I'm on her doorstep.

We are all on different tracks. Some men are desperate for cash in the bank, looking for any way to show they've arrived, to say to their fellow man, you'd better watch out for me as I've got cash in the bank. Another heads for an entirely different deposit box, hunting sexual conquests, saying to himself, *surely I must be better than you, I am incapable of selecting just one of them but who in their right mind would hold that against me.* Others yet strive for domination, in the dubious belief that power will automatically bring them happiness. Me, I'm looking for love, pure and simple.

On the way home from work I stop at the Hackney Baths to prepare myself for the visit. Joe comes too.

'How's it going then?'

'Magic, Joseph, pure magic.'

A man can dream, I tell myself, and anyway, conversations are full of half-truths and lies, it doesn't change the facts.

Joe smiles through a waxy film of white lather, his feet hooked up over the end of the bath in his cubicle. I know this because I am doing the same in mine.

'Where'd you meet her? *More hot in Number Seven, please,*' he calls to the attendant.

'Over at Arthur's, she's an old friend of Ella's, Arthur's girl. Plus we've got history: her nan and my gran were best mates at school.'

I listen as Number Seven receives a burst of hot water.

'Well that should stand you in good stead. And a looker you reckon?'

'Not just me, don't go taking my word for it. Heads swivel as she walks down the street. Why she hasn't been snapped up I don't know. Ella reckons she's choosy. *Hot in Six, when you're ready mate.'*

'And she's choosing you?' I have a picture of Joe's eyebrows bobbing around somewhere near his hairline, a smile creeping across his lips.

'And she's choosing me, Joe,' may heaven look out for me.

'Perhaps there's a dark secret.' He pauses to invent something unpleasantly tantalising. 'You've checked both legs are screwed on tight?'

'Not yet, Joe, early days, early days.'

'If she's as heavenly as you claim, are you sure she's real, not some spectral Siren...' Joe's head disappears under the water and I hear gurgling remnants of his conversation.

'... The Lady of the Lake come to tempt you back into the water.'

'She's been sent to slay my dragons, Joe. I know exactly why she's here.'

'What dragons are they then?'

'What flaming dragons do you think they would be?'

The next door cubicle goes quiet for a few seconds, no longer; Joe's not one to take offence.

'Where did you say she lived?'

'Down Hoxton way.'

'Ah yes, very magical Hoxton. You've not been there yet then?'

'Only as far as the doorstep. I plan to storm the barricade this evening. Hence all the soap.'

'Bearing flowers for the mother?'

'You reckon?'

'I know, my son, I know.'

Where had the days gone when he dived for cover from my clods of earth, when even those that missed claimed his life? You're dead. You're dead. Now he is the one dispensing advice and expertise. To my credit, Joe has turned out something dapper. I might claim to be the making of the man, give me the boy and all that, but I don't say anything, I wouldn't want to take away his moment.

'You've set a date then,' I say, when I can hear Joe has surfaced, leading him on to his favourite subject.

'All arranged, Ray, though it'll be a long time coming. Susan wants a long engagement, to give her time to fill the bottom drawer, and thanks for agreeing to be best man.'

Joe coughs.

'You know, Ray, I only went for the foreman post because of Susan, because of needing a nest egg, so's she'd know I was serious, you know that don't you?'

He's a funny guy. Joe being a foreman makes no difference to me. You might think he would Lord it a bit, I might, if I were in his place, it's easily done, a bit of power, as I've said, can go to a man's head, but not Joe's. If he plays the gaffer just a little in the privacy of his thoughts, for fun like, which he'd have every right to do, then good luck to him.

'Good luck to you, Joe. You've worked hard for it. When I own the factory I'll make sure you're my second in command, you'll have had no end of practise by then. Till then, I'm thinking of getting off the line and getting myself a trade.'

Joe laughs, relieved to have got that off his chest.

Back home, I spruce up nicely, keeping a check on the time. Lily gets off work at five thirty, and I've no intention of arriving late, I don't want to surprise them in their night clothes. It's unusual for me to go out on a Wednesday night, especially smelling as sweetly as I do; Mum lifts her nose as I pass but says nothing.

Charlie looks up. 'I hope she's worth it.'

He's a quiet lad and it is unusual for him to offer comment so I'm pleased he's noticed.

'Impressive eh? Even bought some blacking for the shoes,' I say quietly. I point a toe daintily in his direction.

If Mum is listening she makes no show of it.

Charlie looks at her. 'You bringing the lady home for tea?'

Mum doesn't lift her head.

'What do you think, Charlie?'

I have hidden the flowers under a bush so as not to attract hostility from Mum. Only one tram is needed, and I'm on my way.

Standing on her doorstep in the evening light, a small patch of earth pushing up some hardy spring shoots, I grin, reminding myself of other grins in which my determination to enjoy the moment has got the better of my common sense. This is it, Ray Riley, this is the life for you, what happens tonight could seal your fate. I give the door three sharp raps.

A man in a sage green knitted waistcoat answers the door.

'Yes young man, how can I help?'

'Good evening, Mr Cartwright.' My tongue had grown too large for my mouth blocking the words as they try to get out. 'I'm Ray Riley, I'm a friend of Lily's.'

'You are?' He looks genuinely surprised. 'Your face isn't familiar. Are you from the mission?'

In my stupidity, or nerves, when he says, *are you from the mission*, I hear, *are you on a mission.*

'Indeed I am, sir, and I've brought some flowers for the lady of the house, to help my cause.'

'Well, well, well, well, well, well. Whatever next. Do come in young man.' He calls to another room, 'Lilian, one of your friends has come, from the mission, and he has brought more flowers, how very, very kind. Do sit down, lad. What did you say your name was again? I expect you'd like to see her.' He drops his voice very slightly. 'She's lying in the parlour.'

'Raymond, sir, Raymond Riley.'

Lying in the parlour?

Mr Cartwright beckons me forward. I stand to follow.

The parlour lighting is dim. Net curtains hanging at the windows filter silver threads of evening beams onto a central table. A candle burning on a cabinet against the wall illuminates the small ovals of family portraits. I take in these dainty little details, speckled as if by a twilight haze, then turn with horror to the big event. On the table in the parlour is a pale beech coffin, and in the coffin lies Lily.

I think I'm going to be sick. I place one hand firmly on the edge of the coffin to steady myself, the other over my mouth. Sweat spouts from the pores on my head.

'Lovely isn't she?' whispers Mr Cartwright. 'You look lovely tonight, my dear,' he says to the coffin. 'Doesn't she look peaceful? Such a welcome release, wouldn't you say?'

I'd like to think I don't gawp, but that is exactly what I do. I turn to Mr Cartwright and I gawp. Mr Cartwright studies me for a second.

'You don't look very well, lad. Why don't you sit down. Let me fetch you a glass of water. You haven't seen too much of life passing, I would guess. But you mustn't worry. She's been released from a great deal of pain.'

A noise behind me makes me start. I turn to look and a rush of blood bursts into my ears; there in the doorway stands Lily. I bolt to my feet, my heart beating faster than it can cope with, and grab once more at the edge of the coffin.

'Steady on, lad, calm yourself. Take a few deep breaths. I didn't realise you were so close to my wife. It's always a shock when you first see someone you love, at rest. Here, let me get you that water.'

Wife?

I spin round and stare closely at the Lily in the coffin. It is Lily, but then it isn't. In the pale light I see the dark auburn hair has started to fade to a sandy grey at the temples; the hands, resting calmly on her chest, are speckled with the beginnings of tiny liver spots. But it is in the face, in the smooth ivory that looks more carved than grown, that age and death have settled, changing the living flesh into the waxy sheen of a china doll. Peering closer in the gloom the ravages of age and illness are only too clear. Lily, my Lily, the spectral ghost that Joe had warned me about, glides forward.

'This is not a good time, Ray, she's only here today, for her friends to visit, she's returning to the funeral parlour this evening.' As Lily speaks, two more mourners are shown into the room, their heads tilted in unison to the right, their hands pressed against their chests, each uttering their condolences to the bereaved.

Mr Cartwright returns with three glasses of water on a tray. I swallow the first glass in one gulp, swig the second almost as quickly, and stop half way through the third. Mr Cartwright's eyes have widened and Lily, the living one, takes my elbow and guides me back to lean against the parlour wall. I watch as one of the visiting friends affectionately pats the hand in the coffin and a shiver runs across my back.

'Just a few years ago,' says Lily, her voice barely audible, 'people would stop us in the street to marvel at the likeness.' Her pained face crumbles at the memory, her eyes, swollen and red from the day's vigil, spill tears that creep slowly down her fine cheeks, unchecked.

'She wasn't even grey at the temples a year ago; cancer is a terrible thing.'

The visitors leave and Lily moves to smooth the glossy folds of satin.

'We knew it was there, of course, and even when there were respites, in which she appeared almost normal, it hung in the room, like a cloud, heavy and threatening.'

I stare at Mr Cartwright on the other side of the coffin, he smiles sadly at the dead Lily.

'Pretty as pictures, the pair of them, never has a man been so happy or so blessed, as I have been with my two perfect works of art.'

We stand in silence for a few seconds until Mr Cartwright visibly shakes himself out of absorption.

'Let's go through to the sitting room. We'll leave you to rest,' he adds, somewhat unnecessarily I think, to his wife. I trail closely behind them, eager not to be left alone with the body.

'Now tell me,' Mr Cartwright is saying, 'how is it that you know my wife and what's this cause you speak of?'

In the sitting room I compose myself. Lily disappears and we listen as the tinkling of teacups announces the next in what has probably been a long line of brews. Mr Cartwright and I sit in exhausted silence until she returns. Lily pours. We hug the reviving tea to our chests, clustering in a friendly conspiracy around the embers of an evening fire.

Mr Cartwright is thinking about his daughter, how she will cope with only one parent. 'Are both your parents still living, Ray?' he asks, unaware that such a question might appear impertinent.

Lily tries to distract him. 'Would you like more tea, Dad?' He nods. 'Yes, they are,' she adds, when she sees he is waiting for an answer. She picks up his cup and saucer to take it through to the kitchenette.

'Just about,' I add quietly, so that Lily doesn't hear.

'Poorly are they? No, I mustn't say poorly, that's offensive,' he reprimands himself. 'I mustn't make light of life's afflictions.'

'Well you perhaps could in their case,' I say quietly, 'as their afflictions are self-inflicted.'

'What would that be then? The drink?'

Uncanny. I don't know him, he doesn't know me, yet here he is, going straight to the raw and probing the wound. He looks at me kindly, perhaps registering my reluctance to be tainted by this exposure.

'No need to feel ashamed, lad. What we haven't seen at the mission, Lilian and I, isn't worth seeing. We're a strange and complicated species, we humans, but for all that, we're all there is, so we might as well get used to us, warts and all.'

Still dwelling on his daughter, he continues.

'When Lily was first born, we couldn't believe the wonder of her. We would stand at the crib and stare, incredulous. We'd been told by the doctors that children were not for us, so we'd given up hope and then she came, our own little miracle, a piece of heaven for which we thanked Him every day. We know it's the same for everyone, we all feel that our baby is the most beautiful, pitying the other parents, knowing they must be looking at ours and wishing it was their own. *Your* mother would have done exactly the same.'

I look up, considering whether to raise an objection.

'But that's the good thing about humanity, we each manage to love ours better than anyone else's, that's a great system for any God to invent, don't you think, making us personally responsible for our own, and then helping us to believe we wouldn't have it any other way? He's a clever fellow, you've got to give Him credit.'

Mr Cartwright laughs at his easy familiarity with the biggest gaffer of them all. 'And here's you, knowing my Lilian and me knowing nothing about it. What a wonder it all is.'

I do not reply. His momentary enthusiasm soon lapses back into a solitary grief. In the kitchen I can hear Lily sobbing.

I have given some thought to death. Because of Billy, I have pondered long and hard and found nothing: a mystery, a game, dreamt up by a careless authority that plays by rules I cannot understand. The world gained nothing, advanced not one jot through Billy's sacrifice.

I had read Great Aunt Lizzie's bible. It claimed, with fancy writing and golden letters, that if we sacrificed our first born to Him he would know our faith and return that first born to us, unharmed. This did not happen. The system my God worked by is a far cry from the harmonic, embracing warmth of Mr Cartwright's God.

Lily returns from the kitchen and pats his arm. 'Ray and I might go for a short walk, would that be okay, Dad? Uncle Ernie will be here in a minute, he'll stay with you until we get back.'

'That's fine, Angel. You young things take a stroll, get acquainted; Lilian will be delighted. We'll just sit here for a while and watch the sun go down.'

Lily, the strain in her eyes belying the even tenor with which she speaks, tells me her mother passed away on Tuesday morning. Her father is having trouble adjusting to the past tense. Who wouldn't. When the time comes for me to say goodbye to my mother, warts and all, I will doubtless fall apart.

Chapter 13

A Wife's A Way Of Life

As the months pass the wound slowly, very slowly, starts to heal, and with this, Mr Cartwright's denial gives way to anger. He is furious that she has left him. Furious that he is alone. How could she leave just now when they've the charity book drive to organise, and the teas for the homeless?

He is steered, as always, by the careful hand of his daughter who though in shock herself, guides him safely back to his faith, his resentment gradually softening to recollection. It is only now that I begin to creep into his life, ten months after his wife's death.

I am his audience, the one to whom he can explain her wonders; as biographer of the Cartwright family I soak up his stories like the bandages on the wound.

In the beginning, the stories are miserable, explaining the loss, clarifying the circumstances, but as the months move on, so do the stories. Their mood lightens, their colour returns and what began as black and grey begins to melt to a soft mauve. The Cartwright home becomes my haven, my safe place; the more I go there, the more I need to go. I am an addict.

It is late autumn, 1923. I rap on the door three times, as has become my fashion.

'Hello, Ray,' Mr Cartwright says, flinging wide the door to make room for my entrance. 'We're having a bit of a tidy through.'

The *we* to whom he refers is himself and his dead wife Lilian, though more and more he consigns her to his book of cherished memories, often recalled but no longer interacted with.

'I'm putting all the clothes into the mission's chests, good clothes are always useful, we do see some sorry sights at times and it gives us great pleasure to watch them walk away in one of Lilian's finest. She agrees it's for the best.'

Lily is setting the table for tea. 'Hello, my lovely,' I whisper.

'There's no need for that, Ray. He can hear you whether you scream or sigh. Don't hide it under a cloak. Love should always be shouted from the roof tops.'

Mr Cartwright, I have discovered, is a challenge. Passionate, forthright and blunt. Lily is entirely relaxed about this and I can't begin to thank my lucky stars.

'Hello, my lovely,' I shout, grinning a leery grin.

Sitting behind a pile of egg sandwiches, waiting patiently for me to settle in my seat, Mr Cartwright excitedly fiddles with his shirtsleeve in anticipation of telling today's anecdote. Lily yawns. It is my guess she has been here before, many times. I cross my arms, lean forward and indicate my readiness.

'When I was in the main post office, at Mount Pleasant, I would come home every afternoon, because we started very early.'

Lily pours the tea. I help myself to a slice of homemade cake.

'I would have my dinner, rest, and then read until the evening. I love to read, don't I Lily? I'm fond of the poets, Ray, though that's something I kept to myself down in the post rooms.'

He sniggers at his subterfuge.

'I would sit in that chair, by the fire, and reflect on how many love letters I had distributed that very morning, when the sun was in its heaven and all was right with the world. I'm a morning man, myself. Lilian now, she enjoyed the evening sun, we could never agree on that score.

'At the end of each day she would bring me one glass of ale, as I'll be having later this evening, and what a pleasure it was. Lilian tried sherry once, but it greatly disagreed with her.'

Mr Cartwright lapses into thoughtfulness, his eyes fix on a point beyond the window, beyond the houses on the other side of the street. I remain silent, eager not to distract him from his thoughts. Lily is also quiet, possibly because she is somewhere else in a thought of her own. A small smile creeps across his face as some underlying current tosses a particular incident to the surface.

'Do you know, Ray, Lily is as good as her mother on the piano? The parties we've had would have alarmed the neighbours, if they hadn't been invited to enjoy themselves along with us. We would push the furniture back to the walls, Lilian would make her exceptional egg sandwiches, lots of pepper, that's how I like them, and someone would bring a cake, or some biscuits, and then she would play, and we'd all do a turn. Lilian always sang Nelly Dean.'

To my astonishment Mr Cartwright bursts into song:

There's an old mill by the stream,
Nelly Dean.

We knew all the words. Then, her brother Ernie would stand to take his turn with

Two lovely black eyes
Oh what a surprise
Only for telling a man he was wrong
I got two lovely black eyes.

Ernie was always self-conscious on the singing; he would tug at the bottom of his jumper all the while, his voice cracking at the top notes because he tried to sing an octave too high, silly old fool. As the evening wore on, we danced. Not a lot of space I know, we couldn't be doing with the velita, not amongst all the furniture, and a polka would have sent everything flying, but we could shuffle around to a waltz or two. My favourite, of course, I sang to my beauties whenever and wherever it popped into my head:

She's my lady love
She is my love, my turtle dove
She's no gal for sitting down to drink
She's the only gal Laguna knows
I know she likes me
I know she likes me
Because she said so
She is my Lily of Laguna
She is my Lily and my Rose…

His voice rising to a rousing crescendo for the final lines.

On through the huddling winter months and into the unfolding spring of the following year, Mr Cartwright reminisces and I absorb Lily's childhood like a sponge. How she lost her front tooth at the age of three on an old rope swing that had given up its hold of the branch over which it was slung, and how the sight of so much blood had sent her mother into a frenzy. How she'd torn her ankle shambling around the house in her mother's shoes, getting it caught in the yards of petticoat she had borrowed from Lilian's drawer. Three years running, she had played Mary in the school nativity, much to the displeasure of the other mothers.

'Lilian and I chuckled so. But what could we do? They complained to the teacher, never to us. But when God puts an angel on earth it's only polite that if you recognise the angel, you give her the star part, it would be offensive not to, wouldn't it?'

I nod, dipping a biscuit into my tea, glancing at Lily.

'Given the circumstances, the Angel Gabriel might have been more appropriate?' says Lily.

'Not on your life; everyone knows Mary was God's favourite.'

'Though I've heard Gabriel was quite popular, haven't you Ray,' say's Lily, drawing me close.

She had been kissed and cuddled, stroked and cosseted; when you spring from that much love, when you are nurtured with that much adoration, how can you help but feel peaceful at the core. No gnawing feeling, no yearning, no hole where love should be. You are full. The well inside that craves love is regularly topped up with sprinklings of approval. The happy contentment people spend a lifetime chasing is yours from the beginning.

'You were an utter nuisance, Dad.'

'What do you mean?' cries Mr Cartwright, immediately affronted.

'You know exactly what I mean. Mum would never have pushed the way you did. She would have been happy for me to be a shepherd, or an inn keeper's wife, but not you, it had to be the main part.'

'Don't start that again. What's wrong with a father being proud of his child?'

'You left no space for what I wanted, for what Mum wanted. You had to have it all your own way.'

'Your mother wanted exactly what I did for you, nothing but the best.'

'You were a bully.'

'I was not. That's a disgraceful accusation.'

'Calm down, Dad. You'll be sending me to my room next.'

'Go to your room.'

Lily laughs. 'I don't think so Dad, not anymore. I'm a big girl now.'

Joe has served his time and the wedding is to be next week. I go with Lily to choose her outfit and to collect my hire suit. Lily's nose wrinkles at the smell of mothballs, but I look so dandy in it we can put up with it for an evening. Joe's nuptials have set us both thinking and the conversation turns quite frequently to their marriage.

I look at Mum and Dad and decide it's an institution best left well alone. But then I go to see Lily and her father, I listen to him reminisce the wonder years with his Lilian, and I just can't wait to get there. Joe's marriage finally tips the balance; he looks so foolishly happy that I want to laugh out loud.

'Joe Johnson, I can hardly recognise you. Never has a man smiled so much in one day, and not just for the camera.'

'You have got to do this Ray, it's the most electrifying thing I've ever done. My skin is tingling with satisfaction.' He pushes an arm in front of me so that I might feel the happiness it holds.

'Doesn't she look spectacular?' he says, looking at Susan, who is talking to her parents on the other side of the reception hall.

'She does indeed,' I answer, watching Lily, bending low to tie the sash on one of the bridesmaid's dresses. 'Quite a do, this, Joe. I hope the in-laws are impressed. I think I'll be going for something a little simpler myself.'

'You don't say,' says Joe, his grin expanding an extra notch on its already impossibly wide dimension. 'So you've taken the plunge have you?'

'Well, don't congratulate me yet; Lily hasn't been asked.'

'Well good luck, Ray. No one deserves it more than you.'

He crosses the room to join his new family, carefully negotiating the shuffling couples, stopping occasionally to receive their best wishes for the future, leaving me to ponder his remark. Joe doesn't pity me. He doesn't even admire me, we're too close for that, I'm just Ray to him, and all that that entails is fine by Joe. He's a good man. No one deserves it more than you, Joe.

But let's get real: I'm a best man, and the best come out on top, cream rises. I am decided, tonight's the night.

The evening is warm. I can feel her body through the slippery dress, hugging close to mine as we walk arm in arm along Mare Street, heady with the sweet wedding wine, incapable of little more than a quiet wistfulness. Running my eye along the length of her ring finger, I picture a carnation-like cluster blooming at the joint, a sparkly froth of pink and blue glass. I am waiting for a sign.

A man in a dark raincoat fiddles with a bunch of keys in the shadows of a doorway. The shops, which by daylight are lively with busy shoppers and persistent salesmen, are now closed, their displays enticingly lit to continue the sales pitch long after the proprietor has turned the key and gone home. I draw Lily with me to look into the dazzling fizz of a jewellery shop.

We stare for a few seconds.

'Are you trying to say something, Ray Riley?' Lily smiles up at me, a flood of dark red hair falling across her shoulder.

'Do you think you're ready for it? For becoming the new Mrs Riley?'

She is quiet for a moment.

'I think I might consider myself very lucky.'

'You think you might?'

'I would consider myself the luckiest woman in London.'

'In England!'

'No doubt about it.'

Somewhat overwhelmed by the enormity of what we have said, we return to gazing at the sparkly rows of rings, no doubts about it.

'Lily Cartwright, would you do me the honour of consenting to be my wife?'

'To have and to hold.'

'From this day forward?'

'Ray Riley, I will.'

My chest is stretched tight with too little space to breathe. 'I will too,' I gasp.

We kiss, and giggle, and look into each other's eyes as if to mark the occasion. We've agreed to be together until we die, it's an awesome thought.

The following Saturday afternoon, we return to the same jewellery shop, Lily squeezing my hand to signify that this is exactly right, that the charm will hold, the spell in which we have floated through the week will be magically sustained if we purchase the ring from here.

We stand to look in the window, holding the oath we have taken like a delicate porcelain bowl, carrying it carefully in our hands until the time when we can put it on a high shelf and declare, there, safe as the day is long, sits our commitment to each other.

Had Mum and Dad done the same? Had they believed they were impregnable, enduring? At what point did they admit the lie? I glance at Lily who is frowning steadily at the display.

'That one's nice.' I point encouragingly at a bouquet of glittering diamonds.

'It's fabulous, but so's the price.'

In my excitement I have overlooked this aspect of the ring.

'I can't afford that, Lily,' I say, saddened by the instant smile she turns on me.

'But that's not the ring for me, Ray. I want something much more delicate. I don't like all this show.'

I know she is lying and I am undeniably grateful. 'Well what about one from this tray?' These too are way beyond my means but the sun is shining on her hair, creating a soft halo of gold around her head and I can't help myself.

She turns to face me, a way she has when she wants me to concentrate. 'How much do you have in your pocket?'

I am taken aback by her bluntness. This is, after all, meant to be where the knightly male proves his love to his lady; discussion of the man's means is surely not meant to enter the dialogue.

'£3.15s,' I murmur. 'All I had left after I'd bought Joe and Susan's table linen.'

This is not entirely true. In fact I had only £1.15s left, the other £2 is a sub from Charlie who claims he has no use for it anyway, other than possibly to smoke it away. Charlie has an odd way with money, appearing to disregard it entirely. Wanting for nothing and spending on nothing, he seems content to amble about in threadbare trousers and a shirt worn so thin the hair on his forearms can be seen through the threads.

'£3.15s. Add that to the £2 I've earned from bonuses on the catalogues and we've a glorious £5.15s to spend. Anything in fact on that tray, which holds the very one I want.'

She points to a hoop of the tiniest diamonds ever mined, splinters from a much grander rock, and I heave a small and hopefully indiscernible sigh of relief.

'That's the one for me. Here, put my money in your pocket and let's go in.'

We clang open the door, announcing our arrival for the benefit of the sales staff, one of whom jumps immediately from a back room and dons the serious composure of a seller of expensive goods, as if the value of his stock has in some obscure manner rubbed off onto himself, thereby increasing his own worth.

He has already got up my nose.

I am in the process of formulating an offensive remark when Lily jolts me out of my sneer. Holding herself tall, her chin lifted away from the counter and looking down her nose at the salesman, who in turn looks down his nose at her, she says:

'I would like to see the tray of engagement rings fourth from the left in the window.'

Lily is drawing long, elegant gloves from her slender arms. Needless to say I had not noticed these before.

'Yes, Madam,' returns the purveyor of expensive goods, a little too swiftly for my liking.

Lily winks at me as he unlocks the wooden screen to extract the desired tray. At the centre of the tray sits the outrageously opulent bouquet that we had previously admired. Lily selects a number of rings, placing them on her finger, dipping her hand from side to side to allow the diamonds to catch the light, before turning her attention to what has to be the most expensive item in the shop, if not in London.

'I think this is the one for me, Ray,' she says, spreading her fingers wide and admiring the shards of pink light it throws onto her skin.

Both my own and the purveyor of expensive goods mouths are open, though I like to imagine he is panting a little more heavily than I.

'What do you think?' she asks, holding her hand at arm's length, an action I'm surprised she can manage with the weight at the end of it.

My voice comes out much quieter than I intend, my fingers playing with the small scroll of notes in my pocket. 'It's up to you, Darling.' We'll be in hock for the rest of our lives, but if that's the one for you, so be it.

The salesman has gone pink.

'It suits madam immeasurably.'

'Do you think so? You don't think it's a little…'

'Expensive,' I blurt.

'Heavy?'

'Well, heavy in the sense of grand, as opposed to heavy in the sense of overwhelming, perhaps, maybe a little. But you can carry it off, Madam. Your classical stature can carry the grand design.'

Snotty bloody toe rag.

'I see. But what would one do if one wished to wear gloves?' says Lily, stroking the pair of satin gloves lying on the counter.

'But would one?' counters the salesman, falling happily into Lily's mock nobility. I can't imagine who this bloke thinks he is talking to. It's true, she is regal, queenly even, but let's face it mate, this is hardly the West End, this is Mare Street, Hackney.

'With a ring of this nature one is more inclined to leave it exposed.'

Lily is silent.

The salesman holds his breath and then gives in to a rapid panting.

I stare at him in wonder.

'You are quite right to raise the issue of gloves, Darling. Perhaps you should consider something a little smaller, something that can be worn every day without fear of snagging, or attracting the undesirable attention of robbers.'

We both look at the salesman, expecting him to present a revised tray of less exorbitant designs. The poor fellow is so crestfallen he has taken root, impotent, unable to steer our attention back to the desirable sale.

'I think you are right, Ray. I did see a dainty hoop of stones on the tray to the far left of the window.'

The salesman looks from one to the other of us but does not move. They must be kidding, he is thinking. 'I believe they are set in platinum?' prompts Lily, as if to remind him of the piece.

A shiver runs down his body. Slowly, he slides the fabulous ring back into its velvet slit and returns it to the window. On his way back he snatches at the furthest tray to the left. Apparently, he did know the ring she meant.

'Yes, this is the one,' says Lily, obviously beginning to feel sorry for him. 'This will suit me perfectly.' Then she does something I grow to understand as her most endearing feature. She turns the fullest, warmest smile on the salesman and I am positive she is sincere when she says, 'Thank you, sir, you have been very patient. I am not the easiest woman in the world to please.'

From this I take great pleasure. I have asked a beautiful woman, a hard woman to please, to marry me, and she has said yes.

Lucky doesn't come anywhere near it.

Chapter 14

There Is No Avoiding It;
Lily Must Meet My Parents,
For Better Or For Worse

Lily is enchanted by the ring on her finger, placing her gloves in her handbag and glancing frequently at her left hand to admire its altered appearance. 'We should go to tell our parents,' she says. I have been dreading this moment.

We join the tram queue with the other Saturday shoppers.

'Some of the girls at the factory have mentioned you, girls that come from round your way.'

This is not good news. Any girl from round our way will know that my parents are selfish drunken sots who care nothing for anyone so long as they are indulging their demons.

'Oh yes, good words I hope?'

'Not really. But I told them, Ray is sweet to me, he makes me laugh, he is hard working, he has a good job and he loves me. I'm not going steady with his mum and dad, I'm going steady with him.'

I grin widely at the fat lady stood beside us, whose glazed expression does nothing to disguise the fact that she is listening to our conversation.

'It is no matter to me that his parents are drinkers and fighters.'

Fat lady forgets herself and raises her eyebrows.

'Ray has never touched a hair on my head, not even raised his voice, not once.'

Fat lady nods her approval.

'Of course, what really makes them boil is that they've let such a looker slip through their fingers, that seems to give their meanness an edge, but I don't get nasty in return, in fact I pretend I don't even notice how handsome you are, which seems to infuriate them even more.'

Fat lady turns and slides a slow look from my feet to my head. I smile at her when she reaches the top, whereupon she dives into her handbag in search of something very important.

It's for the best; if the girls at the factory have been bitching about me at least Lily is forewarned.

'And there's nothing wrong with a drink, in moderation, I say.'

I give a little skip, unable to keep the triumph out of my feet. 'So, your place first, or mine?'

'Dad isn't expecting me home until tea time, he'll be in the middle of his crib game with Uncle Ernie. Why don't we go to your house first.'

This is it. I glance up at the clock hanging above the jewellers. Three thirty. They might be home from the pub by now, they might not.

Only Dad and Charlie are in.

Dad, sitting dumbstruck on one side of the kitchen table, stares at Lily who has seated herself opposite him. He looks as if he believes she might evaporate if he blinks. I can't tell if he is befuddled or simply marvelling at her.

Charlie, though obviously nervous, bounds forward to shake her hand. 'Congratulations,' he shouts, the bare floor and walls bouncing his word around, making it sound like a crowd has turned out to wish us well.

Lily laughs. 'Is that just for me, or for the pair of us?'

'Both,' he cries, a little too energetically.

There is nothing in the house he can offer us but he seems to want to mark the occasion. 'Should we go have a drink, to celebrate?'

I glance at Lily, then at Dad. Charlie is not a drinker, he might have a drink once a month, but for his sake, I nod.

'That would be nice,' says Lily, 'though we can't stay too long as we've still to visit my dad.'

'We won't be there long, Lily,' I add, trying for authoritative.

Charlie digs around in his jacket pocket for some money. Dad clears his throat.

'Charlie lad, I think you'll find your mother has borrowed that, until Friday, for bread and milk, and things.' His voice trails off, self-conscious in front of this apparition. Charlie and I exchange looks.

'Back in a sec,' he shouts, and leaps out of the door, springing down the stairs two at a time.

After some crashing and clunking from somewhere deep in the bowels of the house he calls up, 'Ready.'

Charlie obviously has a stash hole; good for him, that's one way to deal with them.

Walking behind Dad, Charlie, Lily and myself, each enter The Dog and Duck with some wariness. It is a dark, cavernous room with one long bar stretching across the back and small, partitioned booths around the walls; we blink until our eyes adjust to the gloom.

Mum is sat on her own in a corner, her face turned away from the bar to watch events out on the street. We will have walked past her as we came towards the entrance, but her expression tells me she is off in her own netherworld.

Charlie has presumably seen her as well. 'What's it to be?' he says, heading straight for the other end of the bar. Dad goes across to the corner where I hear him mumbling something to Mum. She looks up at him and stands to better take in his news, which he repeats to ensure she has understood. Turning her head slowly she looks across the room at us.

'What are you lot doing in here?' she says; she has always found unexpected meetings difficult.

Lily walks towards her, her hand outstretched.

'Hello Mrs Riley, I'm Lily Cartwright.'

I leap to Lily's side. 'Hello Mum. Lily and I are here for a celebratory drink.'

'What's to celebrate?' Her speech isn't slurred and I know she is fully aware of what we have come to celebrate.

'Well,' I take Lily's hand and lift the ring finger as if to prove my words, 'I have asked Lily Cartwright to marry me.'

I am hopeful that this news will prompt at least a small expression of pleasure, a flicker of nostalgic warmth, or even a smile for good manners, but her face remains static. Dad is stood beside her, his focus once again fixed on Lily.

'And I presume from that bauble, she has said yes.'

'I am pleased to say she has.'

'Our Ray's to be married,' whispers Dad into her ear.

She turns slowly to look at him as if she didn't know anyone was there, then just as slowly, twists her gaze back to Lily.

'And you're of the opinion marriage is a good state, are you?'

'And he's going to marry her,' whispers Dad, pointing a bony finger at Lily.

Mum's head wobbles on her neck as it turns, once again surprised to find someone at her side.

'Where will you live?' she says, slowly returning her attention to Lily.

'We don't know yet, Mrs Riley, but we'll find something nice, I'm sure.'

'Huh! How's that then? There's not a spare room to be had round these parts.'

'Something will come up.' Lily persists, determined not to be discouraged. 'I hear of rooms through the girls at the factory or sometimes there are notices in shop windows where the rooms above have become vacant.'

Charlie arrives with a tray of drinks. He lifts his glass in a salute to Lily and myself.

'She's not in the club is she?' says Mum.

Charlie looks appalled, lowers his glass and turns away. Dad is startled from his reverie and spins round to glare at her. 'What the bloody hell's the matter with you? Can't you just for once say something nice? I do apologise, young lady, mother's not feeling herself today.'

Mum looks away, shrugs her shoulders, and backs herself into her window seat.

I am furious with her and start towards her but Charlie grabs my arm.

'Don't.'

I am still hesitating when Lily adds, 'Leave it, Ray, Charlie's right, it doesn't matter.'

Ignoring my mother's intended offence, Lily turns her attention to Charlie. I am relieved to see Charlie's shoulders relax.

'How's your work going, Charlie? Ray says you're doing an apprenticeship now, at the printers.'

Charlie rolls up his sleeves to display a pair of bright blue arms.

'Good Lord,' says Lily, 'it looks like a disease; gangrene, something decomposing. Won't it wash off?'

Charlie shakes his head. 'It's the mark of the trade.'

Lily grimaces. 'That sounds a bit ominous, like the convict's shackle marks or the showgirl's rouge.'

Charlie rolls his shirtsleeves back down his tell-tale limbs.

'Still,' Lily continues, perky as ever, 'at least you're getting a trade, Charlie. There's many would sing to be in your shoes. And wherever there's print, there's words. I expect you see plenty to read, which must make the day more interesting.'

As I listen to their conversation and Lily steers us carefully away from the offending confrontation, my anger subsides.

Charlie's right of course, he's wised up in his late teens, got some necessary distance, but I had expected more from her today. I recall their own wedding photograph, the two sets of parents stood to solemn attention on either side of the bride and groom. I decide I don't want that for me. I want smiles and crowds, rice and streamers, I want the band, the bridesmaids and the smiling cleric, that's the kind of picture I'm aiming for, the whole shebang. If Joe can have it, then I will too.

At four-thirty we take our leave. Dad has stood with us during the whole of the short visit, glaring across occasionally at Mum, drinking steadily, but finally plucking up courage to smile and nod at Lily, with whom he seems oddly overwhelmed. Lily and Charlie are easy together, and I am pleased to watch him making an effort. I glance at the clock above the bar.

'We should be going, Lily.'

'Well, it was lovely to meet you Charlie,' she says, giving him a quick peck on the cheek, 'I don't think I'll mind in the slightest having you as a brother-in-law.' Charlie flushes. 'And nice to meet you too, Mr Riley, no doubt we'll meet again soon.' She walks across to Mum. 'We're off now, Mrs Riley. It was good to meet you at last.'

Mum looks up at her but says nothing.

Lily turns at the doorway and waves goodbye; Charlie lifts his palm in an Indian style salute and then we're gone.

I gather Lily's arm through mine. 'I'm so sorry, I don't know why she's like it, she's never seemed to care about anything we've done though you seem to have made an impression on the men.'

'Don't worry about it, Ray. I would have found it refreshing to be left alone by my parents, allowed my own time. I'd have liked a little of that space myself.'

'She's never shown much affection to anyone.'

Now there's an understatement.

'I'm sure she loves you dearly; some people find it hard to show they care.'

I glance across at her. I don't know what you saw; I didn't see any type of love, not in any shape or form.

We walk on in silence for a while, our footsteps matching; I listen to the neat tap-tap of our rhythm.

'Charlie's nice, Ray.'

'Yes?'

'Yes, nice, he's affectionate.' She pauses and I wait. 'Is he okay?'

'You mean, is he mental?'

'You know what I mean; he's more than simply withdrawn. He's got a way of not hearing some things, of blanking out, he did it a couple of times when we were talking, he sort of switched off.'

Oh, he hears all right, hears and files; I'd noticed this more and more in Charlie. Sometimes, we meet on the stairs, or he's stood at the kitchen sink, or briefly before he falls asleep at night, he acts as if he's the only person in the room. Then at other times, when he feels like talking, the words can't get out fast enough, and none of them make sense. He'll wander off into foreign territory and I've no idea what he's talking about or whether he knows I'm listening. Sometimes, he'll be talking to Billy in St Quentin, just before he goes over the top, advising him where to tread, when to run.

Or, he'll be talking about Mum, he'll get in a frenzy because he can't find where he's put her hairbrush, his hands working overtime as if he's hunting for it, he's tidied the table and he's waiting for the blue fit she'll have when she finds it's missing.

Sometimes, his monologue turns on me, when he assumes a high-pitched la-de-da voice and offers me breakfast in bed. It's something I've heard Dad do, a mixture of spite and bragging, as if he, Dad, was responsible for the high life of my youth, as if he'd put his hand in his pocket and sent me off to some school for rich kids.

And when Charlie's not talking, he can be morose, silent for days on end; I call his name, try to talk to him, but no one's at home. He's gone out to play in the swamp.

'He's okay. Out to lunch at times, but harmless enough.'

At least he never loses his temper, which I'm sure I would, living with those two ghouls.

As we approach Lily's front door we can hear the gusty laugh of Uncle Ernie coming from an open lower window. Lily's aunt had died giving birth to her cousin Moira. Uncle Ernie, having raised Moira alone, with help and guidance from his sister Lilian, regularly travels across London in search of Mr Cartwright's company, now that the encumbrances of wife and child no longer temper his daily pursuits.

They are sat at the table fighting like schoolboys over a hand of cribbage, their teacups, hastily rinsed, stacked to drain at the kitchen sink.

'Are you nearly through?' asks Lily as we enter. 'Shall I make some tea?'

'Almost there, love. I'll finish him off in the next hand.'

Lily kisses her father on the cheek, to which he responds too late, kissing the air as she turns away to kiss her uncle's head. Mr Cartwright looks momentarily aggrieved, an unexpected gloom caused either by his opponents stronger hand or by dropping his kisses carelessly into the undeserving air.

'Fifteen six and a pair's eight!' shouts Uncle Ernie, throwing an attacking hand onto the table.

Mr Cartwright's eyes sparkle. 'Ernie, my son, you'll have to do better than that.' He splays his cards on the table and watches as Ernie's triumph dissolves to a temporary low.

'Pair is two, fifteen-four, fifteen-six, a run is nine, another run is twelve and,' he reaches for the box, 'whoooh, fifteen-fourteen, fifteen-sixteen, fifteen-eighteen, a run is twenty one and one for his knob, twenty-two!'

Uncle Ernie does indeed look crestfallen. I feel right sorry for him. Lily does too.

'Oh, what a shame. Would you like to stay for tea, Uncle Ernie?'

'No thanks love, I won't impose, thanks all the same.'

'Because Ray and I have something important to say.'

He looks up, glancing between us. 'In that case maybe I will, yes count me in. I can live without sustenance, I can even lose the occasional crib hand, but gossip is a way of life, and since my Amy hasn't been here to feed me the daily dose I find I have to hunt it out for myself.' He twinkles at Lily. After twenty-two years he is accustomed to talking fondly of his wife and Lily knows this is good for her father, and for herself.

'What's all this then?' asks Mr Cartwright, clearing the table of cards in anticipation of egg sandwiches with lots of pepper. 'What have you young ones been up to?'

Lily looks at me.

I have been running through my lines since leaving Swan Terrace. Keep it short, I tell myself. Get straight to the point and make it clear. *I'm going to marry your daughter, is that okay?* Sounds about right. Now that the time is here however, I feel less brave and extremely presumptuous. What father in his right mind hands over a beautiful daughter such as this to the likes of me, a non-accomplished doorstep scrubber with alcoholism in his blood, a man whose knit-one-pearl-one level of achievement is never going to win the war.

I am wordless.

He'll say no.

He'll say no for sure.

Lily looks up and takes my arm, prompting a string of words that I hope fall out in comprehensible order.

'Mr Cartwright I have asked Lily to be my wife and she has done me the honour of accepting, we would like to ask for your blessing…' I pause, thinking I am done. Lily leans on me… 'and hope that this makes you as happy as it does us.'

Christ. Now he'll know me for a fool.

The air stops moving.

Mr Cartwright stands up, so still he appears to have stopped breathing. He is digesting the request as he might a fine wine, allowing the sweetly scented aroma to infuse his nostrils, permitting its thick honey texture to caress his tongue. As it takes more shape, he swallows, his Adam's apple pushing the idea deep into his stomach where it generates a warm, generous glow. This is a very good wine; Lilian would have greatly preferred it to the sherry.

I, of course, know nothing of Mr Cartwright's thinking, or taste buds for that matter, I can only guess at what might be going through his mind.

Outrage?

Indignation?

I lean so far forward I am in danger of toppling onto him. I tilt my ear closer to catch the slightest murmur of approval from a man who looks to be in the early stages of rigor mortis.

Say yes before you snuff it, I beg.

'Yes, Ray, you have my blessing,' comes a kindly voice from heaven.

The sound of Uncle Ernie striking his hands together in a single sharp clap shocks little bubbles of air up into my throat.

The room is laughing.

'Did he say yes?' I ask Lily.

Mr Cartwright hugs Lily and Uncle Ernie works himself into a major excitement, pacing backwards and forwards across the small room, which really is beginning to grow unbearably hot. I stand by, gawkishly watching their pleasure as if I am in some way inconsequential to all this activity.

'I do so love a good party, and this will be a fine celebration won't it, Tom? We'll invite the old crowd, best way to fill your bottom drawer Lily. Moira will be happy to help. I'll go and tell her, she'll be so thrilled, you know how she loves to organise everyone.'

Tom Cartwright isn't listening; he is thinking, looking at Lily's smiling face.

'Can you really give something away,' he wonders aloud, 'if you continue to own it as yours?' He turns to consider me. 'How do you receive something, call it your own, and yet always know it belongs to me? It's a puzzle that.'

'I couldn't agree more, Mr Cartwright,' I say, this thought having never occurred to me. She is about to become my wife, end of subject.

Lily looks unsettled, she moves to the table and sweeps her finger through the fine layer of dust. Is something wrong? I try folding my eyebrows to a wavy, questioning, look of concern, but cannot catch her eye.

'*Tom*,' Mr Cartwright is shouting, 'You're to call me *Tom*.' Either my hearing is becoming over acute or there is something about this day that is making everyone bellow.

Then he walks towards me, fixing my eyes steadily and taking hold of my arm in a surprisingly rigid clench. 'What's mine is yours, what's yours is mine; let's all remember that and be kind to one another.'

For a gentle man he makes this sound like a threat. I am left in no doubt that he will break the sixth commandment if, so help me God, I cause a rift between him and his angel.

'I will treat her like the wonder she is, *Tom*,' I say, trying out the name for the first time.

He nods. I have understood him precisely: he will peel back my skin, drag out my innards and throw them in the River Lee if I cause him any grief.

'You'll be wanting to move in here I expect, it's small, but cosy, I'll move into the box room.'

This strikes me as ideal, quite acceptable, newlyweds starting out with a leg-up from their in-laws. I am extremely grateful as this takes a major load off my mind and I rub my hands together appreciatively.

'That is a terrific offer, Mr Cartwright, we would be delighted to accept.'

'And you'll be saving of course, so we'll come to a reasonable charge for your keep.'

119

'Meaning we can set the marriage date for as soon as it suits us, Lily,' I say, hoping this good news will remove the deepening glower spreading across Lily's usually placid features.

'No,' says Lily.

'No what?' both Tom and I say in unison.

'This is a tiny house, with barely enough room for a couple. We'll not all be living here.'

This sounds unpromising.

'Where will you find anything better?' says her father, a smug note unwisely detectable in his voice.

I restrain a nod, thinking he has a point.

'We'll find somewhere.'

Tom Cartwright shrugs his shoulders at me as if to say, this is an indication of what you're getting into. It's not only honey in the beehive! I feel under pressure to say something.

'We'd be foolish Lily, not to think it over.'

'I can be as foolish as I choose Ray Riley, I'm not living in the house I nursed and mourned my mum in.'

Tom Cartwright folds his arms and looks sternly at his daughter. 'Now you listen to me, Lily. What was good enough for your mother will be good enough for you.'

'Here we go again, everything has to be done your way. I'm not marrying anyone to be told I'm a fool, and I'm not living in this house to be leant on by you, Dad.'

'Now you hang on a minute.'

'I didn't call you a fool,' I add peevishly.

'I want my own home, with my own things, modern things, I want my independence. I'm not a possession that you, or you, can pass between you. I thought you were different but you're just the same as him.'

'What did I ever do,' wails her father, 'nothing but the best for you.'

'And you treated me like an expensive doll that you could dress up and turn out for party tricks. A doll that would break if it wasn't held tightly in your tender care. It was stifling; I want some freedom. I want a life of my own, Dad. And if you don't feel the same way Ray, then it'll have to be with someone else.'

I am stunned. 'Now hang on a minute Lily, I only said…' What did I say? Only minutes ago we were happily announcing our decision to marry, and now we're not. My mother had accused her of being a fallen woman and no one batted an eyelid. Tom

Cartwright offers us a roof over our heads and suddenly the wedding's off.

I thought I had the measure of her; I like to think I can read women but perhaps it's not possible. As soon as I think I'm prepared, that I've covered every twist and turn that a conversation might take, out comes some entirely new alternative that neither I nor He could possibly have expected. I've studied women. I remember the quiet persistence with which Aunt Lizzie dealt with the truculent demands of her son. I have witnessed the careful manipulations with which Grandma Bess steered Grandpa along her chosen path. I have seen the resilience and eventual collapse of my own mother. But freedom? Who on earth wants freedom? Freedom means not belonging, drifting, walking away from solid ground to slip and slide on a dangerous scree where nothing can take root. Lily looks determined.

Tom Cartwright's first response is to support me.

'You're being headstrong again, Lily. Listen to Ray, he's trying to do what's best for you.'

'He's trying to do what's best for him.'

No joy there.

He sides with Lily.

'Don't upset yourself Lily, it will all come right for you in the end, we'll see to that.'

'I don't want anyone seeing to that anymore, Dad, I want to see to it myself.'

Finally, his sympathies are with himself.

'Yourself! What about me? What about leaving me, cooking my own tea, making my own fire, doing my own washing. Who is going to look after me?'

'For heaven's sake Dad, you'll manage, people do. Look at Uncle Ernie.'

Tom Cartwright and I both turn to look at Uncle Ernie, as if his physical being might enlighten us. Uncle Ernie, awkward and uncomfortable at being singled out as a fine example of a man who manages, hangs his head like an apologetic dog. All the while I am stood in a bewildered state of uncertainty, afraid to speak in case I fan the flames, equally afraid not to defend my corner. And I had worried about visiting my parents.

Lily looks suddenly exhausted; she slumps into an armchair.

'I don't want you to be upset Dad and I don't mean to sound selfish or bossy but I have plans. Parents are great, of course they are, but they are buffers, between their children and the grave, and

121

it's a short distance. While your parents are alive you feel immune. But when they die you know the Grim Reaper is looking out for you, you're next, he's checking your whereabouts in the crowd.'

She pauses. I'm not sure where this is going. Tom Cartwright and I exchange looks, knowing better than to interrupt.

'Mum's death scared me, as if I was running out of time to do the things I wanted, and living here makes me feel like I'm not even trying.'

I hear a snag in her voice, as if she doesn't know if she should go on.

'Mum told me to get out, get on with life, to enjoy it on my terms, and I feel like she needs me to live it as much as I need it myself.'

She pauses again and looks up at her father.

'I'm being morbid, but the house reminds me of Mum. Some of the memories are lovely, some are not. You can cope, Dad, you've got your work friends, the mission, and you'll have us. But we need us as well. And the two of you will love each other more if you don't fight over me here, where *you* have the advantage, Dad. You have to meet on equal terms.'

She looks at me.

'And you Ray, you're just jumping for the easiest option. When I said I was a hard woman to please, I meant you to hear me.'

I'm still not sure if we're through the worst of this, and I'm feeling a bit shaky, wondering if it's all my fault for not knowing something I was meant to have known.

But it seems I'm to be a man with an assignment, a breaker of new ground and a builder of dreams. All I've got to do is find a piece of ground to build the dream on.

Chapter 15

Solid Ground?
I'd Be Happy To Find The Shingle Scree

Finding the piece of ground doesn't prove easy. Every spare minute of the day I chase the streets, following false leads until, at my wits end, I call in at Joe's.

Flopping into a comfy armchair, I rest my head on the spongy backrest and roll my eyes in vexation.

I've been so busy I haven't had a chance to call on Joe; he is over the moon with our news, oozing satisfaction from every pore. He can't wait for us to join him in happy couples land.

'Where are you looking to live?'

I drop my tense shoulders to a collapsed slump expressing my exasperation.

'It's a nightmare. My feet ache, tramping from one side of town to the other. It's a bloody nightmare.'

Joe frowns, swearing is not allowed in the house of bliss, his mother's house, to be completely accurate. I stretch my legs out in front of me as if to relieve the tramping tension but really to point out that I am looking for slightly larger accommodation. I have in mind the tall windows and dimensions of Great Aunt Lizzie's dining room, though I've seen nothing that comes anywhere near it.

'There are no empty houses or flats to be had anywhere,' I continue, ignoring Joe's frown. 'And then there's the money to pay for it when I find it. We're not exactly flush. Lily has left her job for somewhere that pays more, she's gone to Western Electric in Southgate, at the Standard Cable factory, working a capstan lathe making screws for wireless parts, God bless her.'

Joe nods approvingly and takes a sip of his beer.

'It's only £2.2s a week but she says she saves on fares. And then, she's proving really good at this club holding malarkey, running three or four different catalogues for the likes of shoes, coats, tablecloths, that sort of thing. And working at the factory she's able to take the catalogues in to the girls. She's not pushy mind, you know Lily, she's just altogether hard to refuse.'

I look to Joe to see if he has understood. His face softens to indicate he has.

'I've got to find somewhere soon. She says we can get married as soon as the rooms are settled, so it's in my best interest to get things moving, if you know what I mean.'

Joe knows what I mean.

Susan made him wait near on two years, but did he complain? Not Joe. Not once. At least, not out loud, where I could hear and rattle his cage.

'How's the new job working out?' he asks.

'Perfect. Fully fledged gas fitter now, got my certificate, so I'm taking £2.18s a week. Not as much as you yet, of course, but I'm getting there. I could do with more, but who couldn't. The Gas Company's fine as company's go, and I certainly don't miss the din of the factory, not one little bit, plus I'm a free agent, which I like. It's good to be out on the streets, stretching your legs. It reminds me of my door to door days on the steps.'

Joe grins. 'Do you still get your bags of scraps?'

'More, sometimes.'

He raises a concerned eyebrow.

'The occasional bit of bread and marg, often a cup of tea, perhaps a biscuit, it depends on the street. Though sometimes I'm wishing I'd brought a bag of scraps with me to give to the poor buggers themselves.'

Life with The Gas Company is sweet.

I'm out the door in the morning before Mum and Dad sober up. I take a lunch break in a cafe where I'm hailed as Rollocking Riley, on account, they say, of my rollocking good luck in the looks department. Then I'm back on my rounds, blacking my nose in other people's houses. I'm a natural born chit-chatter and the ladies love it.

It is while I am blacking my nose in Nichols Square, Shoreditch, that I hear of a house next door, a house with rooms from which the current tenants are moving out today.

I keep my head lodged down behind the appliance, supplied new, courtesy of The Gas Company, making out it's a particularly troublesome installation, occasionally banging a wrench against a metal pipe to remind the lady of the house that I'm hard at it, but in reality waiting on the sound of next door's departure. When it comes I am straight out from behind the cooker.

'Back in a minute, Mrs Shepherd. Just popping back to the yard for an extra part. Won't be a jiffy.'

I walk out of one door, jump the four steps, nip down the path, do a sharp U-turn, and trot straight back up to the neighbouring door. Mrs Shepherd is of course watching me from behind her ground floor curtain.

I knock, sharp and business-like. This is it, I tell myself, no one else even knows of this one yet. I have been practising my patter while hunkered down behind the cooker. The woman of the house opens the door.

To my disappointment, she says she cannot comment on the availability of the rooms without her husband, who is himself not due home until six o'clock. I am utterly deflated. I'm sure I must look as if I'm about to sob. Go on, I urge myself. 'Would it be possible for you to show me the rooms anyway?'

Apparently this is not her job either.

Stopping just short of begging her to keep the rooms for me and not to tell a living soul about them until I return in the evening, I race next door, grab my tool bag from Mrs Shepherd's scullery floor and bound off down the road. I am waiting at Lily's by the time she arrives home from work and after a little fuss with her face we are back on the streets, walking as fast as we can. Lily gets a stitch and has to stop and press the sides of her ribs but I march on, determined not to find myself at the end of another queue where for some inexplicable reason I am once again either too late or ineligible for what's on offer.

I reach No. 70 Nichols Square at two minutes past six. Lily catches up and stops me just as I raise my hand to rap the knocker. She tugs down both my lapels, brushes non-existent dust off my shoulders, scrumples her own hair and nods.

Apparently we are now set. I knock for a second time on the door.

Once again the woman opens it and this time she invites me in.

'Good evening.' I thrust out my hand.

'Wait here, please,' she says. After a limp handshake, she leaves us standing in the dark hallway and calls down to the basement rooms. 'Henry! It's the young man who came earlier this afternoon, he's back, asking after the rooms.'

A short stocky man wearing a white singlet appears, wiping a dishcloth across his mouth. We have interrupted his dinner and although he doesn't appear to mind this, he does all the same want us to know we have interrupted his dinner.

'Hello there. Name's Hogg. This is Mrs Hogg.'

We dip our heads and repeat our earlier greeting.

'You've come about the rooms?'

'Yes,' I say, trying to keep exasperation and hope well hidden beneath my tone.

'You'll be wanting to see them I expect?'

'That would be nice.'

Lily gives me one of her looks, warning me to watch my manners.

'Will you be letting them?' I add, doing my best at bright and inquisitive.

'Yes, I'm letting them, but I'm decorating first. Would you like to see them now?'

I clear my throat. 'If it's not an inconvenience.'

Mr Hogg, enjoying the upper hand, leads the way slowly through to the ground floor rooms, two small rooms with folding doors between them. I'm not sure how to react. We were likely to be just as cramped here as we would have been at Mr Cartwright's, but I am learning to withhold immediate judgement in the interest of end result.

'Well Lily, what do you think?' I make sure my eyes are wide, warm, and my mouth is smiling. To me, a room is a room, and a room is a marriage, and a marriage is a life begun with Lily. I'm for the end result.

Lily looks dubious.

'It has nice light,' she says, looking out of the windows. 'Where are the facilities?'

'This way, Miss.'

Mr Hogg leads us to a small room with a hand basin along the corridor, then takes us out to the garden, to the lavatory and the water supply.

'Who lives in the rest of the house?' she asks.

'That'll be me and the Mrs, we're in the basement. When the kids were at home, they preferred the attic rooms up at the top. It's a sort of lodger's sandwich.'

Mr Hogg has obviously used this line before but he rolls his shoulders forward and chortles at us as if this is the funniest image life has ever presented him. Surprisingly, Lily is likewise amused and begins to giggle along with him, managing to glare at me as Mr Hogg wipes the tears from his eyes.

Mrs Hogg and I stand by in silence.

'I think I would like to take it, Ray.'

Bingo!

'How much are you asking, Mr Hogg?'

'Well, as I said, I've to decorate and I've to be sure you'll be certain to come back if I'm holding it for you. How long till you're ready to take the rooms?'

'Well, now that we've got an address, it'll take us six weeks to get the marriage certificate,' I say, glancing at Lily, who I'm relieved to see is nodding.

'Well, I'd like a definite date, you see, as I've to plan the decorating to be finished in time.'

I quickly calculate the weeks. 'September 9th.'

I am twenty-four-years-old and I am leaving home for a second time. 'Our wedding day will be September 9th, 1926, as will our day of occupancy.'

Mr Hogg looks pleased.

'Okay lad. It's a deal. I'll be wanting six week's Duke of Kent in advance, that's £3-12s, and in return, I'll give you the key so's you can come and go as you please, to get your things in place for the day.'

Chapter 16

It Is Unwise To Take Risks With Women, Yet Take Them We Do

Getting things *in place for the day* is easy work: we have nothing. Still, it's nice to hold the key.

Lily is busy organising the church banns, which puzzle me. Hey, now here's an idea. Let's announce out loud, broad and flagrant, that I, Rollocking Riley of Reject Row, plan to marry Hard to Please of Hoxton. They'll be dashing to object to that one, queuing. So just to be real sure, let's do it three times.

Lily smiles but inevitably ignores my wisecracks, putting my jibes down to a male fear of ceremony.

She's wrong there. I'm all for ceremony, I'm simply unaccustomed to it, in fact, I'm ceremony deprived, I tell her.

There's plenty of things you could be doing at the flat, she tells me. Go there and perform manly rituals, install the oven, mend the dripping tap. I'm given my task and sent packing: go forth and build the castle.

Since the engagement life has been a noisy whirl. Sadly, I see less of Lily because she has managed to get some overtime, the cash from which she has already allocated to curtain material. I am using the time productively to sit in the flat and smoke cigarettes, puffing little haloes of smoke late into the evening, some nights sleeping over, lying on my jacket, my head resting on my tool bag. I lie awake, imagining the wonder of a life with Lily.

Although she insists she doesn't need my help, that she wants to organise everything on her own, Lily's cousin Moira arrives and demands entry into the marriage planning conspiracy. When I call to collect Lily for the Saturday dance I am kept waiting for fifteen minutes, watching them in huddled collusion, two little wrens feathering a nest, darting between chairs and paperwork, making lists of needs and secondary lists of who will provides.

I feel excluded, and at the same time thankful; I am not expected to participate in the nesting flurry. When asked my opinion on linen, crockery and furniture, I find I have none. It astonishes me how much stuff is required to furnish two small rooms with folding doors between.

At a loose end, I take my astonishment to Joe, who assures me this is perfectly normal. How would he know? He's gone for the *let's live with Mother* option, the easy route. At least Lily and I are doing it on our own.

I am perfectly aware of the hypocrisy here but I am kind to myself and push it to the back of my mind.

'You've got it easy, Joe. You and Susan have all the furniture you can need here at your mum's.'

'That's true, it's a good way to start. And we're company for Mum.'

'And Susan's okay with that?'

'She's not said otherwise. Why should she? It's a gift.'

'Only Lily has plans. Expectations. She's very modern. She's after independence.'

'Oooh, I'd be careful there, Ray. You never know where that might lead.'

'Where?'

'It can only lead to grief. What would she do with independence?'

'And freedom.'

'Jeez, Ray, that's even worse.'

'Uh-huh. Why's that then?'

'She'll be asking for bird's eye maple next, and expecting you to provide.'

I have no idea what this is. 'Doesn't Susan ask for that?'

'Why should she? We share Mum's.'

This doesn't bear thinking about.

'Lily's not interested in sharing, she wants us to have our own. It might not all be new, she says, but it will be ours.'

'You see. It's started already. Where are you going to get your own? And why would you want it anyway, why lumber yourself with the expense?'

I understand precisely what he is saying and the more he says, the more I lean to Lily's way of thinking.

'You know your problem Joe, you've no ambition, no aims to better yourself.'

'You are probably right,' he laughs. 'I also don't have a millstone round my neck nor debts to repay.'

He can be a self-satisfied git when he wants.

'Dressing table and washstand with jug and basin.'

'A table and four chairs.'

'And armchairs and lino for the bedroom and living room.'

Lily and Moira list their acquisitions to date.

'Where did it all come from,' I ask in wonder.

'Uncle Ernie says we're to have aunt's dressing table set, Dad's work mates had a whip for the lino, our neighbour Iris, one of Mum's closest friends, is giving us a table and four chairs as she's buying new, and Dad says he'll get us a pair of armchairs as a wedding present.'

I run my fingers through my hair. 'Blimey. I thought we'd be sat on boxes for a year at least, eating straight out of the papers.' A romantic image I had grown quite fond of.

'All we've to do is get it all over to Shoreditch.'

Until now I've left Lily to make her own choices but here is a job with my name on it, and something in her expression says she expects me to rise to the occasion.

'That's for me to sort. Pretty Boy's brother is a dog dealer, he has a horse and cart to move his animals around. I reckon he'd lend it to us, for a pint.'

Pretty Boy comes along for the ride. I'm pleased about this as it gives me a chance to show off. It's only two rooms but we have sole use of the front door, the landlord and his family entering the house through a basement door. It makes me feel quite the ticket, calling the flat my own, and entering by our own front door. The rooms look bigger freshly painted and empty so I make sure he has a good look.

'Come in, Denny, we'll get our bearings before we cart that lot up the front steps.'

Lily has given me instructions on where each piece should go. During the week we'd been to Bakers Arms for a bed, a brass top and bottom with spring and overlay, which Lily insisted was the most up to date, and then insisted I pay £7 for it. I baulked at the price but I'd no plans to argue, I have plenty of expectations for this bed and whatever Lily wants is exactly what she is going to get.

The bed is to be delivered this week and the lino has to be down before it arrives. I'll say this for Lily, if she'd been called to The

War Cabinet to organise proceedings we'd have seen more boys returning from The Great War.

'How are you with lino, Denny?'

'No bloody idea but I'll give it a go.'

'Great, we'll start in here first.'

'Yeah. A room this small should only take us half an hour to lay.'

He cannot crush my pride.

'Let's hope so,' I say, flashing a broad smile to acknowledge his envy of me having my own front door key.

Three hours later, having wrestled with the brittle end-of-roll lino that the boys at the Post Office have so generously supplied, we are sweating drops of Bluebell. I am becoming suspicious that my family's inability to show more respect for the postal service is in some evil manner being repaid. Due to much grappling and lunging with said roll, a huge tear has appeared along one side of the mottled grey design, over which iniquity Denny and I have already mentally placed the dressing table, dangerously erring from Lily's designated plan.

'She won't notice,' says Pretty Boy, a cigarette hanging unsupported from his lower lip, sweat running down his nose.

'No. It looks better there in any case,' I say, flinging high the sash in an attempt to clear the room of the cigarette fog.

'And the wood can be retouched.'

I gaze, exhausted, at the scratched paintwork where the animated lino has clawed its way to the ground in a Herculean effort to resist defeat.

'Sure it can. Curtains will cover that anyway.'

'Shall we have that pint now, before we start the other room?'

It's jolly good of him to offer to stay for round two so I'm happy to fall in. We go along to the nearest corner and put away a quick pint. When we return, a little light headed with the beer and lack of food, we decide we need a plan before we tackle the second roll.

'We've got to have a plan,' says Pretty Boy, pondering. 'What we need to do is make a map of the room. Then we can roll the lino out on the road and bring it indoors ready-cut and sweet, to slot in like one great jigsaw piece.'

This sounds a good idea to me.

Denny unfolds his cigarette packet and begins a thumbnail sketch of the room.

'Don't forget this little bit around the gas pipe.'

'Got it.'

'Nor this tiling around the fireplace.'

'All here.'

'And the window bay, about six inches deeper on this side of the room.'

'Done.'

'I'll pigeon step the dimensions.'

'Shuffle away, Sunbeam.'

We unload the second roll of lino and tramp it down on the open street; a fluffy pink sponge that I realise, too late, is the lino Lily intended for the bedroom.

'Nice colour,' says Pretty Boy.

'Wrong colour,' I answer. 'This is the piece for the room we've already laid.'

We stand looking at the decidedly pink rectangle. Denny scratches his chin, then the back of his neck.

'She'll hang you out to dry.'

'Maybe once it's covered with armchairs and table?'

'It'll look pink, but covered with armchairs and tables.'

'We can paint it.'

'What colour?'

'Any colour but pink. No, the same colour as it's supposed to be, motley grey.'

'Maybe,' says Denny, looking doubtful.

'We'll go and ask Mr Hogg.'

No, apparently, there's no such colour as grey, but he's got some tins of black and white left over that we can mix, if our hearts are set on grey. That they are, we insist, it's all the rage amongst the young folk. He wants to know how come we're needing the paint, as he's only just finished all the decorating.

'How come you're needing the paint?'

Denny explains the situation, in too much detail and with too wide a grin.

Mr Hogg's grin is also widening. 'So, you've slid off down the battlecruiser, got yourself a bit Brahms, come back in a two and eight and now you're in Tom Tit.' He laughs.

We simultaneously hang our heads. That's one way of looking at it.

'Here you go then lads, and two brushes, which I'd be pleased to have back clean when you've finished, and mind the new skirting.'

Denny starts to mix the paints as I transfer his thumbnail sketch onto the sheet of lino that is only slightly larger than the cigarette packet: they are surprisingly small rooms to be causing such a headache.

With a pair of draper's scissors, also borrowed from the Hoggs, we hack the floor plan out of the centre of the sheet.

'Time you've fitted your cooker into the front room, she'll be able to serve dinner sat on the bed.'

It's true. It's a forlorn little patch, but I'm growing rather defensive of it.

'But it'll be private,' I say, trying hard to keep gloat out of my voice, but not too hard. 'We'll shut that front door and it'll be just me and Lily. Who needs a palace?'

Denny shrugs. 'Grab a brush.'

We begin to slap on the streaky mixture in great globs, swirling it around, leaning into the centre of the piece on our hands and knees, partly regretting that we have thoughtlessly started from the outer edges and worked in. The neighbourhood kids have no school today so with little alternative entertainment, have gathered to watch.

After a period of silent consideration one of them addresses Denny.

'What you doing then?'

'Me, I'm enjoying a lazy afternoon off with my artist friend here.'

'Well what's he doing?'

'He's being creative. He's creating a patch for the sky, so that when the heaven's open he's got a little scrap to plug the hole with, save us all from getting wet.'

I grin across at Denny who has always enjoyed working a crowd.

The boy looks up.

'But the sky is blue.'

Denny stands, brush in hand, to contemplate the sky, along with six or seven other heaven tilted faces.

'Not on the rainy days, son; on rainy days the sky is leaden grey.'

They consider this. He's right you know. It's only blue when the sun is out like today. But when it's about to rain, the clouds bang together and get all cross and grey. They look back at the patch.

'What's the pink bit in the middle?'

'That? That? That's where the sun is trying to get back through, he's turning the sky pink. You must have seen it?'

133

The lad shakes his head from side to side, wanting to believe but not quite getting there.

'Well you look at the sky the next time it rains. You come out into the middle of the street and stare up at the clouds. Then you'll see a large pink sun struggling to push the clouds aside.'

The boy, his finger pushed jauntily and unselfconsciously up one nostril, turns to the other children to see if they think this is likely.

With their blessing the spokesman decides we are halfwits. 'That's a load of cobblers,' he says, spitting out the words. It's a mistake to patronise kids, I think. 'I don't know what school you go to mate, but even Miss Spriggs, and my dad reckons she's dim as a Toc-H lamp, knows the sun is yellow.'

With this they lose interest. If we can't justify our art to them, they've better things to do with their time, mine their remaining nostrils for one.

Denny and I finish our artwork and sit to have a cigarette as it dries. I'm taking in Nichols Square, mine and Lily's new manor.

'How's your Charlie getting along these days?' Denny asks.

I look at him a bit surprised. 'Fine, I guess. Why?'

He draws on the Woodbine: 'Only I see him round about sometimes, here and there, and I was just wondering.'

'Charlie's Charlie,' I say, squinting my eyes into the smoke.

We stand and stretch our legs: the paint is dry.

We lift the multi-sided polygon upright, walk it up the front steps and into the room overlooking the street, where it slots, far too comfortably, into the floor space. The room is indeed small, but not as small as we have transcribed, distances between lino and skirting varying between six to twelve inches.

Bloody, bloody, bloody.

Denny rakes his hair, looking almost as aghast as I know I must.

'What am I going to do,' I wail.

'I know,' says Denny, after a few thoughtful drags on his cigarette. 'No worries. Go fetch the paint. We'll fill in the gaps between lino and wall.'

I stare at him. Would that work? Any solution, no matter how unlikely, sounds hopeful to me. I tear into the street, grab the grey mixture and return with the paintbrushes. Removing our shoes, we tie our socks around our knees to cushion and protect both them and the freshly painted lino, and we begin to paint the floorboards.

'You'll just tell Lily that the roll was a bit on the narrow side,' says Denny, carefully splicing a line of grey along the skirting edge.

'That in the circumstances, you thought it best not to have a huge gap down one side, but to centralise the piece, where it will get most of its wear and tear. When she looks like she's about to argue the toss, you point out how neatly you've tidied the edges, with matching paint, which will in the main be covered by furniture. In the meantime, you make sure you jump to the top of the list at The Gas Company and install your newest cooker before she's next here. She'll be so pleased with the progress she won't have time to moan. It'll be all hugs and delight.'

I look at Denny, willing myself to believe.

She'll be mad as hell, but what choice do I have.

At Lily's house that evening I try to steer the conversation away from Nichols Square. Tom Cartwright is in an excitable mood, buoyed up by the thought of Saturday's engagement party, but conversation has turned as it sometimes does to his next possible sighting of Lilian.

'So, you don't fancy cremation then, Tom?'

'You and Lily just make sure I'm dressed in my Sunday best, wearing my watch, and that my comb and hair wax are in my inside pocket. And I'll thank you to put me in there in my best suit.'

'And that would be for…?'

'For when I'm walking out, up there. I don't want to look a wreck. She'll have had plenty of time to settle in, she'll be bobbing and nodding to Gabriel and the like, but I'll be all sixes and sevens with the journey.'

'How's the flat looking?' Lily asks.

'And the watch is for…?'

'Well, I wouldn't want to be late, would I? Lilian would only be cross. Though there's a thought. I was wondering if you no longer got cross. If He sort of ironed out all the stress, and you floated around on a wave of patient pleasure.'

'Did you manage to get the dressing table through the front door, the side wings looked bulbous?'

'Yes, Lily. But Tom, what if she isn't up there? What if she's gone somewhere else?'

'You mean down below?'

'And the tables and chairs? Do they fit in the window bay?'

'Yes. Where else?'

They both look at me and decide the question is intended for them.

'There's no mistaking which way she's gone. Lilian was always headed upward.'

'Well, you might have thought they were better in the centre of the room or that they were too large altogether.'

Tom and Lily Cartwright laugh, and I am saved by a knock on the door: Uncle Ernie and Moira have called to receive their instructions for Saturday.

The engagement party is going well. The promised singing is loud and wholesome, the shuffling dancers are squashed and snug, the little terrace house throbs with friends bearing gifts and blessings. Lily sparkles like the child in the front row of the picture house as the organ player begins his descent, the movie about to begin. Every little comment, every congratulatory squeeze on the arm sees her chest swell to irrepressibly happy proportions. Glancing around the room there is a flushed euphoria pinking the guests' faces, even Pretty Boy is sporting an uncharacteristic enthusiasm.

Lily unwraps various pieces of household equipment: a pair of matching egg cups, a set of three tea towels tied in a white ribbon, a cake tin containing a newly baked fruit cake, to warm the cockles our of hearts, we are told, by a smiling toothless old lady who I sincerely hope is a mission guest and not a relative. Lily thanks everyone with kisses and smiles.

I raise my glass to Joe across the room. I would settle to enjoy myself more if Lily hadn't announced she would be bringing the gifts to the flat on Wednesday evening, the day we are taking delivery of the brass bed with spring and overlay.

'I can take them across on Pretty Boy's brother's cart again, if it would help. No need for you to lug this lot through the streets.'

'No, I want to come myself. I want to measure the windows for curtains.'

'Right. Because you can't do that any other time. It's just there seems a lot to carry, it would be easy to drop and break something.'

'I'll be fine. Ooh, these are lovely Moira, look Ray, our first cruet.'

'Well bless me, Moira, and so clever to have found a matching pair.'

Lily looks at me long and close. 'They're perfect love,' she says to Moira. 'Aren't we lucky Ray, to have such lovely gifts?'

She's giving me another chance. Offering redemption.

'Yes, thank you Moira, it must have taken you ages to find them.'

Lily and Moira scowl at me like two cross bookends.

'I'll be over here if you need me, darling, having a quick word with Joe.'

By Wednesday morning I'm a tiger with a toothache: a niggling premonition is making me scratchy and my concentration is all to pot. Pieces of lead pipe get sawn off too short, I leave the yard with the wrong gas valves, which I then try to fit to the wrong appliances. I am preoccupied, and in my defence I blame the lads back at the depot. The ladies stand arms crossed in their sculleries and tut, knowing better.

By seven o'clock Wednesday evening Lily is hurrying up the steps of No.70 Nichols Square. She has reached a barely containable pitch of excitement that I can only watch with a sense of pending doom. I lag a few paces behind, stopping to kick a yellowing leaf out onto the front step.

As she opens the door to our rooms she lets out a piercing scream, dropping the gifts on the floor, which clatter and spring around the hallway. If Mr Cartwright didn't live on the other side of the borough he would be bounding the pavements of Shoreditch waving a machete to put into practice his threat to my person should I cause his angel the merest hint of grief. I hang my head and sidle up to Lily, hiding behind my own armful of gifts, explanations at the ready.

'It was Denny.'

My voice is muffled by a thick, fluffy counterpane.

'He measured it incorrectly, he cut it incorrectly and then he painted it incorrectly.'

She lets out another shriek, which despite my sense of guilt I feel is taking it a bit far. After all, it's a piece of lino. Pieces of lino can be replaced. I can have a new one down before the weekend, if I really have to.

'Ray!' she squeals. 'Quick!'

Quick?

A burglar?

A burglar in search of just that particular shade of grey-tinged-pink lino has raided the flat?

I'll have the police onto that one straight away. It'll be right up there with local man kills future son-in-law in pre-nuptial brawl.

'Get them out!'

Them! Christ, more than one and they're still here!

I step sharply along the hallway to Lily, who has backed away from the door and flattened herself against the wall in horror. Hurriedly placing my parcels on the floor to free my grappling arms, I stride to the doorway to size up the opposition.

There, in the middle of the grey-ish lino, sits the largest, ginger tom cat I have ever seen, his massive onion shaped head smiling happily. From his mouth, wriggling and flaying, hang two pink and white mice, under his right paw is the imprisoned tail of a third, equally keen to escape, scratching away at the painted lino, clawing gouges through to the pink. It looks as if his claws, scratching for so long, have worn away to draw pale pink mouse blood.

I turn to Lily and laugh, overcome with relief.

'Get rid of them,' she cries.

'But he's doing a far better job than I could.' I can hear the ginger tom purring.

'There might be others,' she squeals.

'I'll find the hole and block it up.'

As I enter the room, the onion swings its dinner from side to side, gauging the most suitable window through which to make his escape. He then reluctantly gives up his hold on the mouse beneath his paw in order to escape with his supper through the front window. The freed mouse runs behind the newly installed gas stove.

'There's our mouse hole,' I say triumphantly, in my best Sherlock Holmes.

Lily moves shakily across to the window to sit at the table, tucking her feet up onto the bar of the chair.

'That's right. You sit quietly for a minute and I'll make you a cup of tea, I've some things here in the box.'

I'm going to kiss that cat.

I'm going to take his fat cat face in my hands and rub my nose back and forward across his, both our eyes closed to slits of pleasure at this manly greeting. He'll have sardines for supper and a satin bow for Christmas. I want to adopt him and make him happy.

Lily sits hugging her tea cup, her eyes darting warily around the skirting for warning signs of the mouse family come in search of their late-departed mouse cousins. I bring in the presents, spreading them around the floor to cover the iniquitous lino, quickly unravelling a rag-rug and placing it over the scratched floor.

'I can't stay here, Ray, not until you've got rid of them.'

'That's okay, sweetheart. I'll block the hole while I'm waiting for the delivery men. You run on home. I'll join you shortly. I'll even bring the measurements for the windows.'

'Thank you, Ray, you're a darling.'

Lily is gone in a flash, a wisp of red hair fluttering in her wake.

I love Lily, but at this particular moment, I love Onionhead more.

Chapter 17

I Would Like To Suggest We Elope,
But A Wedding It Is

I decide to adopt him, telling Lily he is our picket against the mice. He will patrol our rooms while we are at work, dine off his labours, and be rewarded for his services when we return.

Onionhead definitely thinks this is on.

He also thinks one of the two armchairs has his name on it, performing a thorough workout on the cushion, circling and circling until he drops, dizzy with effort, into a huge ginger ball. His contented sleep is so heavy I can lift him undisturbed and settle him back on my legs as I take my rightful place in the armchair. His fat paws, the size of apples, spring open into sharp spikes, which he purringly inserts into my thigh, plumping it to an adequate squashiness for his better enjoyment. We do this most evenings.

Most evenings Lily joins us.

She hangs curtains, makes up the bed, eyes the lino sceptically, retouches the scratched paintwork, which she decides was probably caused by the bed delivery men, and piles a small stack of coins on the new shelves in the alcove, ready for the gas meter.

Onionhead and I sit and watch. At the mention of the paint scratches I nod. The cat closes his eyes to knowing slits and spies on Lily through his furry visor: trusting females need so much looking after.

'If you do all this now,' I say, 'what will you do with yourself after we're married?'

'What do you mean?'

'Won't you get bored, all day long, just you and the Onion, patrolling for mice.'

Lily shivers and reaches down to scratch the ball of fur's ear. 'I won't be here. They've said I can keep my job.'

'They have?' I'm astonished. No woman gets to keep their job after marriage.

'Mr Hawks says he'll make this one exception, as I am a good worker. And, he says I can have a week off for my honeymoon.'

'That's excellent, Lily. Clever you.'

'I'm going to take in a bottle of port wine and a tin of biscuits tomorrow, as a thank you. I'm sad they can't be at the wedding. Mr Hawks says, as it's this weekend, he'll let me off early. I can give them all a drink and on the way home I'll pick up my outfit.'

On Friday evening, I call at Lily's to see if she's set for the wedding. I am so excited I can't stay at home; everyone there is determined to stay flat and uninvolved. Mum says she hasn't bought a new outfit but I fetch a dress from her wardrobe and check it for stains. It'll have to do. Charlie sits subdued in the background, smiling vacantly when I talk to him, then dropping back into some private reverie when I'm done. I look at him and wonder what's going on in his head.

I need to get near the action, I want to enjoy the excitement. I know there will be a flurry at Lily's and I spring along the pavement whistling the wedding march, jiggling the hot band of gold in my pocket.

When I arrive the house is in uproar, the front door is open and I follow the noise through to the yard. Lily has locked herself in the outside toilet and appears to be sobbing and shouting all at once. Not quite the excitement I'd been looking for.

Her father is pacing up and down the tiny garden shouting so loud I can't make out his words. Moira has black streams running down her face and her nose is bright red. Uncle Ernie is slamming cupboard doors in the effort to make everyone a calming cup of tea. There is nothing I can do but pitch in.

'Lily? It's Ray.' I knock on the toilet door. 'What's happened?'

'Oh Ray. It was so lovely. I'm so ashamed. They were so nice. Tell him to go away, tell him to go a long way away.'

'Who? Why don't you come indoors and explain.'

'I'm not coming anywhere until he's gone. He's a bully.'

'You watch yourself young lady.'

'Excuse me Mr Cartwright, what has happened?'

'She gets home here, and then I see that outfit and then I know. I wasn't born yesterday, lad. I should punch your lights out, Ray Riley, I really should.'

Tom Cartwright takes a half-hearted lunge at me. Lily, hearing his words, throws open the toilet door and runs at him.

'Don't you ever listen? Don't you ever think? I was having a wonderful day. The girls had bought me such lovely things. Then you frighten Doris away with your shouting, you silly old fool.'

'It's beige! Everyone will know what that means. It's a beige suit! They won't be looking at your green hat and thinking, my, that's a nice titfer, they'll be thinking, we all know what that means.'

'Listen to him. What he doesn't know isn't worth knowing. This is the last time I'll say it: Ray and I can't afford a white gown, we want to put the money into our home. Cream signifies nothing. You scared the wits out of Doris, and she'd been so kind to carry all their gifts home with me. I'm never speaking to you again.'

'Why don't we all calm down. It's a simple misunderstanding. Mr Cartwright, your daughter is as pure as the driven snow. When we looked at the cost of everything it was that, or a decent bed; Lily chose the bed. We know the wedding is an important day and although I haven't seen the outfit, she's not going to look like a scarlet woman, this is Lily we're talking about, with Lily wearing it, it can look nothing but lovely.'

Lily bursts into another round of sobs.

Moira wraps her arms round Lily's shoulders and glares at Tom Cartwright.

Uncle Ernie has finally solved the problem with the cupboard doors. 'Shall we all have a quiet cup of tea?'

'I need a beer,' says Tom Cartwright.

'Have a cup of tea first,' I say. 'Then we can have a drink together later, to wish us all luck, before I go home. I'm sure all our nerves are on edge with the build-up for tomorrow. We want to enjoy ourselves, with no regrets.'

Lily and Moira attend to each other's faces.

'So you're saying nothing's amiss?'

'Nothing.'

'And when everyone asks me if she's okay, I say she's fine?'

'You stand up straight and proud and say she's exactly as Lilian would have wanted her, a beautiful young woman marrying the man she loves.'

'Well, that's all right then. Why didn't you say so sooner.'

Mr Cartwright slinks indoors.

Lily throws herself onto my chest and I indicate to Moira that her services are not needed just for the moment.

The wedding day has arrived; I pinch myself awake to take full pleasure of every moment of my last bachelor day, for by this evening I will be two. Never again me, never again mine, from now on us and ours.

If last weekend's party had been a bouncing celebration, so far this weekend's gathering has all the look of a torpid reluctance. I glance across at Charlie, snoring on the bed next to me and determine to lift my spirits.

Not so, not so, I tell myself, throwing cold water over my head and shoulders and singing loudly to rouse the snoring dead.

I jumped out of the frying pan
Into the blooming fire

Not so.

Last weekend was public, today is private. But what a bedraggled looking private bunch we are.

At mid-morning I inspect the troops. We can't afford any cars, so we plan to walk the fifteen minutes to the church, and there's no money for a photographer, which will upset Lily later on but what's to be done; where there's no cash there's no cake, which is another thing that didn't make it onto the shopping list.

On the plus side, Mum's dress looks presentable and she seems mildly pleased with herself, turning her head from side to side in a small hand mirror, rose-budding her lips at no one. Dad looks at her and smiles. He has been out early and bought four white carnations, his wedding gift to me; I am so grateful I grip his arm in thanks, surreptitiously sniffing his breath to catch the early morning tang of a whisky shot. Charlie walks casually into the room to line up for inspection, what a dazzler. He must have been stashing it away for months to have bought that suit, I could kiss him I'm so pleased.

The wedding is booked for one o'clock. At twelve thirty we begin our way along the road, a few of the neighbours come to their doors to wish us luck, Mrs Wallace placing a cardboard horseshoe into Charlie's hand telling him to hang it on Lily's arm, when the ceremony is over. He nods and smiles at me, apparently pleased to be given this job.

The church is daunting, large and finger pointing, unsuited to my unsanctified soul. I stand in front of the alter, shifting from leg to leg, listening distractedly as the organist making hard work of her programme of cherub knees-ups and seraphim sambas. The pews are empty, save for our few close relatives. Ella, her arm hooked through Arthur's, wiggles her fingers at me and winks; Arthur grimaces and slides an index finger across his throat.

I have no reason to believe marriage can work, few examples to convince me that the state of matrimony can in any shape or form lead to bliss. It is man's biggest act of faith and we have tried every possible route to sustain the belief: bigamy, polygamy, the arranged match, the marriage of convenience, how many make it happily to the end? And yet we all believe we will, we all believe that we are the exception. Indeed, to remain unpartnered would be a stigma, it would suggest unsociability, to be mateless, an ageing bachelor, would be to be unlovable. I used to think I was unlovable: my mother left with Charlie in her arms, while I stood on the step and bawled, begging her to take me also, but she walked away regardless.

Then she appears.

Leaning comfortably on her father's arm, she walks the length of the aisle, smiling at me, only me. She is spectacular. Where before I felt nervous, now I feel alarm. Can I meet this challenge? Can I, Ray Riley, make it happen?

Too bloody right I can.

When she reaches my side I see her lips are quivering, her eyes are shining and wet; I feel for her hand and squeeze it gently.

'Don't be nervous, Lily.'

She squeezes back. It is a pact, as important as the blessing, as important as the vows, greater than the vicar wishing us a happy life together. We leave the church hand in hand. She won't walk away, regardless: this is my act of faith.

As we step out into the sharp autumn sunshine, there is a whooping and a scattering of rice grains. Four of Lily's friends from the factory have come to wish us luck.

'Lily, you look smashing.'

'Gosh, you got yourself a handsome one there, has he any brothers?'

'Lily! Look this way! Mr Hawks lent me his Brownie. I've to get a shot of the happy couple. It's to be his wedding gift to you.'

And there we stand, Lily and I, hand in hand, Mum and Dad, erect and unsmiling at my side, Tom Cartwright and Moira proud and formal on Lily's. Charlie, Arthur, Ella, Grandma and Grampa Riley, Joe and Susan hovering in the background, the lucky horseshoe swinging on Charlie's arm, forgotten.

'And now, just one of the happy couple alone.'

As our unofficial photographer takes her best shot, an autumn wind flicks across the churchyard and flurries what it carries around our legs, swirling the fallen leaves and lifting Lily's skirt to a billowing pillow. In our wedding photo, Lily has one hand on her pillow, and the other, still holding mine, on her hat. We are laughing at each other.

Moira bustles over.

'Come on you two. Dad and my wedding present is at home. Come on everyone, and you good ladies too, on the tram, it won't take us long.'

Two of the girls hook their arms through Lily's and march her out the churchyard gates toward the tram stop. I look doubtfully at Mum and Dad; Charlie has wandered off to look at the gravestones. Joe catches my gaze and saunters after him.

Thank you, Joe.

At Diana Road, Moira wraps tea towels around our eyes, herding everyone ahead of us into their sitting room. Giggles and whisperings make us inch forward gingerly, unsure what trap has been set. Then Moira whips the cloths from our faces.

Surprise!
Congratulations!
Well done!

Where all we have done is hold hands, Uncle Ernie had stayed at home to prepare a wedding breakfast beyond Lily's dreams. A long table is spread with a bright yellow cloth, a splendour in itself after the newspapers on our dining table, which is covered with plates of sliced beef and ham, salad, mashed potatoes, pickles, bread and butter, fancy cakes and a glass of port for each guest. In the middle of the table stands Uncle Ernie's present, a three tier wedding cake, iced and covered in silver balls, wedding bells and orange blossom.

'To the two of you,' he calls loudly, lifting his glass. 'May you always be this happy.'

'May you always be happy,' echoes the chorus.

'It's only a simple sponge inside,' he whispers apologetically, 'but if we don't cut it until they've all gone, no one will ever know.' Looking around at his guests he shouts, 'Come along everyone, take your seats and get stuck in before the riff raff arrive for the evening.

Lily and Ray, you come and sit here at the centre, then everyone else sit yourselves wherever you fancy.'

People shuffle and knock each other to get to the seat they have earmarked. Those with a need for beef, head for the window end of the table; those with a sweet tooth, shuffle towards the fireplace to seat themselves near the fancies. Everyone laughs and jokes as they scramble for their advantage, apart from Mum and Dad, who sit at the nearest chairs and watch the proceedings as if they consider the whole occasion too lavish for their simple needs. Well bugger them. This is my day, and I for one plan to mark it as a new beginning.

Ting, ting, ting.

Joe tinkles a teaspoon against the side of his port glass, and rises. The room falls silent. I sit back in my seat, taking Lily's hand in my lap.

'Ladies and gentlemen. It is my honour, as best man to the groom, to say a few words.' He clears his throat shyly and smiles nervously at Susan. 'Thank you all for coming today to mark this special occasion on the marriage of Lily and Ray. I know they will be very happy together and Lily, you couldn't have picked a better one.'

I small cheer goes up from the lads.

'I haven't got anything very clever to say, it's Ray that has all the clever words, but I want to say thank you to him, for being a good friend, for taking my side when the going got tough, which it frequently did.'

Mum and Dad are sat, their hands loose in their laps, the windows of their eyes closed.

'Ray taught me when to stand my ground at school, which wasn't often, and when to run fast, and he steered me through the beginnings of our time at the factory and then the dole line. He didn't have to sort out my love life, I managed that all on my own, I'm proud to say.'

Everyone laughs and smiles at Susan.

'Ray's the sort anyone would be able to lean on, as Lily will learn in the years to come. And so, I would like you to raise your glasses for Lily and Ray.'

Everyone does as they are bid, offering their congratulations and best wishes, everyone that is apart from Mum and Dad who simply look at us blankly.

Out of the blue, Charlie bounces out of his seat. Mum's eyes turn up in startled surprise.

Silence. Someone clears their throat. Uncle Ernie laughs, a tense, edgy laugh that hopes Charlie won't spill any personal embarrassment onto the sunny contentment of the wedding table.

He hesitates but remains standing.

'To Lily and Ray!' he says, sitting down abruptly.

The company bangs the table and clinks its glasses, hiding a relief with enthusiastic whoops. I look at Lily, who once again has tears in her eyes as she toasts her new brother-in-law. Charlie is smiling at the tablecloth.

Absurd as he is, I believe Lily will welcome visits from Charlie whenever he needs companionship, and I feel he might need it often.

Chapter 18

It Is The Cocktail Hour Of Married Life, And I Have Ordered A Double Smile With A Healthy Splash Of Headache

Food. Nothing gross or overwhelming, simply there and on the plate. Lily cooks breakfast before I leave for work.

I come home at lunchtime to a hot meal steaming into the cool air, condensation rills running down the window, Onionhead sitting with his eyes shut, purring at aromas he anticipates will solidify into his bowl in the near cat future.

Lily and I sit at our wobbly, second hand dining table, which Lily covers with a linen cloth, just for the honeymoon week she explains, and we look out over Nichols Square. We can hardly chew for grinning.

Lily tells me about her morning.

Mrs Hogg has explained where to shop and Lily has taken herself to Hoxton Street market, where she has spent the best part of the morning. 'It's like being in another country. Men dressed in the strangest outfits, long black coats with large fur-rimmed hats, and ringlets hanging down the sides of their faces. I stood staring, amazed, but no one else paid them any attention, and I had to watch my manners, they were everywhere, gabbling in a foreign language, laughing and throwing their arms wide into the air.'

Lily puts down her cutlery and throws her arms up to better demonstrate her market; I think about the gesture all afternoon, my head jammed down the back of Mrs Weil's cooker.

This honeymoon week is a precious oasis in which Lily and I learn the dance of husband and wife. Each day, I depart to earn my wage, which I will give to Lily at the end of the week, an unopened packet for Lady Bountiful to dispense as she sees fit.

Each day she presents me with a gift: a ripe pear, a single handkerchief in the corner of which she has embroidered my initials, a newly darned sock.

I receive these tokens like a blessing, a confirmation, a recognition of marriage as a series of offerings, tenderly submitted, thankfully received and always acknowledged.

I glide through the processes of spanner and wrench, smiling at the bawdy commentary of my workmates, dreaming only of my return home. It is Friday night, Lily has promised a surprise.

As I turn the key in the lock, Onionhead flies out into the chill September air, eager to escape an interior I have yet to be appalled by. I look after him, frowning at his unpredictability. Not the same as dogs, I am thinking as I notice the door to our rooms stood wide, dogs sit beside you, through thick and thin. I am surprised to see Mrs Hogg sat on the edge of our bed, her arm around Lily's shoulder.

The landlady jumps up as I enter the bedroom.

'Thank goodness you're here. Don't be alarmed, Mr Riley, there's been an accident, a nasty accident.'

That's a good start of the non-alarming kind.

'I'm so sorry, Ray,' cries Lily, holding out two bandaged arms.

I drop my tool bag, my face one big question mark. HOW?

'It's the fat pan,' explains Mrs Hogg above Lily's sobs. 'She's caught her sleeve on the handle and tipped it over both arms.'

'Jesus Christ!'

'It was such a nice piece of plaice, and now it will go to waste.' Lily is trembling.

'I took her across the square to The Queen's Nurses and they've done what first aid they can, but they say she must get straight to a hospital.'

'Oh Christ, Lily.'

I want to fold her into my arms, desperate to hold her close, fearful of increasing her pain, tears welling in my eyes. Her lovely skin, torn, just so's she can make a gift of a piece of fried fish. 'My poor darling.'

'She wouldn't leave without you, Mr Riley. I offered to take her straight to the hospital but she wouldn't come.'

'It's okay Mrs Hogg. I'll get her to The Metropolitan on Kingsland Road.'

'She was screaming to wake the dead. I came running as fast I could.'

Mr Hogg wanders through the door in search of his wife.

'Hey up. What's wrong in here? Is someone brown bread?'

'It was all over her hands and arms, Mr Riley, and she's got awful great blisters on the palms.'

'Jesus, Lily, come on, let's get you down there.'

Lily is white with pain.

'She'll not be able to walk.'

Then I'll carry her.

My gift to Lily.

At the hospital the bandages are unwoven to reveal worse than my thoughts have conjured. Lily's flesh is peeling away. I stare, appalled and fascinated, at the sight of bloated, liquid filled swellings and raw flesh; her hands and fingers are swollen to twice their normal size. An old nurse absorbs herself in the routine requirements of her job, moving skilfully around her patient, producing a pair of cutters to remove her rings.

'Don't cut the rings off,' Lily shouts, 'it's a terrible sign.'

'I'm afraid we have to, Mrs Riley, we need to release the pressure.'

'I don't mind it, I'll take pain killers, but don't cut off my wedding ring. It's bad luck.'

'I'm sorry, Mrs Riley.'

A second nurse steps forward and injects Lily, saying it will help her relax and relieve her of the pain.

No doubt about that. Lily slumps back in the chair, her head tipped toward the ceiling, her gaze taking in nothing.

'That's powerful stuff,' I comment. 'How long will that work for?'

'Not long, Mr Riley. Just enough for us to remove the rings and redress her skin. We won't be able to keep her in, there are not enough beds; we'll make her as comfortable as we can, to get her through the night. She'll have to come back tomorrow for treatment. And probably every day this week.'

'Will it scar?'

She looks at me with the weary eyes of someone at the end of a long shift of pain, someone who has seen such ravages many times. She is not unkind, merely blunt. 'What do you think, Mr Riley?'

I don't want to think. Only one week into my role of husband and already Lily is scarred. Why didn't I take a day off as I'd planned, gone with Lily to her market, maybe had pie and liquor in a cafe, or bought the blasted fish and chips to eat from the paper? We might have sat outside on the front wall, watched our neighbours, nodded hello. But I'd been so pleased to be bringing in a wage, I didn't want it docked, I wanted to show her my full worth, show her that I could keep her, I wanted to make my grand offering. Lily burned, and all for a *ta da!*

That night Lily lies in bed, tossing and turning, unable to sleep. She has not eaten. She keeps crying, saying how guilty she feels, how she's let me down, and all the time I'm feeling the same way, and we can't cuddle and make up. With both her arms in slings, I have to wait on her. At least I have the satisfaction of knowing I'm needed.

Mrs Hogg has offered to take over on Monday when I return to work but come Monday morning, I'm jittery.

'How will you manage the journey to the hospital?'

'It's no problem, and I'll stay with her afterward and when I'm cooking Mr Hogg's tea, I'll do an extra portion for you two, it's really no problem. Go to work.'

'What if she faints?'

'She won't faint. She's over the worst. She's a little low, as you might expect. I'll cut some flowers and bring them in for her.'

'I'll pay for the dinner, of course.'

'Get away with you. You just keep your nose clean, I'll sort things here. Go. Or you'll lose your job.'

'Are you sure you'll be okay, Lily.'

Lily looks miserable. 'I'll be fine. Do as Mrs Hogg says. We'll get through. Off you go or they'll be looking out for you.'

I hesitate at the door. Mrs Hogg waves her tea towel at me impatiently.

'Go, lad.'

I blow them both a kiss.

'See you later,' I say, trying for spirit-lifting, achieving careless.

This feels like somewhere about rock bottom. Lily is tired, angry and in pain. I am tired, guilty and frustrated. We get through the evenings as best we can, sadly aware that our bubble has burst and our smiles have spilled, like the burning oil, onto the lino, which, by the way, is now a challenging pink where Mrs Hogg has wiped up. Lily sits on the edge of the chair looking bewildered at the molten floor. Never mind, I say to myself, no use crying over spilt substances, we'll pick ourselves up, shake ourselves out and start over.

Lily is still having difficulty sleeping so it is she who hears the knocking. It is after midnight.

'Ray, Ray, someone's at the door.'

'What's the time?'

'Late. Too late for callers.'

I listen until I hear a voice. Charlie has moved across to the window and is tapping.

'Ray, wake up, I need to come in.'

'For God's sake Charlie, go home.'

'No.'

'Go away.'

'Undo the door, Ray.'

Now I'm cross.

'Charlie, go away or I'll come out there and knock your block off.'

'Lily, let me in.'

'Ah, for Pete's sake!' I throw back the cover and drop my feet onto the chilly lino, a sharp unpleasantness after the warmth of Onion's bulk on the eiderdown.

Charlie is in a terrible state, shaking and stammering.

'It's Dad. He's been killed, Ray.'

I stand very still, rubbing first my eyes, then my ears. 'What?'

'He walked out in front of the bone man's horse and she's reared up and come down on his head. They put him inside The Dog, thinking to nurse him, but he never came out.'

How fitting.

'When was this?'

'Not too long ago.'

'Where's Mum?'

'In the pub, sitting with the body. What are we going to do, no one knows what to do?'

I don't know what to do. Lily is in pain, she can't look after herself even to go to the toilet, but Charlie's eyes are pleading with me.

'Come in Charlie, I'll have to talk to Lily.'

Lily has managed to pull herself up in the bed, both slings resting outside the cover. This is all too much for Charlie.

'Jeez Ray, what's happened to Lily?'

'I'm okay Charlie, it's just a silly burn; I'm on the mend.' Lily doesn't want to cause Charlie any pain. Poor Lily, I'm sure she could do with the sympathy. 'I heard you talking, Ray. You'd better go and see how your mum is. She'll be in shock and Charlie needs your help.'

Charlie, looking even more distressed, starts swaying from one foot to the other and humming quietly to himself. Since the printworks closed Charlie must have been wandering the streets with all the other down and outs looking for work. The last thing Charlie needs is another trauma.

'I've got Mrs Hogg downstairs, she'll look after me while you're gone.'

'No, things back home'll take a bit of time to sort and we can't impose on Mrs Hogg indefinitely. I'll go to the doctor again in the morning, perhaps they can find a hospital bed somewhere else, given the circumstances.'

Charlie and I march back in silence to The Dog and Duck where we are greeted by a wretched congregation of bleary eyed mourners. A knot of gawpers has herded into the corner of the saloon bar clustering around what I presume to be Dad's remains. Charlie and I shoulder our way through the mob, each of which seem reluctant to give up their positions to latecomers. Mum sits on a chair staring at his body, which has been lain along the leather seat. She looks up as we break through the crowd.

'It's funny really,' she says, not smiling, not seeing the joke. 'Rag and bones is what he is, and so the bone man took him.'

'Blimey,' jeers a voice entering the bar. 'Has somebody died? It's like a morgue in here.'

No one in the inner sanctum deigns to respond. 'Come on Charlie, let's carry him home.' The way parts and our passage is cleared.

'Had too many has he son? The demon drink took him in the end?'

'Something like that.' I say.

'Yeah, the trick is to stop while you've got the better of it, before it gets the better of you.'

'You reckon,' I say, as Charlie and I shoulder ourselves one under each of Dad's armpits, dragging his arms across our backs in the affectionate hug he never gave us in life.

'You should tell him to lay off the hard stuff,' calls the sage to our departing backs.

'I'll do that,' I say.

Charlie is looking at me despairingly. Come on Ray, throw me a line, help me, I don't like the smell of this.

I wink at Charlie and smile a gentle encouragement.

'It'll be all right, Charlie. There's plenty to do and I'll need your help to do it. We'll do it together.'

'But what?' he whimpers.

'It's okay, Charlie. We'll muddle through.'

153

'That's all we ever do, muddle through.'

'Don't let it get you down, Charlie. You once advised me: don't let them ruin your day. I took your advice then and now you must take mine.'

'What advice is there, accept them for the drunks they are?'

'Jeez, Charlie, we could have seen this end, in some form or another. I know I sound like a hard git but he never thought about anyone but himself so what are we going to miss? I'm supposed to feel gutted but I don't. It's you and me, Charlie. We've got to look out for each other.'

'And Mum.'

'Right. And Mum.'

He nods, worn out with the effort of shouldering his burden, relieved to receive forgiveness for his inadequacies, thankful to be absolved of his fears.

First thing in the morning I'm at the doctors.

'The burns are bad, she needs daily treatment, look, here's the letters from the Metro, she can't do anything for herself, not even wipe her you know what, how am I going to do this and bury my father. My mother and brother are walking around the house in a daze, useless. I'm the head of the household, they're expecting me to sort everything, and if Lily were in a hospital bed, she'd have help whenever she needed it. I've got a good job, which I could lose by taking time out each day, and they'd cook for her too, I'd feel so much better knowing she was being properly cared for…'

'Hold on, Mr Riley, slow down. There's no need to plead your case any further. I can see the problem. You must have been very close to your father.'

'We were like father and son.'

He looks at me.

In the pause, I straighten my leg, as if to unlock a cramp. I rub the affected area for show.

'And your concern for your new young wife is commendable.'

'Will that get her a bed?'

'No, but it's nice to see, all the same.'

'So you can't get a bed?'

'I didn't say that. How is your mother coping?'

'She doesn't know about the burns.'

'I mean with your father's sudden departure.'

'Oh.' I think about this. 'She'll be worrying, worrying how she'll cope without his dole.'

'Well, one less mouth to feed.'

Dr King smiles encouragingly.

I stare at him. If this was Charlie sitting here instead of me, he would burst into tears. As it is, I do nothing but marvel at his coldness. I stand to leave.

'One moment, Mr Riley, I'll just make one call.'

Dr King telephones what can only be a long lost brother. They discuss their health, their wealth, their families, their friends and then, just as I think I must have disappeared into the carpet, he slips in:

'So, how busy are you at St Leonards, at the moment? Full complement? No room at the inn?

'Wow, and you can cure none of them?

'Oh I see.

'Ahah.

'And this was all down to you?

'Incredible.

'How many?

'And they walked out unaided?

'Congratulations.

'Freeing up how many beds did you say?

'You deserve a medal.

'I'll be sending a Mrs Riley along, she'll be with you by the end of the day, she has severe burns to both forearms and hands, needs daily treatment and a bed allocation of one month. Please give my regards to your wife.'

Dr King smiles at me. I smile back. A big hugging type of smile. We shake hands and I leave in silence, clutching a letter for Lily's admission to St Leonards in Hoxton Street.

Lily is overwhelmed, the tears roll down her cheeks, I wipe them away. She can't hug me or cover her face, which would be the natural thing to do, she just sits there, her arms bent stiff at the elbows, her shoulders quivering. I fold myself carefully around her back, sliding my arms gently into her waist.

My poor Lily.

'I'll make us a cup of tea, Lily, and then you tell me what you want me to pack.'

I hum an old waltz as I gather the tea things, Aunt Lizzie pops into my head, creating a little feel-good moment, a happy laugh. The sweet aroma of her house can sometimes hit me as I walk past the hot wall of the bakery. If I rub against the myrtle bush in the front yard I am spun back into Aunt Lizzie's Christmas. The thought of a walnut or an elegant piece of furniture and there she is, gliding through my head, smoothing her hand along a polished sideboard, blowing the dust from a record. I wonder if she thinks of me, the one member of my family who showed me any care, the one member of my family on whom I turned my back. What kind of fool was I? Lily says I was no fool at all, I was simply too young to know.

I've invented a special way for Lily to drink her tea, in a tall tumbler with plenty of milk, which she sucks up through a straw. She says it makes her feel like an invalid; I think she looks like a girl at a party. I can see that the news of the hospital bed is relaxing into her like a warm balm.

'St Leonards is so near I'll be able to visit real easy. Wednesday afternoons and Sundays it says on the leaflet, for a whole hour each time. That might not sound like much visiting but in between you'll be getting plenty of rest and that's what the doctor says you need.'

Lily smiles.

'And don't say sorry one more time, I'm sick of hearing it. An accident's an accident. We've plenty of time to make up for it, which will be even more fun.'

I tickle her under her chin and am pleased to see she blushes. That's okay then, at least we're thinking on the same lines.

Two days of visiting leaves five days for waiting.

Mrs Hogg is true to her word. When I come home each evening, she has placed an enamel plate on top of a saucepan of water for me to reheat; a rabbit stew, a bit of mutton, piled high with potatoes and carrots. I wolf it down and head straight out to St Leonards.

On the nights I can't go in, I sit on a wall opposite the tall, pink-bricked building, staring up at Lily's hospital window, the blinds are opened or closed by an unseen hand. Lily knows I'm here. I send her up parcels: chocolates, apples, anything I can think of. A magazine would be nice. I try to remember what magazines Lily reads and find I don't know. The last of the sun's rays eventually disappear from the bricks and the night returns the building to a block of grey. The light in Lily's room flickers on, a pale mauve, too bright for poor Lily who I am sure would rather be in darkness.

'Goodnight Princess Mer,' I say out loud, just in case the love wind is feeling benevolent and can float my words up to Lily's window. 'Sweet dreams.'

My nights are long. With only one week of married life under my belt I'm feeling a little sorry for myself. I've sorted what I can for the funeral, now I must sit and wait.

'Shake a leg, Ray,' I reprimand. 'Things could be a damn sight worse.'

I call in on Joe to check out happy house; have a beer with Pretty Boy for comic relief; call round to see Charlie and Mum for duty's sake. Everyone seems to be muddling along, though Charlie often isn't at home, he goes walkabout, Mum says, when she can be bothered to string a sentence; she doesn't see him much these days.

I could be Charlie. We both suffered the same home, or lack of it, both needed the same wallop of love, and were denied it. What he hopes to find out on the streets God only knows but I have to agree with him, it certainly isn't offered at home.

But I can't worry about him for the moment; I've got to get my own house in order.

The following week I'm in Bunhill Avenue, just off City Road, my head tucked down behind Mr Cohen's stove when the conversation turns to Mr Cohen's line of business.

'Me, all my life, I've been in finance.'

'You don't say?'

'Beats ferreting around behind a gas appliance,' he says, grinning the heads-I-win-tails-you-lose grin of the self-obsessed.

'I'll bet.'

I let an amber-black grease globule plop onto his floorboard.

'In the square mile are you?'

'More or less.'

I can hear him pacing the floor behind me, his thumbs tucked behind his braces, his chin lifted to stretch the dewlap. Not much he can do about his conk. I smile.

'What exactly do you do, in finance?'

'I print money.'

'Yeah, right.' I am unimpressed.

'Why would I lie?'

'For the Bank of England, I suppose.'

'Well, no. For the Bank of Turkey.'

'You mean you're in laundry, all nice and legit.'

'Like I'd be telling you about it if it wasn't.'

'You've got a licence to print money?'

I straighten up to relieve my back but stay knelt down on the floor. Mr Cohen laughs, regaining his composure: there was he thinking I wasn't going to believe him.

'My brother owns De la Rues. He got a year contract he couldn't meet on top of his other commitments, so he's put me in charge of production.'

'And that's what you do, you print the money?'

'Turkish £1 notes, to be exact.'

'No jobs going I don't suppose?' I'm joking at this point.

'I'm always on the lookout for examiners, good pairs of eyes are hard to find, if you catch my drift.'

I wasn't exactly sure that I did but I took him at his word.

'What's the pay?'

'23/-, why, you thinking of jacking in the gas?'

'No, but my Mrs has got the best pair of eyes in the business. You'd be a fool not to give her a go.'

'Well, as I say, good examiners are hard to come by. If she isn't wearing bottle bottom glasses when she turns up, I'll put her on the line. Just ask for Sammy at the main desk and I'll see her all right.'

I'm rather pleased with myself: Ray Riley, the smooth talking, wheeler dealer, putting his house in order.

First things first.

The next night, after my hospital watch, I sit down at the wobbly table to write a letter. Onion butts my leg, circling my feet in the cat dance of cupboard love. I rub his forehead with my knuckle and settle to write. Onion joins me on the table top, his braying purr thrumming into the silence.

Dear Mr Hawks

I stop to suck the pen top. Onion opens his eyes to inspect me, his gaze focusing somewhere behind my left ear.

You might have already noticed that Lily Riley, Lily Cartwright as was, has not returned from her honeymoon to take up the promised position with your firm. You might think this is a sign that married life is so good she's decided to stay at home, ha ha, but joking apart, things are not so good. Lily has had an accident and is, as I write, in St Leonards Hospital with two burned arms. The hospital cannot say when she will be recovered, in fact, they say she is very ill.

In the circumstances I think it best to let you know so you can find someone else. Thank you once again for loaning the girls the Brownie. I know Lily will be pleased to see the photographs, if they came out well.

Yours
Raymond Riley

It's only fair to let Mr Hawks know. And perhaps Lily'll take a liking to a job in Shoreditch, instead of traipsing off to Southgate each day.

What I've done hangs in the air like a cloud. The more I think about it, the more I fret: what if Lily doesn't thank me for handing in her notice at the old place? What if she's no fancy for another job, a better, nearer job, when she gets home? Lily's been through the mill: there were a couple of nights of delirium when the nurses wouldn't even let me onto the ward, and they say she's now on the long haul to recovery, fragile and exhausted. Will she miss her old pals? Have I moved too fast?

I won't tell her just yet, she needs bringing back to life first, she doesn't need me punching above my weight. Nurturing and cosseting is required, all of which I'm more than happy to do.

Though I'm reluctant to share her, and concerned that she'll feel self-conscious in front of others, I ask if she would like to see anyone else. Tom Cartwright has been in once but apart from that, it's only me at visiting hour.

Lily shakes her head, no, she doesn't want to see anyone else. So I sit at the edge of the bed, holding her bandaged hand, talking about our rooms, how I've mended a few things, the handle on the saucepan, the doors between that scrape on the lino, anything amusing that I think might lift her spirits. I'm pleased when she nods and smiles, delighted when I raise a giggle, tickled pink when she laughs.

'She's coming on nicely,' says the doctor as I am leaving one afternoon. I wonder if this could be the miracle worker that Dr King tricked into giving Lily a bed.

'All thanks to you and the grand job of your nurses,' I say, spreading a thick slice of gratitude onto my words.

'No, an awful lot is her own grit, and your constancy. You don't see many men in here with their wives every visiting hour.'

I hadn't thought of that and spread my shoulders wide to receive the full weight of his praise, then I skip off down the stairs. Lily's going to be fine, and it's down to me. For better or for worse, we'd said. In sickness and in health, we'd promised; well, I'd kept my side of the bargain.

Chapter 19

Just Who's Planning This Party,
Me Or The Onion?

It is December 1927 and I'm to be a dad; I've a mind to have myself a Great Aunt Lizzie Christmas, or the shoestring version at least. Lily is spending most mornings with her head wedged inside the rim of the lavatory seat. 'Parties don't come cheap,' she points out in one of her rare moments of verticality.

After a wobbly start at De la Rues, Lily schmoozled her way up to the higher rate of pay and is now settled in nice and sweet. What with The Gas Company and the Turkish Pound we're doing fine, we don't have to scrimp, we're even putting away a pound a week, so a party is possible, plus I'm in the mood to celebrate.

I've told Lily I'll be taking some of the money out of the Post Office for Christmas. I've got my eye on a fur coat and a velvet dress and I plan to give her one last fling before the dribble and smell of children drag her down.

In between Lily's visits to the outhouse we plan our party.

Lily's going to bring home the contents of De la Rues' waste paper bin for us to paint and hang as chains. I'm going to talk to Mr Hogg about lending us his piano, which has never once had its lid lifted in the whole time we've been in Nichols Square, though I don't doubt he'll find a reason to use it or a means of charging me for the hire, once he hears I need it.

Lily sets herself to drawing up and mailing out the invitations, and then she concentrates on worrying about where we'll put everybody. My tasks are sorting the booze, fetching in the long list of ingredients for the Christmas cake, and making the paper hats out of rejected sheets of Turkish pound notes. I finally get round to fixing the wobble on the table leg so it can take the weight of the advocaat and cherry brandy, and I've even found some walnuts. Lily can't see why I need to paint them gold and string them up with lengths of red ribbon stolen from her sewing box, but she doesn't question each and every foolhardy thing I've a mind to do.

Onion on the other hand does.

He winds his way amongst the growing herd of beer bottles to investigate their place on his floor, which he decides must be a mistake on my part, one that I will correct as soon as I've noticed the blunder. He skids his fat paws through the slithers of falling paper, remnants from my paper chains and party hats: snow flurries of paper swirl into the air expressly for him to grapple and kill.

The price of hire for the Hogg piano is an invitation to the Christmas festivities for Mr Hogg and his lovely wife. I think this is a cheek, but what the heck, he'll have the devil's own job getting that piano back down to the basement, and Mrs Hogg'll be so pleased with the extra floor space I'm sure we will be musically enhanced from this time on. All things considered, I believe we won the toss.

The piano has been left in our hallway until I decide the best place for it, which is definitely not where Onion thinks it should be as it provides cover for his quarry. He stands guard, dolefully eyeing the large black beast with exasperation and distrust: what exactly is this that has walked into his hallway and plonked itself down over his dinner?

He approaches carefully and slides a tentative arm beneath the belly of the beast, casting his paw from side to side in the hope of catching a passing meal. He suspects the mice of laughing at him. I watch through our doorway until he becomes self-conscious, shakes himself out, and jumps up to pick a jauntily jarring tune on the keys. Put that in your pipe and smoke it, he says to me, and when you're done, shift this fool.

On Christmas morning the piano is still stood happily in the hallway, Onion perched on top presumably to show he has conquered it. I have festooned the hall with further paper hangings in an effort to increase our floor space. By the time Mr Hogg notices my liberty he'll be three sheets to the wind and won't notice when I disregard his objections. The day of the party has arrived and we have been blessed with a fresh fall of snow.

'Perfect, couldn't be better. If they spill down the steps they can sober up in the snow.'

'We'll get slushy indoors.'

'Then we'll put down newspapers and blot them up.'

'They'll be freezing getting here through this.'

'Then we'll stoke the fire to a furnace and put boiling water in the punch.'

Great Aunt Lizzie used to sprinkle cinnamon on the top. There can be no more potent memory of Christmas than the smell of Aunt Lizzie's whisky and cinnamon brew. I don't suppose Lily has any cinnamon but I rifle through the cupboards while she is out taking another close look at the lavatory bowl.

The decorations, pinned from the cornice to the rose, hang like great hammocks of confetti, twisting and glinting in the thermals of the fire. I pace between the rooms, grinning at the sparkling canopy. Onion views the ceiling with a mixture of suspicion and malice, his tail flicking at the glittering birds dancing around his heaven. The rooms are so hot I remove my waistcoat, then thinking of a better idea, I race out to the garden on the pretence of checking on Lily, but really to cool down, and to chop yet more logs for the fire.

'This is it, Lily,' I call through the slatted door, excitedly jousting the snow-sparkled air with my wood axe. 'We're ready for our first *at home*.'

Chapter 20

At Home For Christmas

Lily emerges from the lavatory, her face strained and colourless, her recovering arms hidden beneath the long sleeves of the velvet dress. A party is just what she needs to lift her spirits.

'I don't fancy this party, Ray.'

'You look great. I'll tell everyone you've come as the ghost of Christmas present.'

Lily smiles. 'I feel dreadful. The nurse at the clinic said it must be a girl, all those female hormones rushing about making me feel ill.'

'No, Lily, it'll be a boy, a feisty little feller, making his presence known before he's even popped his head out the door.'

Lily doesn't appreciate this image and returns to the toilet to eject it.

The front door announces our first guest with a loud clatter of knocker on wood.

'We're off!' I call to Lily, bounding over the snow covered log pile and up the back steps. 'Don't hang around in there too long, Lily. You'll miss all the fun.'

'Believe me, Ray, if I had a choice, I wouldn't be in here at all.'

But I am gone, already flinging back the front door and throwing my arms around Joe.

'Merry Christmas, Joe. Come in. Lily'll be up in a minute; she can't wait to get going on the piano. Come in.'

The door knocker announces the next guest like the herald at Cinderella's ball.

'Ernie! Splendid. Nice hat Moira, from Santa?'

Pretty Boy wanders across from the other side of the square, a girl hanging on each arm.

'Hey up! Did they come in your stocking? I only got the waistcoat.' We shake hands and grin.

'You win some, you lose some, Sunbeam. Meet Gloria,' he motions to a pretty little brunette on his right, 'and this is Anne.'

The negative version of the first. 'Distant cousins, up staying with the family for Christmas. Say hello to Ray, girls.'

'Come in everyone, there's plenty to drink. We've a good hot punch to warm you.'

Arthur and Ella scamper up the front steps ahead of Grandma and Grampa Riley. As usual, Grandma arrives mid-sentence.

'Lord, what a journey we've had, Ray, it's enough to freeze the, oh hello Joe, how are you, we haven't seen you in a while, are you keeping well? And look at Susan, you look fit to burst my dear, when are you due? I hope you're looking after her Joe, lots of milk, and cod liver oil, they do make the prettiest maternity smocks these days, look at this Bert, doesn't Susan look pretty.'

But Grampa Riley has slipped away to the warmth of the fire.

Charlie slides up the steps and along the wall to stand beside the piano.

'Goodness Charlie, what's up with you? You've lost weight, you're not ill are you? What with the influenza,' Grandma says to Susan, 'and the TB, you don't know where to turn in these winters, I say to Bert these pea soupers will be the death of me. Are you eating properly Charlie? You look like you could do with a good meal, get inside lad and warm yourself next to Grampy.'

Charlie is still in earshot when she adds conspiratorially to Susan, 'I don't suppose their mother'll be joining us. Did you hear about my poor John, tragic it was, and she was drunk even at the funeral, disgraceful.' I hover in the doorway, collecting coats and dispensing Christmas cheer.

Joe sits down to pick out a carol on the piano. Grandma Bess trails to silence, swaying gently backward and forward to the haunting melody of In the Bleak Mid-Winter. 'One of my favourites,' she advises Susan, presumably despite the influenza and the TB.

I shut the door and throw the coats onto the bed. Charlie is stood beside Grampa Riley, his hands pushed deep into his pockets, his hair sticking out abruptly at unlikely tangents. A flick with Mum's hairbrush wouldn't have gone amiss. I offer him a hot whisky but he refuses.

'Do you think Mum might join us later, Charlie?'

Charlie's cheerless eyes focus on the rag rug. He shrugs.

'Doubt it.'

His voice doesn't rise to scorn but it hovers somewhere nearby. I picture her sat alone in the attic room, a jug of beer at her side, her eyes vacant.

Charlie's indifference hangs in the air.

Well, we can all do that, if we choose, Charlie boy. We can sit around and mope about it, or we can get out and get on, though I don't envy his living alone with her, that might be enough to tip anyone into the back of beyond.

Lily comes into the room bearing a small gift for Charlie. He unwraps it warily, embarrassed for people to see him in this private moment. Lily has found a leatherbound copy of The Christmas Carol on one of the market stalls: she's all for happy endings is Lily. 'Merry Christmas, Charlie,' she says, kissing him on the cheek.

He nods, looking dolefully at the book.

'My goodness, Joe,' I call across the room, eager to distract attention from my brother's inanimate Christmas spirit, 'do you only know the morbid ones? Shift over and let Lily give some zip to the proceedings.'

Joe slides across on the piano stool and Lily joins him for a rousing Good King Wenceslas, prompting gusty vocals from the room.

Two of Lily's work friends arrive, their young men draped on their arms. They stoop to kiss Lily then weave their way towards the fire.

'We're here, at last,' calls a voice from the door. 'We went to the wrong house, but we've brought the Brownie, again. Mr Hawks says he can't get away, his wife has been cooking a turkey since last Sunday, but he wishes you all a very merry Christmas and he's sent this as a Christmas gift. Isn't that nice of the old man?'

No one in the room knows either Mr Hawks or the conveyor of this gift but Lily calls out above the *gathering of winter fuel*.

'Open it Ray, let me see.'

Lily doesn't miss a beat as she watches me untie the string and remove the paper from what turns out to be our wedding photo: a happy couple smile out at us from the frame, the wind puffing up Lily's outfit to make us laugh.

'So, it's true then,' says Lily, her fingers sliding up and down the keys. 'We're really married.'

'Happy Christmas, Lily,' I say, kissing her on the crown of her head. I prop the photograph on top of the piano before Gloria swoops to claim me for a dance. Lily raises her eyebrows quizzically. *Pretty Boy's*, I mouth, shrugging my shoulders in cheerful resignation.

The volume rises and the party begins to bubble and fizz with the annual exchange of news. I'm beginning to enjoy myself. I'd had a panicky sweat about mid-morning, worrying that no one would come. Had I bought too much booze? Had I bought too little? Had Lily cooked too much food or not enough, making us look cheapskate? But here we are, panic over, everyone merry: Arthur rolling back his head in laughter at something Ella has said, Pretty Boy standing toward the back of the crowd, oscillating between a cynical smirk and a surprised pleasure, Lily and Joe thumping out a duet. We might only have a hallway and two small rooms with doors between but we can certainly entertain.

Tom Cartwright falls into the hall bearing a huge parcel in his arms, sweat dribbling down his face.

'I never thought I'd make it, Lily,' he calls above the noise. She waves mid-plink. 'I've walked all the way with this balanced on my shoulder.' My father-in-law Tom is looking very pleased with himself. He pauses to remove his overcoat then shuffles his way into the middle of the room.

'Excuse me ladies and gentlemen. Can we have a bit of hush.' He sets down his parcel and begins to open what I presume to be Lily and my Christmas present; we grin at each other.

'You see,' he announces to the attending crowd as if he were hawking in Hoxton Market, 'it's all in the detail. I said to myself, my Lily won't want anything ordinary. She'll be wanting something with a bit of character.' Tom pauses while an inadvertent lack of attention at the drinks table is shushed to silence. 'And so I set to whittling spindles, carving the lattice for the sides, setting in the batons for the canopy, sanding and varnishing.' He runs his hand across the treasure hidden in the box, 'Moira made the covers and the padding until we had, drum roll please,' he calls to the wings.

Joe performs a drum roll on the bass notes as ordered and Tom Cartwright triumphantly hoists a satin ribboned cradle out of the box, beaming broadly around the room.

'For the coming baby!'

I am stunned. My mouth drops open; my eyebrows collapse in on each other in a deeply furrowed frown. It was my job to announce the baby. Lily doesn't show yet so nobody knows; this was meant to be my big *ta da* and he has stolen it from me. I have a speech prepared. I was going to declare a race between ourselves and Joe; with Susan already seven months pregnant that was my opening joke.

The crowd bursts into applause: I don't know if this ovation is for the cradle or what will go in it. There are squeals of delight and congratulation from the girls who crowd round Lily; there are grunts of manly approval from the men, who push forward to slap me on the back, offering to get me a drink, which is a bit rich as I bought the whole bloody bar myself. I glare pointedly at Tom who turns his palms to heaven and feigns confusion. Joe strikes up a rousing *Pack up Your Troubles in Your Old Kit Bag*, everyone refills their glasses and the show goes on. Just wait till I get my hands on him later.

Tom dives off to chat with Uncle Ernie.

You might well scurry, I say to myself, but you'll pay.

'Have we missed anything,' asks Mr Hogg, breezing into the room with a fat cigar smouldering between his rubbery lips. 'Merry Christmas lad,' he says, producing a similarly plump torpedo from his top pocket and poking it inside my new waistcoat. 'For you to have a laugh 'n' a joke on later.'

I've only ever smoked one cigar and I felt ill all evening.

'You'll come to know Christmas by its smell,' he adds, taking a long, hearty draw.

'It and oranges,' says Mrs Hogg over his shoulder, producing a large golden globe from behind her back and offering it with the flourish of a conjuring trick. 'Scarce as hen's teeth these are…'

'…and twice as expensive,' he interjects, 'But we thought you'd appreciate it.'

The sight of Mrs Hogg makes me step back in shock.

Usually, when people make an effort for a special occasion they surprise you into seeing them anew, all polished and pristine, as if you are seeing their glory for the first time. Usually, the preparations are designed to make improvements on the original. Mrs Hogg has somehow created directly the opposite effect.

The matronly cosiness of her floral pinafore has been replaced by a hip hugging bust plunging green satin dress, around which she has thrown a dead fox. Her lips are slashed with crimson, and two fuzzy pink circles either side of her nose mark the spot where she supposes her cheekbones to be. Bright green eyeshadow has been liberally scraped from beneath her lower lashes to her eyebrows, nestling in the bowls of which are the two tiny black currants of her eyes.

Lily, who has been inspecting the cradle with her father, rushes across the room. 'Hello Bella, Merry Christmas. How splendid you look.'

She kisses the landlord's wife, laces her arm carefully through Bella's, and guides her across to the cherry brandy. Mr Hogg and I stand side by side and watch as Bella's ample rear parts the crowd, the thick blue worms of her varicose veins bulging from beneath her nylons.

'Fine figure of a woman,' he says, taking a satisfied draw on his Christmas indulgence. I glance sideways at him to see if he is in jest.

'A fine figure indeed,' I echo, my eyebrows jiggling busily somewhere above my hairline as I enjoy the realisation that love and desire can survive our early twenties.

'Listen up everyone, it's time for games,' calls Ella from deep in the crowd. Arthur and Ella have been busying themselves in our cupboards, emerging now to push the mob back to the edges of the room. Arthur has a suspicious white powdery smudge on his jumper.

'Those of you who can find a chair, park yourselves on it. The remainder find a space. Lily, strike up something we can sing along to.'

Ella places a chair in the centre of the room as Lily launches into The Beggar's Rhyme: *Christmas is coming, the geese are getting fat.* Mr Hogg takes her up with a surprisingly competent baritone. *Please put a penny in the old man's hat.*

'OK everyone, listen up.'

On the chair Ella has placed an inverted bowl of flour.

'Keep singing everyone. When the music stops, whoever is holding this knife, which I'm passing round now, will slice a careful line from the top to the bottom of the flour mountain, scraping the flour to the edge of the plate. On the top, in the centre…'

If you haven't got as penny, a ha'penny will do

'…in the centre is a tanner. If on your slicing the tanner falls, it is your task to remove it from the flour, with your teeth! Get back in here Denny Pell, Christmas games are compulsory!'

If you haven't got a ha'penny, God bless you!

Uncle Ernie slips in beside me, his eyes glistening with delight as the music stops and the first unfortunate is caught with the knife in her hand. She steps up to slice a fine line through the flour mound. The tanner remains safely perched.

'Grand show, son,' he says. 'You and Lily have set up real nice.'

'Thanks Ernie. Can I get you another?'

'I wouldn't say no to a topper.' He's thinking about saying something else but he doesn't know whether to carry on. I wait to see which way he will go. 'Sorry to hear about your father, Ray. I bet your mum's taking it bad. Is she coming over?'

'Later. Maybe.' I glance at Ernie; he's no fool. 'You know how busy it can get at Christmas.'

Joe and Lily fumble with the knife as it passes along the piano keys. Lily plops it smartly into the hand hovering at her right, the music tinkling on without pause. The flour mountain has been carved by respective players to a craggy peak; the sixpence precariously holding its own on the summit. Lily watches over her shoulder.

When whippoorwill call, and evening is night
I'll hurry to my blue heaven
You turn to the right, you find a little bright light
That leads you to my blue heaven
You find a cosy place, a fireplace, a cosy room
A little nest that nestles where the roses bloom
Just Molly and me, and the baby makes three
We're happy in my blue heaven

The room sings, and then whoops as the music suddenly stops, the knife falling flat into the palm of Tom Cartwright. This should be good. Tom swaggers forward, kneels for a more precise angle and attempts to shave a sliver of flour from the mountainside. Oh dear, oh dear. The sixpence falls. Everyone claps with glee, it now being Tom's unpleasant duty to retrieve the sixpence, with his teeth. Couldn't happen to a nicer chap, I think to myself.

'Drum roll please,' I call to Lily who frowns at me.

What? It's a bit of fun. He'd have been just as delighted if it had happened to me.

Lily performs a short drum roll as Tom inserts his lips into the flour. Sadly, the sixpence has wedged itself beneath a flour snowdrift and Tom has to use his tongue to hunt it out. I look across at Arthur who gives me a thumbs up. Arthur doesn't miss much.

The flour is cleared away and Lily and Joe move the gathering into sing-a-long. The power of the piano is at its peak, controlling and guiding the crowd in a careful choreography intended to lift the spirits and gladden the hearts.

God rest you merry, Gentlemen,
Let nothing you dismay,
For Jesus Christ our Saviour
Was born upon this Day.
To save poor souls from Satan's power,
Which long had gone astray.
Bringing tidings of comfort and joy
Comfort and joy...

My eyes seek out Charlie, who has moved into the window bay, sitting down with his back to the room to watch the snow falling outside. There are some hearts beyond the reach of music, I think. Denny leans down to Charlie offering him a plate of food, Charlie shakes his head. Thank you anyway, Denny.

By nine o'clock in the evening, the revellers have had their fill of Christmas cheer: their excitement and energies spent, the party begins to thin. Lily slumps exhausted into an armchair, flicking her tired fingers round and round the silky snake of a red hair lock. Joe and Susan have already left to let Susan rest. I didn't notice Charlie's departure. The ivories have been handed back to our landlord Henry Hogg who again impresses me with his musical capabilities.

'Well done, Lily. You were superb. Everyone had a great time. Your cake has all but gone, and there's not an egg sandwich in sight.'

'Well I hope Dad got one. He'll be complaining if he didn't.' Lily stifles a yawn.

'He is doubtless the principle reason the table is bare.'

'Now Ray, don't be like that.'

'Well. He spoiled my fun.'

'I know he did, but he's probably just as excited as we are. He didn't mean to steal the show.'

'Yes, he did. That is exactly what he meant to do.'

'And look at the lovely work he's done on the crib. It's precisely the right present to receive at Christmas.'

'I suppose,' I say grudgingly, 'though not so good as Mrs Hogg.' I whisper. 'Imagine getting that in your stocking.'

'You're being unkind.'

'What? I'm shocked. Me? Pretty Boy and I have never been so inspired discussing a woman's attributes. Never.'

Lily glowers at me but she hasn't the energy to be serious.

I remember Arthur and Ella's game. 'And thank you for letting the music stop where it did.'

'I don't know what you mean,' she says, but I am happy to see the playful glint in her eye telling me she knew perfectly well that her father would be fishing in the flour, reminding me that we are fighting from the same trench.

She changes the subject to stop me pressing home my advantage. 'There was only one person missing.'

'You didn't really expect Mum to come, did you?'

'I'm not talking about your mum. I had planned a special Christmas present for you. I sent an invitation to your Great Aunt Lizzie. I thought it would be a lovely surprise for you to meet again. And with everything you've told me, I'm curious to meet her myself.'

I draw back and look closely at Lily. 'When did you send it? She didn't write back? Explain why she couldn't come? She didn't write and ask how we are? You must have introduced yourself as my wife, did you tell her you were pregnant? Won't that set her smiling. What a thought; snotty little no-pants Riley, stood tall and ready. I bet she enjoyed that.'

I smile at the thought until another less cheerful thought pops into my head.

'Perhaps she didn't write because she can't, perhaps she's dead. She must be,' I do some quick calculations in my head, 'she must be in her mid-sixties by now. I thought she was ancient when I knew her, probably the effect of all that silky hair piled elegantly on top, and the long slim dresses.'

I wish I'd been to visit.

'Poor Aunt Lizzie, you would have liked her. She gave me the train set one Christmas, I must have been about ten: junior will be playing with it in no time soon.'

Lily squeezes my hand in consolation.

Eventually Mr and Mrs Hogg slip off downstairs after crooning contentedly to one another for a while, leaving Lily and I to flop onto our bed, dead beat and delighted with our endeavours.

I've to go back to work tomorrow but when I return, I'll set up the train set, and get it running for Lily to see it in all its splendour. It'll feel good telling the nipper where it came from, describing the house in Tottenhall Road, explaining how we were once related to readies. I could take him to Palmers Green, show him the road, maybe even knock at the door to have a few words with the owners, so's he can peep inside. He can tell his mates at school how his dad once lived with the gentry.

Chapter 21

'The Universe Is Not Hostile, Nor Yet Is It Friendly. It Is Simply Indifferent,' Said John Holmes, And I Can Find No Fault With That

In the bleak mid-winter is just about right.

After the feathery frilliness of the Christmas snow comes the raw edged bite of icy sleet, driving into your face as you hunch along, biting at your skin as you turn a corner. Nobody talks, conversation is reduced to throaty snipes into the wind.

'Right?'

'Mate.'

'Cut?'

'Ta.'

We hunker our necks down into our shoulders, slipping and skidding on the treacherous footpaths. There is nothing elegant about this. No picture postcard muffled skating scene here. The weather puts you in a raw mood for the day. And then it puts you in a rare mood for the night.

No matter how much coal I pile on the fire, the wind slides beneath the door and through the window frames, freezing any point in excess of a yard from the blaze. Onion presses so close to the flames I swear some nights he is ablaze and couldn't care less, as long as he is warm.

Lily no longer fits her clothes and has moved into her first smock, over which she piles a double layer of my jumpers. I think she looks cute, but that's about as much enthusiasm as I can muster: I am too bloody cold.

January shifts into February and still there is no let up. The days are dark and thankless. No delicate hoarfrost, no quaint wisps of wintery ether: the heavens push down on the earth and let their heavy bellied weight hang oppressively over us.

At the end of February Susan gives birth to a bulbous red smell with swathes of skin no living thing can possibly have need for.

They name it Rose, presumably in the hope that it will grow into something beautiful. I can't see it myself, but there is no matching Joe's elation.

At the christening Joe takes me to one side. I suppose I'm to be given the this-is-even-better-than-marriage speech, oh and did you notice, it happened to me before it happened to you, again, but that is not his intention. As it turns out, he is painting on a much larger canvas.

'Have you been home recently, Ray?'

When did I last go home? I was in and out sorting Dad's funeral arrangements but nothing much since.

'Yeah, I pop over all the time, keeping an eye on my inheritance.'

Joe guardedly doesn't look me in the eye. Instead he talks generally to the middle of the room. 'Only I saw your mum in the street the other day.'

'On her way to The Dog?'

'Possibly. She was a bit het up.'

'She was probably on her way home then,' I say too quickly, trying to prove I'm not concerned. It's not like Mum to show any emotion, least of all to the likes of Joe. I take a slow sip of the christening sherry. 'In what way, het up?'

I can see Joe feels uncomfortable. My gaze shifts to join his in the middle distance. 'Well, she took my arm for one, hung on it like she needed support.'

'That'll be the gin.'

'Then, she asked if I'd seen Charlie, and I told her not since Christmas at your place, what with Susan and the baby and all. She looked startled. She said it was a fine state of affairs when a son can visit acquaintances at Christmas but not his own mother.'

I stare at him. 'What did she mean by that? Do you mean he wasn't living with her at Christmas? Did he say anything to you at the party?'

I'm casting around in my mind to remember anything he said to me.

'Nothing I took much notice of at the time, it all seemed a bit obvious.' Joe lifts his glass to salute his pink ball of blubber. 'He told me how cold snow was, but that wind was the worst. He said unless you found a brazier on nights like this, you could freeze to death. I just nodded and agreed with him; we were watching the snow clinging to the myrtle outside your window.'

Why hadn't I spoken to Charlie? I'd been on the verge of commenting on the state of his dress but it didn't seem right to bring it up in the middle of a crowded room.

'Anything else?'

'Well, your mum says she hasn't seen Charlie since just after the funeral, since November.'

'That don't sound right. How did he know we were partying? How come he was there if he hadn't seen Lily's invite?'

'I don't know, Ray. I just thought you should know what she said.'

'She's talking rubbish. It's the drink. Don't think any more on it, Joe. He's tucked up safe and sound in our old bed, no doubt about that.'

I'm full of cobblers I am, and Joe knows it. What the hell is Charlie playing at? I get slung out the house but he, not waiting for the expulsion, walks out of his own accord. What's the matter with you, Charlie? What am I supposed to do now? Leave you to drown? To wander back each Christmas, a little more vacant, a little more vagrant, or do I come and get you, yank you back into the here and now, set you on the path?

I don't like the picture of Charlie sleeping rough, on park benches, in shop doorways, becoming ever more tattered, stinking of urine, begging. It springs into my mind at odd moments of the day, an unwelcome warning, a bad omen. I mustn't worry Lily with it. She's all bound up in baby thoughts.

I call on Pretty Boy, who suggests we go to his local, to chew the cud.

'I had a cousin went AWOL in the war; they brought him in and shot him.'

'You know Den, that really helps.'

'No, I'm sorry Sunbeam, all I mean is, it happens. Things get too much. The easiest thing to do is disappear, take yourself off, alone, and fend for number one.'

'That might be fine in war time, and I'm not saying life's been all peace and poppies for Charlie, but Swan Terrace is hardly the bloody front line.'

'Ah well, that all depends where you're coming from. For Charlie, maybe it is. Maybe he was dealing with something alone that he couldn't bear. Perhaps he felt he'd been deserted. First you, then his pa. Leaving him in charge. Some blokes, you and me maybe, can cope. Some blokes can't. There's no shame, it's just a different perspective.'

I look at Denny Pell and consider him anew.

'You want my reckoning? He's gone to ground. He's done what any sane man would do who's on the point of going mad. He's run. I'd do, no, have done, the same. I cloak it in ways-of-the-world jargon, but when it gets tough, I scarper. I'm not about to put myself down over it, and I'm not about to think any the less of your Charlie as I'm sure he has his reasons. All you've to figure is, whether you leave him to row his own boat, or whether you haul him in. If you haul him in, you become his keeper. That's a tall order, Ray, a real tall order.'

'I should have been there for him. I thought I was. I thought he could depend on me.'

'You're busy, Ray, a pretty wife, a coming baby, you can't play the Good Samaritan to all and sundry.'

'He's not all and sundry, he's my only brother. I've already lost one.'

'Well, you sound like you've made up your mind. Where are you going to start looking?'

I have no idea.

The fact that he was at the Christmas party still jars: how did he know about it if he hadn't seen the invite?

'You don't think he could be nearby? Watching from a distance? Like a shepherd keeping an eye on his flock. It's the sort of dumb thing Charlie would do. Having completely lost it, he'd turn himself into my look out.'

'You don't strike me as someone who needs to be looked out for, Ray.'

'Too bloody right I don't.'

But something is niggling at the back of my mind, something I don't like the look of and would rather ignore. Something suggesting that Charlie, for all his madness, might have a better handle on what's good and right than his big brother, but I sweep that thought away. Here's me, someone who has everything, and there's Charlie feeling sorry for me? Feeling I need protection? Where does he get off?

Denny Pell stares into his glass and smiles. 'What about we organise a hunt? We could hire some of the lads from the printworks. They're all laid off, walking the streets themselves most days. We could form a possy.'

'I don't know, Denny. I don't want our dirty laundry fluttering around for all to see. Charlie would be mortified.'

'Charlie would be bloody relieved to know you cared. You can be a selfish, self-centred git most of the time, Ray, that's one of the things I like about you, but they're not the sort of things your Charlie goes for.'

Am I offended? I think I'm offended.

'Like you know anything about me! I took care of Charlie I did, I was the only one that did.'

'No you didn't, Ray. You took care of yourself. If I remember rightly, you were off swanking it with M'Lady for most of Charlie's childhood. I don't mean to be disrespectful but your Charlie grew up with two cantankerous old sots who most likely beat the living daylights out of each other and him more evenings than not. I'm not judging them, it's the way it goes sometimes. I don't imagine for one minute Charlie looks on you as his saviour.'

'I was sent away! They didn't want me!'

'What a load of bellyache. Okay, so you were sent away. You were sent to a silver spoon and a jelly mould. You weren't exactly down the pits, Ray. And as I recall, you had the high and mighty nerve to run home like you were charging in to save the day. Course, when you got here, you realised the day was long gone, so you left again, running to your gran's. And then you finally left altogether. Where you get off thinking you were there for him, I don't know. You were somewhere on that horizon, a puff of smoke, looking out for number one. That's where you were.'

I am more than a bit stunned. 'I got married! Everyone leaves home when they get married!'

'True. But usually they remember to visit.'

'That's a load of tosh. Where'd you get the idea I don't take care of my own? From Joe? From the factory?'

'I don't need to hear things Ray, I've got eyes, I can work out the lie of the land.'

'Well you've worked it out wrong. Charlie doesn't think I abandoned him. He's a grown man, he doesn't need his big brother wiping his nose.'

'In that case, let's forget the whole thing. You're right. If he wants to go wander the streets with a piece of string tied round his waist, newspapers and sacking for bedclothes, you're right, that's his own damn choice. Who are we to interfere with a man's free will.'

'Is that what you reckon? You don't think he might have found himself somewhere else to live?'

'Maybe he has. You're probably right. He's found himself a nice pile of bricks set in parkland, trap and ponies coming extra.' Denny Pell taps the rim of his beer glass. 'What's the matter with you, Ray? You know that's not likely. If it bothers you, do something; if it doesn't, shut the crap up.'

I stare at the yellow speckled mirror behind the bar. Denny won't let it rest.

'When he slunk into your bash, dishevelled, his clothes hanging on him like they would a coat stand, I thought his number was up. I thought you'd be telling me the TB had him and we'd be hauling him down the parlour six months after doing the same for your old man.'

I swivel my eye back to Charlie at the party. He was jittery, nervous, sloping back into the night without saying goodbye. Probably Lily, myself and Joe were the only people he spoke to in three hours, and then it was hardly more than a sentence, as if he'd forgotten how to string words together. But then, Charlie's never had much to say for himself. Look at that terrific wedding speech. Yet still I thought he was managing. When I'd seen him stashing away money at the house, I decided he'd found a way to hack it. At least, I wanted to believe he'd found a way, or else I'd have to do something about it.

'What do you reckon Charlie wants, Ray?' This problem is Denny's red rag, he can't stand indecision or dithering, for Denny it has to happen now and it has to be decisive, right or wrong you stand by what you do, and my hesitancy is irritating him. Short of thumping me he tries to cajole some action out of me.

'If you could sit down now with Charlie and ask him what he wanted, what do you reckon he'd say? To have everyone back at home together? Not very likely. And it's not your leaving that's thrown him off balance. He must be lonely, he's grown up entirely alone: maybe he would ask for your friendship. Or maybe he wouldn't: you don't necessarily take yourself off on walkabout if you don't like the solitary life. Put yourself in his shoes. He has nothing. He has no one. Jesus. I think I'd slit my throat, put myself out of my misery.'

I am shocked at this thought. 'He wouldn't do that.'

'How do you know what he'd do? You hardly know him. Your mother probably knows him better than you do and she's away with the fairies most days, if you don't mind my saying so.'

Denny is getting pretty near the bone but what can I accuse him of? Truth Telling? Calling spades spades? 'If we went to these blokes, from the printworks, what would we say?'

Denny looks interested, as if he's been waiting for me to wake up: he's ready and willing to play. 'You don't have to be specific. Tell them your brother's been unwell, that he took your father's death badly, they probably know him enough to know he's the sensitive type. They'll go for that. You could even offer a reward. Five bob for whoever finds him; they'd be more than pleased with that, and you'll have bought yourself a little police force.'

Five bob. Lily wouldn't notice if I took five bob from our savings, and if she did, I doubt she'd mind.

'You don't think Charlie means to disappear?'

'I wouldn't put my wages on that horse, Sunbeam. I reckon your Charlie could just drift away, judging by the state of him a couple of months ago.'

I'm getting scared now. I tot up how long Charlie might have been on the streets through this winter: eight weeks in the ice and sleet. He was always cold in bed: I'd have to drag an extra coat on top of him to stop his chattering teeth from keeping me awake.

Denny wants action. 'Why don't we go hunt them out now? I know where a few of them drink.'

'You don't think we should talk to Mum first. See if she knows anything?'

'What's your mum going to say at this time of night? Charlie who? It's up to you to sort this one, Ray.'

'Maybe I should go tell Lily.'

'She'll be in bed long ago, leave her to her beauty sleep.'

'Is it going to be any use, hunting at night?'

'For Christ sake, Ray, do you want to find him or not? If not, just say so, I'm happy to go home to a warm bed.'

'It's not that. I just wonder if we'll see much.'

'Well at night at least they're still, they'll have found a place to kip down. All we've to do is lift the newspapers from their heads. In daylight they'll be shuffling all over the place, we'll be chasing our own tails.'

He's right. He's right. Stop wasting time Ray. 'Let's go.'

I down the remains of my pint, slap Denny on the back and rush out of the bar, Denny close on my heels.

'This way, Ray, they're over by the station. We'll be there in under five minutes.'

179

We charge into the night; and what a hell's night it is. Fast though I'd like to move, pleased, finally, to be sorting this, the going is slow and difficult. On the way to the station, I am glancing into dark corners, eyeing likely doorways.

'He won't be round here,' calls Denny over his shoulder. 'He'll be up on the heath, on the benches, or further in town, where it'll be warmer. We'll have to ask around.'

Denny's voice trails into the fog. Nice one Charlie, you couldn't scare the bejesus out of me on a warm, balmy evening, oh no, you have to choose the coldest night of the bloody year.

My toes are numb by the time we reach The Station Bar. Denny has already located the old printworkers.

'Over here, Ray,' he calls. 'Come and tell them your story.'

They're a nice bunch of lads, oohing and arrhing and scratching their heads in concern. Denny's right, they are particularly interested in the five bob and one of them steps forward with a plan.

'We'll split up, into pairs, six of us, and you two makes four pairs. We'll take different areas so's we don't waste time, and we'll come back together by say midnight, to see what's what. Okay lads?'

The lads nod.

'Right. You two head east, check all around the Crooked Billet and Printing House Yard, go as far as Old Market Square; he might head that way in the hope of finding leftovers from the traders. You two head south, down as far as Broadgate, don't forget to check inside the churches, St Marks, etc., the tramps often go into them for a bit of warmth, makes sense on a night like this. You two head out west, over as far as Finsbury if you can. That leaves us; we'll head north, from Sherpherdess Walk across to Kingsland Road. It's ten o'clock now. Two hours will just about see us done in. We'll meet back at my place, No. 10 Bevendon Street, around midnight. My Mrs'll make us all a cup of tea. I'm Harold, by the way.' He thrusts his hand out to shake mine. 'Don't worry son: I didn't live through the war only to lose one of our own in peace time. We'll sort you out.'

Who is this guardian angel? If he can rally such immediate energy to the cause, why couldn't I?

'Thank you. Thank you, Harold. All of you. I'm grateful.'

'Okay lad, that's enough blathering. Let's get off.'

And off is what we get, separating into our allotted districts, slithering into the night. Harold has rounded up some torch lights for us to shine into doorways.

As I slip in and out of alleyways, shining my torch behind coal bunkers, I reprimand myself for my lack of care. Charlie, lonely little Charlie, a picture of his burnt foot flashes up: he would have felt Lily's pain. I should have gone and told him about her arms: he would have wanted to help. I'm not much of a guardian. Am I capable of being a father? Will I see what is needed? Will I know how to protect a helpless baby? I begin to feel sick. Finding Charlie takes on a bigger importance than I mean it to. If I don't find Charlie, it'll be proof that I'm not cut out for this guardian lark. If I don't help Charlie back to the land of the living, show him how much he means to me, I'll be judged. God will point His finger and say: *You must be joking. Put a child, a hapless infant in your care? Not so ruddy likely.* And He'll be right. I'd be a laughable, despicable father, no better than my own.

'Come on, Ray. Shift yourself.'

Denny has reached the end of the road.

'We'll nip through the park, see who's on the benches.'

Denny goes up to one bench where two down and outs are in a grizzly row over a bottle of whisky. No, they hadn't seen no young feller with blue arms. But if they did, they'd give him a wide birth. They chuckle together, their brawl forgotten with this outside interference. Denny repeats his question at various benches around the park but with no joy. One woman thinks she saw him once, months ago, over Bethnal Green way, but she can't be sure. She thinks she could remember a little more if we could spare a few coppers.

I put my hand in my pocket.

'Forget it, Ray. There's no way her pickled brain can remember anything past last Thursday.'

I should know this! Hadn't I learnt anything from living with Mum and Dad. What'll I say to Mum if we're too late? She'll say it was my fault; and she'd be right. Come on Charlie, where are you?

By twelve o'clock we have nothing. We make our way stiffly back to Bevendon Street. The others are already there. No one has anything to report.

'Don't worry, Ray,' says Harold. 'We're not licked yet. We've nothing else to do but walk the streets so we'll keep doing it until we find him. And we will. Mark my words. When Harold Pontefract makes up his mind to do something, he jolly well does it.'

I tell Lily immediately I get in. She's worried sick, in part for Charlie, but mainly for me walking the streets in darkness, talking to the drunks and beggars at night, though she agrees I have to do it.

We continue for a further six nights. It is ice cold and miserable; the wind eats into our hands and cheeks like it is scratching away the top layer. On the seventh night we get some news.

Harold has got himself a job in a bakers. During the day he's been doing his usual trawling of the streets, looking for work, and this morning he saw a sign in the window of Da Mario's Bakery in Pitfield Street, asking for a general handyman, someone who was willing to learn the trade. Harold Pontefract was in there like a shot, he tells us. Anyway, to cut a long story short, he started straight away and in the course of his sweeping he told the baker about our night time hunt for Charlie Riley. It turns out the baker has seen Charlie, first, warming himself against the outside wall, and then, coming in to enquire after the job.

'He nice boy, Harold, but I could no give job him, my wife no like blue arms in dough.' Harold Pontefract grins at his impersonation of his new boss.

'When was this? When was Charlie in the shop?'

'The baker says he's only had the sign in the window for two days and he's been inundated with people but he reckoned Charlie were one of the first, so some time early yesterday morning.'

Thank God, thank God. The relief is overwhelming. I can feel my heart racing.

'Bingo!' shouts Denny. 'A result. We can probably bring the search in a little closer, we don't need to spread so far afield. We had a hunch he'd be hanging around Nichols Square.'

The group look quizzically at me. If that's the case, why had they been traipsing off to Broadgate and the like?

'Nichols Square is where I live,' I explain. 'Denny thinks he comes to check on me, see I'm okay.'

They nod.

'I didn't think it was likely, me being the older brother, and he being the one with the problem.'

'Ah,' says Harold knowingly. 'Only in *your* eyes, Ray. From Charlie's viewpoint, there might be a completely different picture.'

Lily is thrilled with the news.

'We're not there yet, mind,' I caution. 'We've still to find him, and once found, he's still to agree to come with us. And then, come where? What can I do with him? I can't send him back to Swan Terrace, not yet anyway.'

'Well, while you've been out, I've spoken to Bella and Mr Hogg. They reckon there might be room here, up at the top, for a short time, until he finds his feet.'

'That's great, that's so good. You're a wonder Lily Riley. It'll give me time to sort him out. Maybe there'll be something going at The Gas Company.'

'Slow down a bit, Ray. You've got to deal with Charlie first. He's got to feel comfortable, you can't thrust a life on him just because it's a life that suits you.'

She's right. She's always right.

'And, while you've been out, I've had some other news.' Lily hands me a letter. This had better be good.

Dear Raymond and Lily,

What a truly delightful surprise. I was thrilled to receive Lily's letter, and so sorry to miss seeing you at Christmas; Christmas has not been the same since you left, Raymond. For a start, I have no dance partner.

I look at Lily and grin.

Thank you Lily for your lovely news; I can hardly believe Raymond is old enough to be a father. The last I knew him, he could barely remember to fold his clothes at the end of the day, instead of dropping them in a pile on the bathroom floor. Now, he is preparing to teach his children the same. What a responsibility for such young shoulders. But, if there are any shoulders that can bear the weight, it must be Raymond's.

As soon as the weather turns a little brighter, perhaps you would call on me. Wednesday mornings suit me best, but no doubt you work during the day Raymond. I am at home most Saturday afternoons. Please write soon and tell me when would be convenient.

My best wishes to you both.
Elizabeth Delaney.

Chapter 22

There Can Be No Greater Loss

The evening after Harold Pontefract tells us of the baker's sighting, Denny and I head straight to the bakery. The wall's bricks, which never cool entirely, exude a dusty warmth into the night air, clearing a patch of snow beside the baker's shop. On Harold's request, the baker has agreed to meet us.

'Mr Riley, your brother, he blue arms not the problem. He smell, the problem. And my ladies, they come in, they no have three farthing to rub, but they particular about being clean. One smell your brother and poof, I lose my ladies. I sorry, Mr Riley. He nice boy, but I can't have work here.'

'Did he say if he was staying anywhere?'

'No, Mr Riley, he no say, and he no look like he either. He hair!' Mr da Mario flicks his hair up into the air, 'all stick up. And he face, dirty. That wash, I know, but he smell so, I open door when he gone, to let smell creep out.'

'Was he thin?'

'Very thin, Mr Riley. I give him yesterday bread. He pleased but not too much pleased. Sad eyes, Mr Riley, sad eyes like you.'

'What time was it?'

Mr da Mario slides a mealy finger up the side of his nose to indicate that he is thinking. 'Ooh. He here 'bout six thirty in morning, it not even light when he here. We empty ovens.'

'Where did he go when he left you?'

'We watch him. He go stand by hot wall to eat bread. Then he turn into alley, behind bakery, and we no see him no more. I sorry Mr Riley.'

Denny has already been round the block while this conversation is going on.

'I didn't try the alley, Ray. Let's go.'

'Thank you, Mr da Mario. You've been a great help. And thank you for giving him the loaf.'

'It okay, Mr Riley. I do it again he come.'

The two round figures of Mr and Mrs da Mario stand in silhouette like a puppet show in their brightly lit doorway, mealy dusts of grain swirling in the air, the heady aromas of yeast and ginger floating into the night. Denny and I skid off into the darkness.

We flick the torch lights from side to side. The alley is full of dustbins, mounds of dirty, caked snow, rills of greasy slime where slops have been tipped over the back walls. A cat spits at us and slips out of the wavering pool of light. About a hundred yards into the alley Denny finds a body.

'Ray. Something's here. Do you want to take a look.'

Curled into a ball behind a dustbin is a heap of human remains, putrefying and rank. I turn the body over to see a skeletal Charlie, his head lifting from the stench of his own vomit, his body cold and stiff. I place it gently back on the floor.

'Too bloody late. Ah Charlie, how did this happen?' I groan, and sit heavily onto a pile of rock-hard snow, my head in my hands.

'How do you know it's too late? You're no doctor.'

'Can you smell him, Denny? Don't you know decay? He stinks like a polecat.'

'Doesn't mean he's dead. Just means it'd be better to stand up wind.'

I leap up to punch Dennis Pell.

'Are you making jokes?' I swing my fist into the air; Denny blocks me with his arm.

'Hold on, Ray, take it easy. I'm telling you you're jumping the gun. You've been expecting and fearing to find this and so you've found it. Didn't you know you could make mistakes?'

'He's dead! My brother Charlie, like my brother Billy, is dead!' Denny is shouting now.

'Too bloody clever by half, you are Riley. Rollocking Riley, Always Sodding Right Riley. You say he's dead, so he must be. Well, I'll be off then. Let me know if you need a bearer.'

I stare after Denny, who starts to pick his way out of the alley.

'I don't know how to check him, Denny.'

'Put your bloody hand inside his shirt and feel if he's warm? That would be a good sodding start.'

I gaze back at the slumped bag of bones. Can I do that? Can I tell from that? I slither across to the body, pull it over onto its back, and force my hand between layers of clothing. I hold my breath.

'He's warm!' I shout.

'Now, can you feel a heartbeat?'

'No. Nothing.'

Denny is back crouching beside me.

'Yes, yes, yes! I can feel it. He's alive.'

'Thank Christ! Come on Ray, let's shift him. We can carry him between us, he's only skin and bones.' Denny grimaces as he picks up Charlie's head. 'I'll send you the bill for the whistle.'

'Thanks Denny. Thanks.'

With both arms entangled in the spindly sticks of Charlie's limbs, neither I nor Denny have a spare hand for the torch lamps. In the foggy darkness, we skid across hummocks of ice, losing our footing to scrape our knees along brick walls and rough fencing. Denny grunts as his elbow knocks against a telegraph post.

'It's like carrying a rigor mortised spider,' he groans.

Out on the main road the gas lamps light the way; we slither between the murky haloes, falling quiet in the struggle to negotiate the uncertain terrain.

What will Lily say when I present her with this offering?

I hunch my shoulders, hoiking Charlie's body higher. Charlie's body, light at first, has begun to feel like a dead weight. Mr Hogg's promise of a room is taking on the pallor of a mixed blessing: what can I do for him while I'm at work all day? I can't ask Lily to look after him, not in her present state. I'm working up a sweat, my breath freezing to the snort of a steam train on the night air. Denny's boots trudge heavily behind me, his crunchy step echoing in the darkness. We might have left him in the alley. He might have ended his life as he'd lived it, alone and misunderstood.

Well blow that. Perhaps the nurses across the square will know what to do with him. They did well for Lily's arms. He'll be wasted away for want of food; perhaps they'll know a cure for that.

Back in Nichols Square Lily's hand covers her mouth in alarm.

Denny drags the tin bath to the fire and throws an extra log on the flames.

'Have you any spare blankets, Lily?' he asks.

I rush around, pulling out trousers and jumpers for Charlie to put on after he's cleaned up.

Lily collects blankets and goes to the back room to sit on the bed. 'Pour the water right over his head, Ray,' she calls, 'scrub him with carbolic. Bella won't want him in her rooms like this?' She falls silent, then adds, 'Do you think he'll wet the bed?'

'Probably,' says Denny.

Charlie appears to have no idea what is happening: he hasn't spoken since we found him. As we pour the hot water over his head he lets out a gasp, but no words.

186

Lily goes upstairs to the room Mr Hogg has indicated we can use. She lines the mattress with an old newspaper, just in case, and pulls a blanket onto the mattress.

Then she takes Charlie's discarded clothes and drops them into the outside dustbin, some of which we have had to tear off him.

'God Charlie, what a mess.' Lily looks up bleakly, hoping for a hint of moonlight from the matt black sky.

Scrubbed until his skin is raw, we place Charlie in the bed, and there he lies, torpid, empty, unresponsive. Lily keeps herself at a distance, conserving her energies for the baby.

After two evenings on which I return from the attic bearing unwanted trays of food, she becomes a little exasperated, imagining the fault lies in some mysterious way with me, Charlie's inability to heal himself is a response to my inability to nurse him. She follows me to the attic room where she stands in the doorway, staring in at Charlie, looking rather cross that his long sleep is not over. She wants to concentrate on her baby and Charlie is a distraction.

On the third evening she can contain herself no longer.

'I'll take Charlie his food this evening.' Her tone of voice doesn't welcome any truck from me, her mind is made up.

She has made a soup. On the tray she places a small vase of flowers and a ripe pear. 'If he can't eat, at least he'll be able to smell what he's missing. I'll coax a reaction from him yet.'

Of course I'm hopeful that Lily will have better success, I'm also relieved to have the chore taken from me for the night; and I'm a little smug when she returns half an hour later with the full complement of aromas still on her tray.

'We're going to have to get him to a doctor soon, he can't live on thin air,' she says, her bullish mood changed to one of anxiety.

Three days pass and Charlie's emaciated body grows thinner, his ribs protrude through skin that has become transparent, the tiny traceries of blood vessels lethargically moving weak, anaemic blood around his uninterested body.

Lily boils a piece of fish, which she mashes into some buttery swede. On the tray she places the same vase of flowers, though they have begun to droop.

Tonight she stays upstairs for over an hour. I can hear her murmuring to Charlie through the floorboards. I throw a couple of coals on the fire, which fall back out onto the hearth, the over-stacked grate in a small way compensating for my own nurturing needs. I settle myself with Onion in one of our armchairs.

'Okay Buster? Warm enough?'

Onion lifts his head, his eyes drawn to slits to protect them from the melting heat of the flames.

'I don't know how to break this to you boy but Lily has taken your fish up to Charlie. What do you think about that then, eh? Bit of a cheek?'

Onion drops his head heavily onto my scratching finger, stretching his neck like a tortoise to better enjoy the massage.

'Well, don't get yourself in too much of a fix, no doubt she'll be bringing it all back down in a few minutes.'

I listen for Lily pulling his door closed. My heart skips a beat when I notice the empty plate.

'Well done, well done.' I take the tray and hug Lily tight. 'At last. How many days has he gone since Mr da Mario's loaf of bread? Far too many that's for sure?' I am so pleased with Lily.

'Sadly, it's not true. Each spoonful I tried to coax him with, ended up in my mouth. I'm sorry, Ray, I'm not having much luck. He must have been awake at some point because his water glass is empty. It's a start, I suppose.'

This makes me buoyant. Lily hasn't brought him back from the dead but he's not yet on death's door. We can celebrate, just a little.

'Come into the warm, Lily, snuggle up and enjoy the fire. You've been wearing yourself out up and down those stairs. I'm sure just hearing your voice has been enough to cheer him. I'll take over again tomorrow, we'll get through, don't you worry, we Rileys are made of stern stuff.'

Lily looks doubtful.

The following evening when I return from work, Lily is flushed with excitement.

That morning, in desperation, she had enlarged the teat on the bottle she has bought for the baby, to feed Charlie some milk and honey. At first, the liquid had dribbled in one side of his mouth and out the other, he was too pathetic to swallow. But after a while, she watched as the Adam's apple in his neck began to flex and the amber nectar trickled down his throat. You'd think from her reaction she'd had him up dancing the fox trot and I am caught up in her pleasure.

'This is so great.' And I really mean it; illness is exhausting. 'What now?'

'After an hour I went up again and he took another third of the bottle. By four o'clock he'd drunk almost a pint of milk. Go up and see him, Ray, see if he can take any more.' Lily holds out the warm bottle. I wash my hands quickly and climb the stairs two at a time.

When I enter the room Charlie's eyes are open. He looks awful, cadaverous, skeletal; I look away.

'Well, what do you know, the wanderer returns. Are you ready for your tea?' I ask, awkwardly offering him the bottle.

Charlie doesn't move.

'Shall I hold it for you?'

He doesn't say anything but his lips part and I take this as a sign. As the liquid spills into his mouth, I regale Charlie with news from the world.

'You've been pretty clever, Charlie, you've missed a blinding few weeks. We're not quite out of the ice yet but I think we're breaking its back. The snows are melting and the wind doesn't tear the skin off your face as it did a few weeks ago.' The little vase of flowers has been placed on the mantelpiece, changed to hold three sprightly yellow crocuses.

'Lily's stopped work.' I am about to add so that there is someone in the house to keep an eye on you, but I think better of it, 'and she's not feeling quite as sick as she was at the start, though it hasn't been easy, but then, what Rileys are?'

I look to his face for an amused response but there is none. He is concentrating on swallowing and that seems to be enough to do for the moment.

'We're busy at work, everyone wants their gas fixed in the winter.' I kick at a cinder that has flipped out onto the floorboards.

'I went across to have another look at Joe's nipper the other evening, it was bawling a racket to wake the dead, colic or something Susan called it. Joe and I went out for a bit of peace and quiet. I've told Lily that if she ends up with one like that I'll be finding myself out with Joe more often than is good for me.' I laugh at this, to indicate to Charlie that I'm joking but I can't tell if he has heard.

'Anyways, you've guzzled that down nicely. I'll take it back to Lily. You rest, no doubt she'll come and see you again before long.'

As I descend the stairs a sense of relief warms my chest. It is March, spring is almost here, and Charlie will mend.

Progress is slow. Some days Lily reports a leap forward, a piece of bread chewed and swallowed, other days he slips back to milk and honey. I watch as Lily's maternal instincts swell. I suppose it's natural, though it strikes me as an unrewarding task. Charlie has become Lily's practice run at motherhood and I can see that she is pleased with her accomplishment. And why not.

189

I lie on the bed at night, waiting for her footsteps on the stairs, explaining to Onion how good Lily is, but Onion and I know: Charlie needs to get better soon, we're both missing our penn'orth of love. It isn't Lily's job to tend my brother, but perhaps there's someone else that can help. I explain my plan to Onion who is in full favour; he looks up at me, smiling the proverbial smile.

The plan, to which Onion has consented, involves a long hard talk with Mum; I don't know why I hadn't thought of this before. Charlie's been home a month, during which time Lily has washed him, changed him, fed him, and all but burped him. After Mum's scene with Joe, she'll be relieved to know he is found, she'll come directly to see him, take over from Lily and nurse her son back to health.

The following week I find myself near Swan Terrace, working on an installation in the next road. The lady of the house has insisted I stay for a cup of tea so that her husband can check the work before I leave. She's not too sure about these new gas appliances and she wants to be safe. Better safe than sorry she tells me at least three times. Her clock says five o'clock and I am itching to get across to Mum but I sit patiently, thrumming my fingers on their kitchen table, waiting for her husband to complete his inspection. As soon as I am given the all clear, I thank them for the tea and tear from the house.

I rush along the street, eager to bring the good news to Mum, rehearsing the conversation; it is already dusk by the time I arrive at our old door. When I enter the rooms I realise my mistake.

The walls, reeking of an acrid fungal growth, are cold and wet, a steady stream of water trickles through a hole in the roof the size of a dinner plate; I fish out a bucket from under the sink to catch the fall. The rest of the roof is peppered with peepholes, the night dropping a steady patter of rain through the colander.

For a moment I stand, my hands on my hips, in awe at how low things can fall, then I start down the stairs and head toward The Dog and Duck where I find Mum, sat with a tankard of beer, on the same bench she had lain Dad. For a moment I wonder whether I should bother but I'm here now.

I nod to the landlord and cross the bar to Mum's favoured bench. She has grown thin. A large grey hat has slipped to the side of her head, stray strands of hair fraying from its rim.

'Hello Mum, how are you?' I sit myself on the bench beside her.

Her wobbling head shudders unsteadily to upright. 'Is that you, Billy?'

Billy's name surprises me and I stare at her.

'No Mum, it's Ray.'

'Oh. Ray. How are you, son?'

'I'm fine, Mum.' I slide my work tools under the bench. 'And yourself? You're looking well.'

Mum doesn't answer. She places her fingers on the edge of the circular table, beer dregs seeping unnoticed into her gloves. I try to gauge the level of her sobriety.

'I've come to tell you about Charlie, to tell you how he is.'

'Charlie's gone, Ray.'

'I know, Mum, but now…'

Mum's thin hold on the conversation hangs on the thread of Charlie's departure.

'Charlie's been called to the front.'

I consider the confusion, not knowing whether to correct or collude. After a pause I say, 'No, that was Billy, Mum.'

'He's gone to fight for the king.'

'No Mum.'

'And Raymond, has most likely gone with him. He's just disappeared; one minute he was here, then he was gone.'

'Mum, I'm Raymond. I haven't gone anywhere.'

Mum's eyes turn to look at me for the first time, their clear blue shine washed to an opaque grey.

'The war's long over. We won the war, don't you remember? We had a party in the street.'

She continues to hold my eye. 'Billy's hurt his hand, but Raymond is writing to the king to sort it out.'

I look across to the landlord who is wiping an oily rag across the bar. On the floor lies a dark pool of beer spillage, oozing its way towards the canvas tool bag.

'I've been to the rooms, Mum; they're damp. Has the landlord said anything about fixing the roof?' She stares at the table. 'Would you like me to fix the roof?'

She seems to think about this possibility. 'No. Your dad's promised to fix it when he gets back.'

I lace my fingers together on my lap.

'I'll come by next week, Mum, one lunch time, I'll do the roof if Dad hasn't had a chance.'

'Okay son. That's good of you.' Her head wobbles off in the direction of a new arrival in the bar. She regards him for a moment.

'That's old man Bones, that is. It was his horse that killed your father.' She takes a sip from her tankard then points it at old man Bones. 'I should have the law on him I should.'

I look up, interested to see the perpetrator of my own father's passing. Bones lifts his hand in a hello, Mum returns his salutation, her grievance forgotten.

Sitting back against the worn leather settle, I calculate how Mum has spent more hours in this bar than she has in her own home. I remember another winter, rushing home expectantly from Great Aunt Lizzie's Christmas splendour, the pathetic presents I had brought. The disappointment that my homecoming went so unmarked, made so little impact. Charlie had commented on my defection and all I'd done was look on home with distaste.

I sit with Mum in the bar until the landlord suggests we might like to go home. Go home, that's a laugh. I slide my arm through hers but she shakes me off, preferring to stagger alone, so I walk beside her, listening to her mumbling conversations, first with Billy, then Charlie, then with the lost Ray. A lump rises in my throat: she appears to have more to say to us now we're not around than she ever did when we were.

I go with her as far as the door and watch as she mounts the first flight of stairs, her hands crawling along the walls to guide her way. Mum couldn't nurse Charlie as a baby any more than she could nurse him now.

It is pitch black by the time I leave; I trudge across town, my shoulders hitched high around my neck, my thoughts buried low in my stomach.

When I reach the house in Nichols Square it is eerily quiet. Lily is not in our rooms and no dinner is bubbling on the hob. I go upstairs to check on Charlie, perhaps he's taken a downturn, but he is sleeping, his body turned toward the wall, gently snoring. Where is Lily? Mrs Hogg isn't cooking. Mr Hogg isn't singing. Onion moons around, stopping pointedly in front of the hearth to remark upon its lack of warmth.

As I stand looking out of our front window I hear Charlie move upstairs and run back up, not knowing who else to ask.

'Where's Lily, Charlie?'

Charlie stares at me, then his gaze wanders to the black square of the attic window.

'Lily must have made this fire.' I point at the embers still smouldering in the hearth. 'How long ago was she here.'

Charlie's eyes follow my finger to the fire, then he becomes agitated.

'What? What happened?'

Now I'm afraid Lily has burnt herself again.

'What happened, Charlie? Is Lily all right?'

Charlie looks at me, anxious and fearful. 'Lily's hurt,' he mutters.

'What do you mean? Where is Lily?' Where could Lily be? 'Has she gone to the hospital?'

Charlie thinks for a minute then nods.

'She's gone to the hospital? At this time of night? Are you sure?'

Charlie's eyes return to stare at the flickering embers.

'You wait here, Charlie, I'll be right back. I'm sure it's okay. Stay here in the warm, I won't be long, I'll be back and tell you about my day. Have you got water? Right, you have water. I'll go find Lily, we won't be long.'

I fall down the stairs, pulling the front door shut behind me, locking Charlie in. For a second I stand on the roadside; where shall I go? Has she gone to the doctor, or to St Leonards? I decide on the hospital, if there is anything serious to worry about, that is where I'll find it. A light flickers in the downstairs rooms.

'Mr Hogg!' I call. 'Mr Hogg, is Lily in there?'

Mr Hogg throws wide the basement door. 'No lad, nor my Mrs. What do you reckon?'

'I'm not sure.' I look vainly up and down the street. 'I've a mind to try the hospital.'

Mr Hogg follows my lead and inspects Nichols Square.

'I'm with you, lad. Let's get moving.'

We set off at a trot through the back doubles, Mr Hogg keeping pace as best he can. When I have the hospital in sight, I forget to worry about his wheezing and make a dash for the entrance. He arrives seconds later, gasping and panting.

The doors swish back and forward as softly creped nurses glide in and out. The SILENCE signs are clearly being observed.

'Excuse me.' I tap urgently on the counter to attract the desk clerk's attention. 'Can you tell me if my wife has been admitted?' I whisper loudly.

The clerk smiles the tired imitation smile of the night shift. 'And you are?' she asks, not speaking, merely pointing her finger at me and raising her eyebrows.

'Riley, Raymond Riley, husband of Lily Riley.'

'What has she been admitted for?' murmurs the clerk.

'She's pregnant. Nearly six months. I don't know what the problem is. She might have burned herself, on the coal fire.'

The clerk runs her finger down a list of names, tapping the ledger lightly with the end of a pencil. Mr Hogg and I lean silently onto the counter, our fingertips turning white as they grip the counter edge. We concentrate our gaze on the clerk.

'Ah. She's on D Ward. Do you know where that is?' She indicates a sign above the corridor on our right. 'She's under Dr Freedham, ask for him when you get to the ward.'

We rush along the tunnel toward D Ward.

So, she's here, under a Dr Freedham. I've not heard her mention the name from previous visits.

The pungent smell of disinfectant seeps inside my head reminding me of Lily's burns. Please God, don't let it happen again, anything but that. She should have left Charlie to get cold, he's strong enough to be making up his own fire now, he doesn't need her fussing over him every which way. I'll give him a piece of my mind if I find the coals have burnt her.

At the end of the tunnel is D Ward. At the entrance to D Ward is a small, glassed office, the walls of which are piled with files and document envelopes.

'Hello, hello,' I say, knocking in charade on the non-existent door.

In the cubicle are two starched nurses dimly lit by the yellow glow of a desk lamp, engrossed in the paperwork on their desk, their heads leaning together to study their notes.

'Is Dr Freedham here? I've come to see Lily Riley.'

One of the nurses pushes back from the desk, the name finally invading her consciousness.

'Mr Riley? Hold on a moment, sir. Take a seat and I'll fetch Dr Freedham for you.'

'Can I see my wife?'

'Please take a seat, Mr Riley.'

I watch the nurse glide silently across the tomb of the ward. The long mound of a body is stretched uniformly and neat on each of the beds: the ward is in darkness but for the soft glimmer of moonlight through the high institution windows.

She approaches a doctor doing his rounds, leaning up to whisper in his ear.

The doctor glances over and takes a moment to contemplate the clipboard in his hand. He says something quietly to the nurse who disappears into the darkness at the far end of the ward. Then he removes his spectacles and pads towards us. By the time he arrives, a distance of some ten paces, his hand is outstretched and his head is tilted sympathetically to the left.

'Good evening, Mr Riley, I am Dr Freedham. Your wife will be in my care while she is with us at St Leonards.'

He is younger than I imagined and has the plummy voice of a newsreader on the radio: I take an instant dislike to him.

'How is my wife, Dr Freedham?'

'She is going to be fine.' He glances down at his hands. I follow his look and observe the smoothly sanded texture of his skin, his nails are immaculate. I wonder if the hands have touched Lily.

'Well thank God. She gave me a bit of a scare.' I lean back against the wall. 'Did she say what happened? You've probably found her old notes. She's been in here before for burns: she'll be getting herself a name for arson if she's not careful.'

I grin apologetically at the doctor. Mr Hogg, who has followed behind us, laughs nervously and pats me on the back. Dr Freedham looks blank.

The doctor waits until he has my full attention. 'What exactly have you been told about your wife's condition, Mr Riley.'

'Well, nothing, as yet. I'm waiting for you to give me the details.' I raise my eyebrows at Mr Hogg to indicate how absurd it is that the medical profession is in the hands of someone apparently this incompetent.

'Your wife said she left a message with someone at home.'

Now it is my turn to look blank.

'Well, it didn't get through. She'll be talking about my brother probably, but he's not the most reliable of messengers.'

'He might not have guessed the full story, anyway.' Dr Freedham pauses, choosing his words with care.

'Unfortunately I have bad news for you, Mr Riley. Lily hasn't burnt herself as you appear to believe. She was admitted to St Leonards in the early hours of this evening because she began haemorrhaging, not much at first, but by the time she was on the ward, she was in a bad way. Blood loss, as you might know, is the first sign that the baby is in difficulty and I'm very sorry to have to tell you, though we worked on your wife for forty minutes or more, we were unable to stop her losing the baby: it was all over by nine o'clock this evening.'

Not burns? Not serious burns? Something far more awful, far more incomprehensible? A ball of heat rises in my chest escaping in a low, rumbling groan. My arms go numb. The thudding in my ears is so loud I think everyone can hear it. A wave of panic climbs from my bowels to my throat. I clench my fists tight. Lily lost the baby?

'She was very sensible,' the doctor is saying. 'Your wife came in as soon as she realised something was wrong and we were able to help her through the process. She hasn't torn and will make a full recovery. There will be no problem having further children, Mr Riley, though she won't want to do that immediately, her body will need time to recover.'

'How? Why did it happen?'

'That is the question we all ask, Mr Riley, but there isn't always an answer, it just happens sometimes.' He glances back at his notes. 'I expect you would like to see her.'

I shake my head. I can't face Lily. What can I possibly say to her? What can she say to me? The doctor takes my elbow as if to guide me forward. 'Doesn't she need to rest?'

'Well, she is sleepy, I've given her a sedative, but I'm sure she would like to know you are here.'

I stare at the doctor. How wrong can he be? In the space of eight months I've given her a chance to remove the skin from her arms, I've landed her with a beyond the pale brother to heal, and a baby not strong enough to stay latched inside her womb. I'm not exactly the sort of person she'd be desperate to see.

The doctor walks off down the ward. If I don't catch up with him I'll lose my way in the dark. I creep with dismay between the shrouded bodies on the beds, my heart racing. I feel so feeble I have to stop to hold the end of a bed to steady myself. In the darkness I hear Dr Freedham's footsteps slowing down to wait for me.

'She's through here, Mr Riley.'

Lily is in the end cubicle, hidden behind screens of cheerfully floral linen. I follow the doctor, who walks to the end of Lily's bed to look at her charts. Satisfied with the map of Lily's progress, he moves to lift her eyelids, shining a torch onto each pupil. I draw back from the glare.

'Just for a few minutes please, Mr Riley.'

Standing at a distance from the bed, not knowing how to introduce myself, I struggle to find words that are appropriate for the moment. A few minutes? What can I possibly say with any effect in a few minutes?

Lily registers my presence and turns her head to look at me, pools welling in her eyes.

'Hello, Ray.'

Moving to sit on the edge of the bed, I stroke a loose red curl from her forehead.

'The doctor says you're going to be fine.'

She nods, biting at her lower lip.

'We'll have you home and rested in no time. Don't worry, Lily, it's going to be all right.'

'It was a little boy, Ray.'

My neck tightens and I gulp back the plum stone rising in my throat.

'They could tell, could they? That soon?'

Lily nods. She presses the knuckles of her hand to her lips.

'Did you see him?'

Lily's eyes open wide; she shakes her head. 'They bundled him away, wrapped in a sheet.'

I don't know what to say. No doubt she would want to see her baby, just once, but would she want to see him like this? At least she won't have the awful picture of a dead baby to haunt her.

'I expect it's for the best, Lily.'

Lily looks down at the bedclothes. I fall to hug her, unable to keep the quiver from my voice.

'A little boy,' she repeats, her chest rising in silent sobs.

Chapter 23

Some Homecoming

It is May when Lily finally arrives home in an ambulance, the six-month foetal lump sliced from her body by an indiscriminate act of nature. An infection had led to complications and the hospital had kept Lily in for observation.

I want to tell her how much I've missed her, how sorry I am about the baby, but the sight of her makes me shrink to mute, a self-accusing penitent. I am the child who having pulled the limbs from the Daddy long leg to watch it circle in vain, lies in bed cringing at his own cruelty. Can a father lose a child that easily? Is it really that simple?

Mrs Hogg puts Lily to bed and tells me she must rest; the hospital has given her sedatives and she needs to sleep. She usurps my role as Lily's carer, telling me it's women's work and that I'm to go look after Charlie, as I should have been doing in the first place. I am conscious of her implied blame and take myself guiltily upstairs, bearing the stewy broth prepared by Mrs Hogg.

Charlie sits down on the bed when I enter. His eyes, now alert, follow my pacing of his room, waiting for me to speak.

Lily is lying in bed, absorbed with grief, though I'm not sure I want to say this; I don't like the tone of guilt that is creeping around in my head. Charlie is watchful, smoothing the blankets rhythmically with his long fingers, waiting for me to emit anger, frustration, melancholy, all of which he might digest like the asbestos panel soaking up the heat at the back of the cooker. In the end I say nothing. I move Charlie's clothes onto the washstand and sit on his chair looking out of the window. Charlie picks up his spoon and begins the broth. I leave having not said a word.

When I arrive home in the evenings I check in on Lily and Mrs Hogg. Mrs Hogg reports on what Lily has eaten, how much she has slept and if she has managed to get up to throw water on her face. Lily smiles, grateful to be relieved of the effort of speech. I feed Onion the bone that has been left to cool in the pan, and leave the ladies to their recovery programme. Mrs Hogg, sitting beside Lily, is reading snippets from *Woman's Weekly*. On the table are the coloured squares they are crocheting for a bed jacket to keep Lily's shoulders warm. I am not needed for anything so I climb the stairs to Charlie.

More and more I have heard Charlie moving around upstairs. The attic window is squeaked open, the fire is prodded with a poker, clipping the grate with a dull metallic twang. The fresh change of clothes left draped across his chair-back are exchanged for soiled ones, which he folds meticulously into a pile on the seat.

This evening when I go up, Charlie is lying on top of the blankets. He is dressed, and yesterday's well-thumbed newspaper is folded on a stool beside the hearth. The attic window is set ajar and the room no longer smells of invalid. The eyes that greet my entrance reflect his return to the world, marking his change from indifference to tentative curiosity.

'She's better this evening.' I say in response to his unspoken question. 'Mrs Hogg has got her doing a bit of needlework, something to distract her. It seems to be working.'

He lowers his head, shifting his weight higher on the bed to receive his meal tray. I place the tray on his legs and start straight in.

'I feel bad all the time. I want Lily to be better immediately, so that she can forget about it. Tom Cartwright was round last night, railing at me that I'd put too much on her. I expect you heard him.'

I frown gloomily out of the tiny attic window onto the rooftops; a light spring rain has washed the tiles to an oily blue that the sun is reclaiming back into the atmosphere. Charlie doesn't acknowledge whether he heard the row or not so I kick out half-heartedly at the washstand for want of any other response.

'Lily felt well enough to carry on as usual: how was I to know she should have been resting. Old Cartwright's acting as if it's my fault, as if I've been thoughtless, inconsiderate.'

So far, I've managed to lose Billy, Dad, Mum is lost, I nearly lost Charlie, and now apparently it's my fault the baby is lost. Things don't come much more slipshod than that. I turn again to contemplate the steamy outdoors.

'If I hadn't been paying so much attention to you, she probably wouldn't have lost the baby.'

Behind me looms a silence, loud enough for me to feel guilty about passing the buck to Charlie. I know it's not fair and I rake my hands through my hair, pulling my forehead back to stare at the ceiling. Of course, it wasn't me that had been paying all the attention to Charlie, it was Lily. Charlie is probably thinking the same. What the hell, it all boils down to the same thing, the baby is lost.

I hear Charlie carefully replace his spoon on the tray. I still don't look at him but I can't quite let it drop. 'I've messed up everything.' I'm waiting for Charlie to feel sorry for me. I'm waiting for him to take the blame. But he doesn't.

'Surely I'm due a bit of good luck. I've done my bit. Didn't I come back to you all? I didn't have to, you know. I was living tickety-boo up at the Aunt's; I didn't have to trade that in for Gin Street.'

Charlie clears his throat but still says nothing. I pick up the poker and prod at the embers, rattling the cage a little.

'There was no one else cared for the family, not as much as I did. No one. So where's my reward?'

He looks past me, vacantly inspecting the jug on the washstand.

'I leave a perfectly good, clean, home to reunite my family, gather the Rileys round the hearth, and what thanks do I get? I did it for the Rileys. And what did they care? Nobody said, *Thanks Ray, you're a great guy*, because nobody cared.'

Charlie exhales heavily as if my presence is oppressive. He pulls himself up higher on the bed, adjusting the tray balanced on his long skinny legs.

'And I'm expected to be okay about this. After all, what's to be unhappy about?'

I fling the poker back into the companion. 'Mum's a drunk, Dad's singing with the angels, Billy's pushing up roses, Lily's downstairs without a baby, you're in bed watching the clouds skit by. I can be happy with that, who wouldn't be?'

Charlie looks at me, respectfully waiting to see if I've more to say. He decides I haven't and spoons in another mouthful of broth.

'And friends? They've turned out about as good as the relatives. Joe pops up just every once in a while to bring news of misfortune; Denny crawls out from his cave like a hyena to enjoy the carnage; they're buzzards, not friends. And what was that charade of a Christmas party? Eh? They probably only came for the free booze.'

I'm too busy enjoying being unloved and put upon to accommodate friends. I look at Charlie to see if he's taking any of this in and decide he isn't; I slump down on the end of the bed. Charlie picks at a hunk of bread, dipping it carefully into the broth.

'Lily loves you,' he says, his mouth slushy with soggy dough. 'Lily loves you.'

I look at him guardedly.

'Did she say that?'

'No.'

I stand to look blindly at the rooftops. A few wisps of smoke curl from chimneypots, rising from firesides around which families sit waiting for summer to begin. Slippers rest against the grate, next of kin and distant relations call on Sundays to pat the heads of children and remark upon the similarities of one's issue, looking for proof in the tilt of a nose, in the slant of an eye, that their line will continue, that their family collateral is in good health. Charlie's simple words, *Lily loves you*, ricochet in my head.

Pulling the door closed behind me, I make my way quietly downstairs to our rooms, where Lily lies staring at the ceiling. I go to her and place my head alongside her stomach. I am not the centre of the universe. Lily has lost her baby. Poor Lily.

We lie together and weep.

Chapter 24

In The End, People Mend Themselves

We cry, we smile, we cry some more. We've lost our baby.

Lily won't let it pass, she wants to talk; what would he have looked like? What would we have called him? Would he have been clever like Lily, sharp like me or short of a few cogs like Charlie? He would of course be clever, though he wouldn't have Lily's red hair, he wouldn't like being called Carrot Top at school, so he would have my dark brown hair, and brown-black eyes like mine to match. We sit together and imagine our son a grown man, the shape of his hands, the length of his stride when he walks. Mourning is exhausting: it's a relief to get back to work on Mondays.

On the way home, I collect pie and mash, dividing the fare into three equal portions. Onion resigns himself to licking the papers or scavenging. Habitually he slinks upstairs, attracted by the remnants of Charlie's half eaten meals. From below, we hear Charlie murmuring to him but we are unable to decipher the words. Onion talks back, meowing in the gaps left by Charlie: they appear to have plenty to say to each other.

One particularly bright morning the pattern takes a new turn: Charlie returns his supper tray.

He washes the plate and utensils in his washbowl, places them silently outside our door, and carries on past to slip out onto the street. Lily stops me calling after him, apparently he'll knock when he's ready.

She fidgets up and down the room, asking in an attempt at humour if I suppose he could have gone for good. I watch her. I could be jealous of my brother, it could irk me that she pays him so much attention, but it doesn't. Maybe it's for the best. Maybe Charlie was never meant to be an indoor man. If he wanders off again, would I track him down?

Lily's eyes are glued to the corner around which he disappeared. I'm not sure.

She dusts the window ledge for twenty minutes until he reappears at the corner of Nichols Square when she darts back into the shadows. I am relieved to discover I am relieved.

Charlie's excursions become more frequent and Lily settles to listen for their coming and going with less alarm. Sometimes he returns carrying a small package of books; it's my guess he has discovered the library and has set himself to learning the English language in order to take advantage of speech.

I am amused by this idea but Lily frowns, knowing I'm being mean, knowing I'm wrong, but not wanting to take Charlie's part against me.

'It's your turn now, Lily.'

'Turn for what?'

'To be brave. To take some steps outside.'

Lily shrugs her shoulders.

'Why don't we pay your dad a visit?'

'What, after that row? I didn't think you'd want to see him again.'

'A little squirt like your dad doesn't scare me. When I get back tomorrow evening, grab your hat and we'll go call on him. We'll only stay a short while, for a cup of tea and such, to see how his egg sandwiches are coming along.'

Tom Cartwright is both tickled and sheepish when he opens the door.

'About time you paid your old dad a visit,' he says, launching into the lonely parent's wail. 'How are you feeling, love?' The silent implication being that she can't possibly be well as she is still living with me.

'I'm fine thanks, Mr Cartwright,' I say before Lily can answer. 'Though if you plan to make a scene I should let you know Lily's still not feeling the full shilling and she won't take too much aggravation.'

Tom Cartwright looks at me, relieved that I am making light. I hope he thought I'd come to give him a thump.

'Come on in, lad. You always were a stroppy feller. I'm sure that's what she most likes about you.'

When we get back home, Lily seems exhilarated. She busies around the rooms, tidying away clothes, checking the cupboards and chatting to Onion, who shouts back as best he can, upholding his end. Lily begins to prepare our meal.

'You should go and talk to Charlie, Ray. He can't keep sliding past the door like this, we won't recognise him when we bump into him in the hallway. Go and ask him to have a cup of tea with us this evening.

'Do you reckon he's learnt to speak already then?'

'Get up those stairs Ray Riley and stop making fun of your own.'

Lily throws a runner bean at me. I jig around pretending to be scared, squeezing out the door to save my bacon.

I climb the stairs noisily to announce my entrance to the attic.

'Evening, Charlie.'

Charlie lifts his head and smiles; his boyish face is innocent and unlikely on a grown man. I won't pussy foot around.

'How you feeling?'

His eyebrows lift to an arch as if considering this for the first time. 'Okay,' he concludes.

'Lily would like some company this evening; the visit to her dad seems to have lifted her spirits and she's in the mood to be sociable. Are you free?'

I reckon Charlie sees the irony in this question: I wait for him to mentally check his diary. He crosses to the chair to inspect the clothes wrapped around the chair-back.

'Is it formal?'

A joke!

Charlie Riley has cracked a joke!

I laugh loudly.

As far as I am aware, Charlie hasn't held a conversation with anyone for the best part of two months, apart from Onion.

'Lily and I are having something to eat, Charlie. Do you want to join us or will you come down afterwards?

He looks a little unsure, as if he's painted himself into a corner. 'After.'

I nod, patting him on the back.

'We'll see you later then.'

Two hours later there is a soft knocking at our door. Lily looks up, alert and expectant. Onion pins his ears back ready to expel any unwanted disruption to his calm. He hisses.

Charlie slides in the door, his head tilted in enquiry, his expression asking, am I intruding?

Charlie's hair is slicked flat to his head, his parting, deep on the left side, cuts a sharp white line through to his scalp, his hair must have been combed for at least an hour. He is wearing one of my white collarless shirts, admirably hiding his bony limbs, over which he has pulled a home-knit Fair Isle waistcoat, another cast-off since Lily bought my Christmas waistcoat.

Lily looks pleased to see he's made an effort. She too has pinned up her hair and removed her apron.

'Charlie! It's good to see you up and about.' Her voice is casual and easy, it says, she hasn't been worried, she hasn't felt troubled, it's a casual greeting from one neighbour to another.

Charlie shuffles forward self-consciously, Onion rising to wind himself around the recognised intruder's ankles. As Charlie bends down to stroke Onion's head I stare intrigued at the rake marks of the comb, his head a deeply ploughed field. Lily reaches out to take his hand.

'Come and sit in the armchair. You could probably do with a comfy chair yourself upstairs. We were lucky to get these as wedding gifts; I don't doubt we could pick up another one second-hand somewhere. We'll see what can be found, won't we Ray?'

He looks fondly at her and I feel like the spare chair-leg.

'Tell us what you've been doing up there while Ray makes the tea. There are biscuits in the cupboard, let's celebrate.'

Seeing Charlie is really giving Lily a lift. 'Celebrate what?' I ask, bemused.

'Invalids everywhere,' she declares.

'I'll drink to that,' I say, sloshing milk into three cups and handing them to Lily and Charlie. 'To the indisposed, chronic and complaining; may they soon get up and get on with it.'

We clink cups in a tribute to rude health and hearty constitutions.

With some coaxing from Lily, and much input on her part to the conversation, they begin to swap recuperation stories, tricks that they played on themselves to fool their bodies, distraction techniques to pass the long dull hours of staring at the ceiling. Lily makes suggestions, Charlie nods rapidly in agreement. Being of sound body and mind I am excluded from even this limited excuse for a conversation but I can see they are a tonic for each other, taking care of each other's suffering, knowing without having to explain. I am simply the biscuit bearer.

'Ey up! More tea!'

Lily and Charlie look up at me and smile.

Charlie's conversational style doesn't give much away; he is the prop, the fall guy. Lily needs him, someone she can relax on, someone who is likewise recovering. She doesn't want to talk about the decrepit or the sick, she focuses hard on the brightness of the daylight, the resurgence of flowers and the sounds of life in the square. It seems that Charlie too has listened and they have heard the sounds simultaneously, as if for the first time. The early morning milk cart clattering around the square, the whoosh of tram and omnibus running in the distance, the honk of a factory hooter, signals from the real world.

I have been out amongst these things and can add exciting titbits, colourful details that they can carry back to their beds to ponder at leisure. The recent news of car bandits attempting a smash and grab raid on the furniture store in Balls Pond Road; it's all the talk at the works. Lily is shocked at the thieves' audacity, and then saddened to hear they weren't successful. I laugh. The court case of the barrister defending eight Dartmoor convicts at Princetown Town Hall on the charge of incitement to mutiny. Lily bewails the thought of their incarceration, likening it to being reduced by convalescence, but the convicts' bid for freedom cheers them both. There seems to be nothing like the recovering invalid to flip from one extreme to the other, especially Lily, who wilts with laughter almost as easily as she weeps with sadness.

I hunt around in my head for more stories of mirth: Stan Laurel and Oliver Hardy are to visit London, sailing from New York in June for a three-month holiday in Europe. Lily tells Charlie that Laurel's father, a Mr Arthur Jefferson, lives in London, she has read about him in *Woman's Weekly*, and that Stan Laurel is indeed English! So there you go; we learn something new every day. Not that I'm interested in Stan Laurel's lineage, but if it touches a chord with Lily it's okay by me.

And The Queens Nurses, they have a new summer uniform, very perky, their skirts are shorter and their hats smaller; Charlie and Lily can watch their coming and going from across Nichols Square to verify this fact, should they so wish.

Lily carries her teacup to the window, smiling equally at the trees, the front gardens and the people in the square.

Chapter 25

New Beginnings

It is June. Lily is looking out on Nichols Square over a newly built window box. Charlie has constructed this from the remains of a broken wheelbarrow carted home from a rubbish tip. His time on the streets has left him unpredictably curious about other people's junk, occasionally appearing on the doorstep with a torn wire chip pan, or a piece of shattered drain pipe. He squirrels these treasures away to the garden, or up to his room.

Onion, sitting on the windowsill to guard the box of sweet peas, takes an unprovoked swipe at a hovering bumble bee.

There are no jobs at The Gas Company, they are full to capacity, but Charlie isn't bothered; his hoarding and foraging are enough to occupy his mind for the present.

Mr and Mrs Hogg have spoken to Charlie: 'You can stay up in that attic room young feller me lad rent free on one condition: you're to make sure that lass has a smile on her face at least once a day.' Charlie grins. He can do that.

But this morning, Mr Hogg has taken one look at the sabotaged view from his back window and climbed the stairs to the attic to rail at Charlie before he heads out to work. Charlie's scavenging is getting on Mr Hogg's pip and he demands to have his view restored.

'There is now a pile of junk higher than an omnibus right outside my kitchen window. The basement is so dark I don't know the sun's up! Curb your kleptomania son, get rid of that crap heap and sharp or you'll be in Barney Rubble.' He twangs his braces. 'And bring something useful into the garden for God's sake.' He is exasperated. 'I don't know…what about plants?' he suggests phlegmatically.

After Mr Hogg has slammed the front door, Charlie goes to stand in the back garden, where he continues to stand for a full hour, staring at the pile of unwanted cast outs, looking occasionally between Mr Hogg's sunken back window and the garden.

'What do you think he's doing out there?' says Lily, watching him from our bedroom window.

'He's doing a Charlie,' I say dismissively, wiping my mouth on the teacloth. 'Gotta go, love. Don't get it into your head to go and join him or you'll both end up with a chill and back in bed.'

'Don't be silly, Ray, I'm not foolish.'

But apparently she is, as Mrs Hogg reports to me when I return from work.

Less than an hour later, Lily has drawn on a pair of my old work boots, wrapped a pink scarf around her red hair and taken Charlie a cup of tea, three sugars, guesses Mrs Hogg, who has become accustomed to Charlie's sweet tooth.

Mrs Hogg has then positioned herself inside her back door, out of sight but commanding a warden's view and within earshot of their conversation.

'All right?' Lily had asked.

Charlie's eyes had flickered, his thoughts probably somewhere down in his boots the landlady surmised. He took the warm mug into his hands and hugged it close to his chest.

Mrs Hogg is having a ball, delighted that snooping has become an entirely legitimate pastime, given the present circumstances. She fluffs at her hair, straightens the thick woolly stockings around her bumpy legs and continues.

Lily had tried again.

'Don't let Mr Hogg worry you,' she'd said. 'I'm sure he didn't mean it; he probably didn't fancy work this morning, you know how it can be when the sun is shining.'

Bless her, Mrs Hogg had thought. He *can* be a bit grumpy in the mornings, it's quite true, it's brought on by a touch of arthritis in his knees, you see; he's not as young as he used to be, well we none of us are.

Charlie had seemed not to hear Lily. He had put his back to the house wall, forcing Mrs Hogg to step deeper into the shadows of her kitchen, and he had paced long steps down the length of the garden, slopping tea onto his jacket as he stomped. Forty-six steps there were, Mrs Hogg had counted, in case I needed to check on her detective skills. Lily had sighed, and gone back indoors.

I thank Mrs Hogg for her attentiveness and go upstairs to our rooms.

My dinner is bubbling nicely on the stove, two places have been set at the table with a little vase of flowers in between, and Lily is still at the window.

'Come and look Ray, he hasn't stopped.'

I join Lily and am astonished at what I see. At the end of the garden Charlie has built a towering bonfire that is crackling into the sky, plumes of dark grey smoke drifting up to the heavens.

Onto this he has thrown the bulk of his collected rubbish, stacking any non-combustibles against the side wall. The garden has been cross-hatched with string, the corners of which are pegged deep into the earth by fallen branches. A pile of good bricks is developing behind the junk pile; smaller chipped bricks have been thrown into a rusting dustbin, one that had originally found its way into the garden as an essential component of his metallic rockery.

Charlie dashes inside, his feet thundering up the stairs leaving tell-tale trails of mud in his wake for me to clear up later. He bumps and clatters back down the flight, appearing at the garden door with the chair on which his clothes had been carefully piled.

'Aw Jesus, he's going to burn the furniture.' I grab at my boots to get downstairs to the garden before the landlord finally pops his cork and throws us all out onto the street.

'No wait, Ray. It's okay.'

I hobble back to the window. Charlie has set the chair in front of the coal bunker, the top of which he wipes clear with a handful of dry leaves. On the bunker he spreads a double sheet of newspaper and with a piece of charcoaled wood hooked from the fire, he sits to divide the paper into square and rectangular plots; large arrows are drawn from each plot to little drawings that decorate the border of the page.

'Well, what do you know, he's setting the garden in order.'

Susan has heard that Lily has lost the baby and sends Joe with a letter of sympathy and a box of bulbs. She's sorry she can't make it herself, the baby is still troubled with colic and she is worn to a frazzle, but she'll come across as soon as she can.

'I expect she feels bad, bringing the baby. It is awkward for her,' says Lily.

'Do you reckon?'

Lily can't possibly know how ugly Rose is, in which case, how does she know Susan will be embarrassed. Beats me how women pick up on these things.

Charlie works like a man possessed; he digs, shifts, uproots, turns, scrapes and burns for three full days. The rubbish stack gets smaller as he carts barrel loads back to the dumps he has previously pillaged. He is in the garden when we rise in the morning, and we can hear him trundling his wheelbarrow as we lie in bed at night.

When the garden looks turned and ready for planting, Lily carries her box of bulbs downstairs with me following close behind, curious for this first inspection of his industry.

Charlie looks into Lily's box and turns the bulbs over, squeezing them slightly, and checking his newspaper drawing; he points to a small cleared patch in front of Mr Hogg's window where Lily takes them to begin planting. I linger behind, intrigued to get my first look at the map.

Charlie's latest drawing is a grid of coloured boxes and arrows, with a border of tiny sketches indicating the planting expectations of each box. The garden, 150' long by about 40' wide, is to be reinvented as a vegetable patch for marrows and beans, with side walls of hollyhocks skirted by a fringe of primroses, and a wide rectangular plot in the middle to separate the veg from the blooms. On this plot he has drawn a bench against a screen of roses. When I look closely I can see the picture of two women, one a longhaired redhead, the other a mousy brown. They are sat on the bench, their faces tilted to the sun.

Lily has picked up a trowel and humming to herself, she pokes at the freshly churned soil. I settle myself on the back step to smoke and they beaver in silence, making holes, filling holes, tamping holes to hide where holes have been.

After only a short while I am bored.

'Anyone for a cuppa?'

Charlie scrunches his foot down heavily on a fork, scooping up a sluggish clod that he turns and stabs at. He doesn't answer.

'Do you need a cardigan, Lily?'

She shakes her head.

I light another cigarette and wander across to look again at the map, to see if I can decipher the key to what she is planting. It is beautifully drawn and I remember his early obsession, pressed tummy down on the bare floor boards of Lorenco Road, coloured pencils stolen from Kyle's Pencil Factory tucked behind both ears, in his hair, across his mouth.

Peering closer at the drawing, miniature sketches of turnips and carrots are easily distinguishable. Well Charlie, there's nothing wrong with your eyesight even if your vocal chords don't get much of an airing, which is handy, as gardening is a decidedly silent affair, a world of grunts and nods, watering cans and muddy footprints. I am caught in reverie when Lily asks:

'What about a chicken coop?'

Charlie shrugs his shoulders, pulling his hat down low over his eyes.

I strain towards them. Was that a yes? Or was it a no?

'A goat would a nuisance,' she agrees, 'but chickens would be useful.'

Did I miss something? Did he speak?

As soon as the days are thoroughly warmed, Mrs Hogg joins Lily and Charlie in the garden.

This evening she is lacing the beginnings of a sweet pea through a newly built twig teepee, advising Mr Hogg to mind where he stands and if he's looking for something to do, he can shift that bucket of stones to the path behind the rose trellis, by the old apple tree.

Mr Hogg thinks he's just fine where he is, thank you. He places his feet squarely on the small slab of stone he has found and there he stands, until I invite him to join me on the back step for a bottle of pale ale.

The weeks pass. The sun, churning the air in our sheltered refuge, has turned the workers' cheeks to a flushed pink: it has been good for them to get the air to their lungs.

I suck deeply on one of Mr Hogg's fat cigars and puff fat rings into the sunshine. Mr Hogg and I have been left on the benches, both wondering when it's going to be our turn to play. Mr Hogg had been tasked with purchasing the seeds according to the map, which he had done with pleasure, but tonight Mr Hogg has had enough.

'Let's have a garden party,' he says, more as an announcement than an invitation, 'to mark the new apple-pie order of the garden.'

Charlie places his wheelbarrow carefully onto the path and pushes his cap to the back of his head. He looks up at the cloudless sky and waits, possibly for Lily, checking her response; I look to them both but within a few seconds I get impatient.

'That's a great idea. The garden's looking shipshape, sprigs are sprouting everywhere, shoots are poking through, it's all looking splendid, and I think we're ready to toast the gardeners.'

Lily is hesitant.

'How big a party?'

She is not in the mood for a knees up.

'How big do you want it to be?' asks Mr Hogg, sucking deeply on his tobacco.

'About as big as the five of us?'

'Then that's what it will be,' he says, winking at Mrs Hogg, who smiles broadly at her leafy embroidery. 'And what say we have it this evening, on the patch of earth you plan for your grass?' He pokes his cigar at the brown rectangle indicating the grassy area.

'But there's no grass yet?'

'All the better. Nothing to spoil. We'll shift that old dustbin into the middle, dig a few more holes in it to make a brazier, and burn off today's rubbish, and we'll put some of Bella's fat potatoes into the fire, and a few bangers, and Bob's your uncle, a party.'

This idea seems acceptable to everyone.

'Come on Raymond, lad, let's get started. I know these gardeners, they get engrossed and before you know it, it's morning and we're half starved to death.'

I follow Mr Hogg inside, pleased with this turn of events. He sits me down in his kitchen and hands me another ale. On the griddle is stacked a small pile of potatoes, already scrubbed of earth, and on the table, an iced cake with candles on top.

'What's the occasion?' I ask, revisiting Mr Hogg's conspiratorial wink.

'Oh, nothing important, Ray. Between you and me, it's Bella's fiftieth birthday, only she's a little shy of announcing it. So she was rather hoping something like this might emerge, only she didn't want to press it on your Lily, she wanted Lily to walk about in the idea a bit before she made up her mind. You know how they are. I just went along with it, and as it turns out, she's happy as Larry; she gets her party and she doesn't feel she's imposed herself. Worked out nicely for us too; we get some food, for a change.'

I consider how the arrival of the Rileys at number seventy must have changed Mr Hogg's life. There he was, rattling around with his adored lady Hogg, not a care, when along comes a tornado of grief for them to deal with. Late night dashes to the hospital, forays out to recover near-dead relatives, the upheaval of losing Mrs Hogg first to nurse, then to cook, to bedsit and now to garden, and all for the Artful Dodgers, as he calls us. Mr Hogg must have had his fair share of cold suppers over the past few months and I feel a rush of warmth towards him.

I look up to see Mr Hogg has donned a ruffle-edged pinny. 'What are we cooking?'

'I've been told to check her meat loaf,' he says. 'We're to bring that out at the last minute to spice up the potatoes. You grab the bangers, prod them a bit with the fork to stop them exploding, and we're ready for the off.'

I like this.

Lily is blooming in the garden, supervised by the ever-watchful eye of Mrs Hogg. Charlie is lurking in the shadows, a secondary convalescent for Mrs Hogg's mothering instincts. I am indoors sharing a bottle with the landlord, who is perfectly happy to accommodate my oddball family, providing he doesn't have to starve to death in the process.

Chapter 26

Rebirth

Charlie, self-communing as always, locks his thoughts into the garden, seemingly bewitched by his ability to pot and grow. He presents his achievements to the household like offerings on a sacrificial alter, placing his produce in crumpled newspaper on the gentle slope of the coal bunker.

Things come slowly at first, the early offerings generated from the tidying of existing wildflower and rambling rose: two small posies of Michaelmas daisies, a long shoot from a pendulus rambler, three slender sticks of rhubarb.

The apple tree, though gnarled and sickly looking, produces a good crop; one evening Lily and Bella peer into a bucket at twelve small but waxy skinned apples, plucked before the birds can pierce their skins. The carefully raked grass seed has sprouted to a carpet of green baby hair. Bella and Lily select an apple from the bucket, cross to a bench made from a plank of wood supported by two oil drums, and sit to drift their feet rhythmically through the grassy mane.

He offers the ladies the fruits of his labour, to me he offers his thoughts. Slowly, his mumblings take the form of words, and these words appear to have some logic. As his unique conversational style becomes a little more transparent I decide, good on you, you cure yourself Charlie, you'll be the first Riley to go to the edge, look over, and think better of it.

Out he treks to the library, armed with a list of enquiries about Rosy Mantle climbing roses, Ruby Chard and Torch Lily red hot pokers, all of which he draws beforehand to show the librarian. What she must make of him I can only guess: she obviously understands his requests as he returns with weighty tomes beneath each arm, sits himself near me in the garden and flicks through the pages, stopping at illustrations to run his mud-tipped fingernails along the lines of words. He jabs his finger at particular species.

'Ray!' he demands.

I glance down at carmine red Lobelias; dull, claret coloured loganberries and spiny branched Firethorn.

'Nice.' I agree.

He carries the books across to the master plan, a newly drawn newspaper map that he redrafts every two to three days according to his development plans. He is creating a new section and his research appears to be untangling the medicinal qualities of herbs: now there is a subject to keep me riveted.

Through his intensely magnifying eye, Charlie maps a landscape to explore every hue of the red spectrum. In his drawings, maroons, deep burgundies and crimsons bump and jostle against green grasses and foliage, each shouting for dominance on his page. This must be how it is in Charlie's world. He must try to marry likely objects, and then stand back, and wonder why there seems to be such friction, so much discord. As the maps progress, so does Charlie's style, moving from meticulous, closely observed drawings, to thickly laid down colours, with no attempt to smudge away the signs of his crayon or lead. Charlie is inviting me to feel his sensation of colour and I am grateful for his trust; we stand together, looking at the map. I lay my arm across his shoulder and feel him relax under its weight.

July runs into August, proving to be warmer than the radioman had predicted, who sounds breathily surprised by the rise in temperature. Lily hoists the windows to allow a floating breeze to waft the summer's fragrances through the rooms. I watch this action from a window across the square, from where I also spot Charlie returning from Hoxton Market with the five slim slivers of haddock.

I know this as I have seen Lily's shopping list before leaving the house this morning: Lily is preparing a meal for the inhabitants of number seventy.

I am at work in a large double fronted house on the far side of Nichols Square: I am with The Queen's Nurses who are cranking their accommodation into this century by having a gas oven fitted.

'How is your wife now, Mr Riley?'

I return to tinkering and tightening. 'Fine and dandy,' I say, squashing my words between the cooker and the wall.

Silence.

'We can't wait to get one of these new ovens, they're so convenient.'

The voice pauses again, unsure whether to continue, then decides to take a chance.

'Did she scar, Mr Riley? We've often wondered.'

Scar?

Undoubtedly she did.

She is afraid of the oven.

Never fries our food.

Has switched all her saucepans to short handled pots or casserole dishes.

She rolls her sleeves up past her elbows when she cooks. She tends the fire wearing large canvas gardening gloves.

Did she scar?

Yes she did.

I pop my head out from behind the stove.

'No. Not at all. Not a mark anywhere, thanks to your expert administrations she has perfectly beautiful skin.'

The two nurses smile broadly at this knowledge.

'Only, we've always wondered. And we're so sorry about the baby, Mr Riley.'

I realise that like me, they can as easily watch our house from across the square, a magnet for interest, as we can theirs. I stand slowly, brushing away the fluff and dust that fills the hidden spaces of every household.

'Yes. It was very sad. But she's feeling better. Thank you for your concern. I'll tell her you asked after her.'

'And your brother, Charlie? How is he bearing up?'

I look from one nurse to the other. They fidget a little nervously.

'He's fine. Why do you ask?'

'Oh no reason, nothing at all, Mr Riley. We just wondered. We've seen him, of course, around the square. He seems devoted to you all.'

'Yes, he is. He's been very busy recently, renovating the garden, he has blue arms and green fingers it seems, he can magic flowers out of flotsam.'

They look at each other and nod at the value of this talent. 'That's good to hear. He needed something, something to involve him.'

I feel uncomfortably exposed. I hardly know these girls, apart from the occasional wave across the square as I come and go, but they appear acutely familiar with the Riley goings on.

'What else has he provided?'

I look at the nurse and wonder how to answer.

A rethink of married life?

A distraction from marital bliss?

A responsibility where one was not asked for?

'Pardon?'

'What have you added to your menu, now that your brother is providing from the garden?'

Up to this point, I haven't thought of it quite in that light. Charlie has been the dead weight, the burden to carry, the dependent to keep. But she's right, he has found a way to pay his dues.

'Well, we do a very good Queen Charlotte Pudding, from the apples, there's an old eater and a cooker in the garden which, before Charlie, were dropping their fruits for the worms, and rhubarb crumble is often on the menu, and now, he has hopes for any form of marrow, onion or herb you might need, so Lily is collecting pickling jars, in readiness. And salad stuffs, mustn't forget those: he's built a tiny glass tent under which he's growing lettuces and tomatoes.'

The girls seem genuinely delighted. 'We knew he could do it. All that thought and wondering had to be put to some use. We've seen him sometimes, in the reference section at the library, pouring his way through great volumes, completely engrossed.'

I am smiling at their enthusiasm, believing they know very little about him, when a wicked thought pops into my mind. Perhaps they would like a closer look, perhaps they would like to see what sort of fruit cake we're dealing with here.

'Ladies, I know it's short notice but are you by any chance free this evening? Only Lily would be pleased to have a proper chance to thank you. Perhaps you would care to join us, for our meal?'

The girls glance quickly at each other.

'Oh, we couldn't, Mr Riley. We wouldn't presume. Your wife will only have catered for the household.'

I smile at the first nurse, a pretty brunette called Connie who looks to be about Lily's age. She has been very attentive it seems. I wonder if Lily will mind, then brush the thought aside: 'It's no presumption. You saved Lily's arms, don't forget. If not for your quick response to the emergency Lily might be sporting two very different limbs. Thanks to you, she's fine. She would be pleased to do something, no matter how small, in return.'

Connie looks out of the window, across at number seventy, I look as well, to allow her the privacy of gauging a response. 'Well, if you're sure.'

I raise my palms to indicate the matter is settled. They cover their mouths in excitement.

'Five o'clock then?'

'We'll be there, Mr Riley.'

It's a little late in the proceedings but I offer my hand for a formal introduction.

'Ray. Call me Ray.'

They giggle again; you've still got what it takes, Ray Riley.

'We'll be there, Ray.'

Well, what do you know; a gift for Charlie.

Lily is cross as a bear in a trap.

This is her first hosting since losing the baby and I've rocked her by inviting two nurses we're just about on nodding terms with. Apparently, it was to be just the five of us, no outsiders, no surprises, no one to perform to, and I was supposed to know this. My response is, where are the rules? Can't see anything pinned to the door? Why don't we just live our lives like lepers, detached from the rest of mankind!

It is our first row and we are exhausted. Lily is probably nervous about the meal and I've gone in like a bull and caused havoc where none was needed.

'I'm sorry Lily, I'll go across and say you're not feeling well, they'll understand.'

'No you can't do that,' Lily wipes her eyes and blows her nose. 'They can probably see the table from their front parlour, we would have to cancel the whole thing.'

'But I've made a mistake, it'll be too much for you, I can see that now.'

'They'll have planned their hair and put on new stockings, you can't go now.'

'I'm sure they would understand.'

'They've probably had to rearrange their shifts so that they can come.'

I dither at the door. Having made the mistake of inviting them I could get myself into hotter water by disinviting them.

'Would it really be such a problem? It's not as if they don't know us.'

'But they don't know us. They might have bandaged my arms, for which I am grateful but they don't know anything else, how I feel, how Charlie feels.'

'I think you're wrong, Lily. I think they know pretty well how you are. And I think it would be good for you to receive them. They helped you, now you can thank them. It's no big deal, it's only a meal.'

Lily looks at the potatoes bubbling on the hob. 'Charlie won't like it.'

Well blow Charlie.

'Charlie will just have to lump it, won't he.'

At five o'clock we are all stood smiling at one another in our front room, introductions over. Lily has laid a board on top of the table, covered it with a white linen table cloth, an engagement present, and set places for seven; it looks grand and I can see she is pleased with her efforts, smoothing her palm over the cloth to encourage away the final fold creases, smiling at the polished knives and forks. Charlie has crept back to the market to get two more slivers of haddock. Then, having inspected the pans on the hob, Lily asked him to return to the garden for another bowl of Sunset Beans, which she explains to Connie, have a beautiful blushed pink flower. Connie smiles across at Charlie and tosses her hair, bashful and interested. We take our seats.

The fish, which has been baking in the oven in a knob of best butter, is ready to serve. I decide it would be nice to say a few words of welcome to our guests and tap the table with my fork to bring everyone to a hush.

'Thank you all for coming; it's nice to have you here. It's been a tough winter but we're looking on a good summer and, we're pleased to be spending it with you.'

I raise my water glass.

Lily smiles, places her hand over Bella's and clears her throat; I hadn't realised she was going to speak.

'It's true, our first months in Nichols Square weren't easy, but we're putting them behind us.' She flicks a stray red lock behind her ear and loops her spare arm through mine. I hadn't noticed before but I see now that she has painted her lips a pale coral and her eyelids hint at a soft green tinge. She looks lovely.

'But that isn't all.' Lily turns her gaze to me, as she still does when I'm to pay attention.

'I wanted to have you all here to make a special announcement to friends that have helped me through this winter. To tell you that my recovery has been so complete, I am, though I can hardly believe it myself, pregnant again.'

The two nurses let out a gasp of delight and instantly start to clap, which prompts Mr Hogg to burst into song, which encourages Mrs Hogg to burst into tears.

Lily laughs. 'Only this time, I feel good, no sickness, nothing but pleasure.'

I collapse down in my chair, at once excited, scared and sorry to have anyone here, never mind outsiders, to share our news. 'When did you find out? Is everything all right?'

'I only found out yesterday for certain. I didn't want to get your hopes up, knowing how badly you felt after the first baby.'

I fold myself around Lily, giving Charlie a broad smile over her shoulder; he is making a showy display of blowing his nose and I'm not sure if he has heard what Lily has said. When he looks up there are tears in his eyes and I know. I grin at him again.

'Should you go and lie down?' I whisper to Lily.

'No. I'm perfectly fine, in fact, I feel great.'

The table erupts into conversation. Mr Hogg stops singing to talk to Daphne the young nurse serving him a creamy pile of mashed potato. Mrs Hogg stops crying to talk to Lily: she'll be coming with her to the hospital in future, that's not something to be undertaken alone. Charlie stops fidgeting to listen to Connie, who wants some advice on Sunset Beans. Charlie for the present has none to give: he looks at her warily, trying to see if there is a catch. You plant things, they grow, end of Charlie's story. Leaving me, a broad grin on my face, to deal with Onion, whose claws are piercing my kneecaps in the expectation that fish is about to be diverted his way.

Chapter 27

How To Love Your Skeletons

The August sun carries with it a social contract: it will give you sunshine, a reason to strip down to your shirtsleeves, if you promise to shake those shirtsleeves with other shirtsleeves to warm the cockles in the hearts where the sun can't always reach.

Everywhere you look people are taking heed of this bargain: in Victoria Park, in Hoxton Market, over hedges to houses next door, people are finding trivial reasons to venture away from the security of their homes and to enter into liaisons with their neighbour.

Mr Hogg lifts his cap at old Mrs Shepherd, who is out manicuring her privet as a guise for inspecting Mrs Jones' new red gate.

'Fine morning for it,' calls Mr Hogg, pleasantly familiar with an equally senior member of the square. I follow him down the path.

'Do you see that, Mr Hogg? Do you see that? There's no knowing what the young ones will be doing next. All the others are green. I should send my George to complain.'

I stop beside Mr Hogg and we look in the direction of her wrath.

'You mean the gate, Mrs Shepherd? Well, there's always a new way of looking at things, in my book. My bricks and mortar is always up to something new, and these two young uns gone and invented the colour grey! I ask you! Just when you think you've worked it all out, along comes a conundrum, something to buck the system, and off you go again, seeking the rights and wrongs of it all. Don't let it worry you, Mrs Shepherd; there's more to take up your day than worrying about the colour of that gate. My, look how wonderful your Camelia is this year. It's been blooming since May I've noticed, you're the envy of the square.'

Mrs Shepherd blushes with pride, her hand rising to scratch behind her ear in an effort to hide her pleasure.

'Get away with you Henry, do you think we can't see your garden from our back window? George and I marvel at that lad's industry, at everything in the right place, every colour dancing with the colour beside it, every shape echoing another shape, a tonic for the eyes...' then she stops, pleased and embarrassed by her own unexpected eloquence.

Mr Hogg and I stand tall, allowing the praise for Charlie's work to fall happily on our shoulders.

'Ay, it's a grand job; we're mighty proud of him,' says Mr Hogg, picking up speed again now that he has smoothed Mrs Shepherd's feathers. 'We'll be off now though, but we'll be sure to pass on your praise to young Charlie. Have a good day now. Splendid Camelias!'

Mrs Shepherd giggles and waves us off to work.

On my way home, Mrs Shepherd is still in her garden, twisting and tweaking at the various shoots. She straightens her back at the sound of my footsteps, smiles and nods her head. I am one of the young uns and haven't yet risen to the conversational status of the older members of the square, but I am the beneficiary of Charlie's gift to Mrs Shepherd and I acknowledge her appreciation with a returning nod of the head.

The sun has been warming the garden all day and the plants have built a wall of scent thick enough to wade through. Mr Hogg has beaten me home: he sits with the ladies beneath a bower that Charlie has constructed from two fencing poles. Mr Hogg is sipping tea and soaking in the sun. Charlie is digging behind the trellis of roses, at work on his herb garden.

'It's too hot to be indoors cooking; we should be eating outside,' says Lily, fanning herself with a rhubarb leaf.

As I flop down onto the grass I notice Mrs Hogg and my mouth falls open, almost too late I glance and catch the warning in Lily's eyes. Trying hard not to stare, I dip my head low and peep at Mrs Hogg from below my fringe.

Due presumably to the heat of the day, our landlady has peeled off her beige stockings, exposing the lumpy knots and dykes of her legs, and pushed her blue green feet into a pair of pink furry mules. Her rollered hair is wrapped in a white spotted headscarf that has bled into her skin to create a pasty, washed-out sweatiness. A white, summer skirt, pinched tight at the waist, springs wide in a volume of cloth that would be excessive on a prima ballerina; the matching blouse, clamped to a fierce tourniquet on her upper arms, billows out a worryingly white bouquet of flesh. I glance at Mr Hogg who is smiling happily at her.

'If we weren't off out tonight, we could picnic in the garden,' Mrs Hogg says to Lily, 'but we're catching the omnibus down to Henry's brother and his wife; they're always such fun. We're hoping they'll suggest a little dancing, hence all the effort,' she adds, indicating her ensemble as final explanation of their evening plans.

'Handsome,' murmurs Mr Hogg appreciatively. 'Well, best start to get myself ready. Don't want to miss the bus.'

Mr Hogg springs up out of his chair, the thought of dancing with his lovely wife having put a zing in his step. Mrs Hogg collects the tea things and I stare at Lily while the landlady's back is turned. Lily is determined not to look at me.

'You know Ray,' she says as a diversion, 'maybe *we* could go out this evening? For a stroll, or perhaps to visit. What do you think?' We grin widely at each other, pleased to have sidetracked our thoughts to a legitimate topic.

We wave goodbye to the Hoggs, Mrs Hogg presenting us once again with her ambitious face painting skills, then sit back to discuss our own evening.

Lily is a sight for sore eyes; you can keep the pleasure of looking at a garden, I'll take Lily any day of the week. Her hair has grown longer, a thick downy blanket that floods over her shoulders in waves, trickling through my fingers like fine silk. The sun has tinged her face to a flushed gold, her dainty pearl teeth glisten as she talks, and I have missed what she is saying.

'So, that counts out Susan and Joe, they won't want us there at the moment; and as it's Friday, Dad is at the mission; Denny is busy with his new lady friend; Moira will be at Tottenham Palais trying to catch that lad she's got her eye on; what a shame, I really feel like some company.'

Lily has turned the corner: her animated interest in others, their needs, her desire for news, is reawakening.

'Are you feeling up to a ride, Lily? Do you think we could go and call on Aunt Lizzie; it's a nice journey up on the bus.'

Lily sits up. 'It won't suit her visiting days, but as it's on the spur of the moment, we could excuse ourselves, say we were out walking because it was such a lovely evening.'

'She'll see straight through that.'

'Then we'll just say none of our other friends were available and she was our last choice.'

Lily grins; fine by me, if anyone can pull it off, she can.

But on the way to Aunt Lizzie's Lily gets the jitters.

She has dressed herself in an aquamarine suit and looks like sailor's heaven. The neckline sits high at the back where she has tucked a white scarf, softening the jacket on her skin. Her hair is pinned up with tortoise shell combs. I'm no judge: Lily could be sat next to me dressed head to foot in Bella and I would think wow! Much the same as Mr Hogg.

'She'll think we're presumptuous, turning up unannounced, she'll know I know it's not the thing to do.'

'She'll take one look and forgive you.'

'Like your Mum did? Please God let me do better than that introduction.'

I am cross to be reminded of Mum at this moment and shake her out of my thoughts, replacing her with memories of Aunt Lizzie, and anticipating the forthcoming introduction. Aunt Lizzie's genteel pastels meets Lily's shimmering vibrancy: what if they conflict? Despite an underlying nervousness I am excited, I stretch my toes in my shoes, clench my thighs and squeeze Lily's hand until she yelps a complaint. I'm proud of Aunt Lizzie; I like the idea that I can show her off to Lily, proof that at least one member of my family isn't hanging in the cupboard with the rest of the skeletons.

It is with hesitancy that I mount the steps to Aunt Lizzie's door. The last time I saw these steps I was running hell for leather in the opposite direction, sneaking away like a thief, no note, no goodbye.

Tottenhall Road has diminished in size since then, and the house itself, while still well to do, isn't as imposing as it is in my memory, but I am suddenly cowed by our audacity, by arriving uninvited, and I shuffle on the polished doorstep, pretending I am waiting for Lily to be ready. Lily puts her hand on my arm.

'Ray, knock on the knocker.'

When the Great Aunt opens the door I am taken aback to see she is no longer taller than me; she is a delicate little thing, standing bolt upright in a pale blue brocade nipped close at the waist beneath a child-like ribcage. When I move forward to embrace her, she barely reaches my shoulder.

'Aunt Lizzie, it's good to see you. It's Ray, Ray Riley.'

Aunt Lizzie pushes away from me to stare at my face, her hands covering her nose and mouth, her eyes peering hard into mine. She fumbles in a small satin purse looped at her side to produce a pair of silver rimmed spectacles. I move forward again to take one of her tiny hands in mine, pumping it like a crap player rousing the dice. She seems bewildered.

'Is it really you, Raymond?'

'Of course it is. Who else would it be, and this is…'

'I've looked forward to seeing you again for so long. Since I first got a hold of Lily's invitation.'

'This is Lily, Aunt Lizzie.'

Lily offers her hand. Aunt Lizzie drags her eyes reluctantly from my face to turn to Lily. She steps back again to focus more clearly.

'Why, she is lovely, Raymond, perfectly lovely. How nice of you to visit. Come in both of you. Let's go through to the sitting room, I need to sit down, to get over the shock.'

My eyes linger in the hallway, so very different from when they were here before. For a start they can see, they're not glued up with snivel and gunk. The large chandeliers still drip from the ceiling though now their sparkle brings pleasure rather than fear. The clock that had ticked so ominously on my first entrance, smiles at me from the side table. Every surface glistens as it always did. But more than anything is the smell, a complicated blend of cloves, cashews and camphor, all hanging in the air like individual remembrances from my childhood, little packages of memory, waiting for me to flip them open and revisit.

Aunt Lizzie leads us into the sitting room where Lily remarks on the orange cascade in the garden.

'Yes, they're lovely aren't they, they bloom right through to autumn.'

Aunt Lizzie studies Lily again, her voice trailing away as she seats herself on a long sofa and indicates that we should sit opposite. She cups one hand inside the other and looks between our faces; she can't be bothered to talk about the flowers, she just wants to look at us.

I smile back at her, wondering if she is trying to place this tall, slender man with the writhing and twisting tumbler that used to skid and roll on her polished floors.

'Heavens, I'm forgetting my manners. You've travelled all this way, I must offer you a drink. What would you like? Something cool? It is a very warm evening, or perhaps a sherry? I think it would be permissible on this special occasion, don't you?'

Aunt Lizzie suddenly looks worried. 'I hope you'll stay for some tea.' She looks disconcertedly between the two of us and adds, as if to convince us to stay, 'I've so many things to ask. I've an old lady's ear for detail and I'll want to know every last fact so that I can relive it later when I'm alone.'

Aunt Lizzie leans forward and squeezes my arm as if to reassure herself that I am real.

She must be lonely, I think, looking around the high ceilinged room, the only sounds the echoes of her own footsteps.

As if she has read my thoughts she adds, 'I have my bridge on Mondays, and my ladies on Wednesdays, and Lawrence on Fridays, that is enough to keep me on my toes, but I don't sleep as well as I used and there are so many more hours of the day to fill. The more news I have, the more there is to do when I'm at liberty. And things move so fast when you are my age: I fear I miss much of what passes before me and I need the extra hours to unravel everything.'

I notice the well-thumbed newspapers in the rack beside the fire-grate: I can't imagine for one minute Great Aunt Lizzie misses much.

Aunt Lizzie continues to look at me, then sighs. She tinkles a high-pitched brass bell and for a confusing moment I wait for Grandma Edna to sweep through the doors. Instead, a young girl appears. She bobs down beside Aunt Lizzie who whispers in her ear. When she has left the room I venture, 'Is that little thing now chopping your wood, Aunt Lizzie?'

'Good gracious no,' she laughs, 'though she would probably make a good job of it. No, for that task I have to coax and bribe my Lawrence. He's a little short tempered at the best of times and manual labour constitutes the worst of times, only recoverable from by a large brandy, it seems.'

It is such a delight to be in this room. I look across to check that the old wind up player is stood in its usual place, the records stacked neatly in their brown paper sleeves in a nearby rack.

Young Alice returns, carrying a tray of the tiniest biscuits I have ever seen, accompanied by the smallest stemmed glasses on the planet. There is also a cut glass jug of iced lemonade. She places the tray on a low table before taking further instructions from her employer.

I look at Lily to see that she is okay. Lily is watching the young girl receive her orders, at Great Aunt Lizzie running her palm rhythmically up and down the bare skin of the young girl's arm and the girl patting her hand in return.

'May I offer you a drink, Lily?'

Aunt Lizzie's hand shakes as she pours the lemonade into a small tumbler.

'Look at me,' she says, embarrassed. 'Anyone would think I'd been tippling.'

'Well, we have some news that will justify a tipple.' I want to give her something good to think about, something that she can enjoy. Aunt Lizzie looks up, places the jug down on the tray and flicks her eyes backward and forward across mine and Lily's faces.

'As you know from Lily's letters, we lost the baby, when Lily was six months pregnant.'

Aunt Lizzie's hand rises to her mouth.

'Raymond, I was so sad for you.' Moist pools glisten at the edges of her eyes. 'You know, Lily, you mustn't give up hope. Losing a child doesn't mean you won't have children. You must feel dreadful.'

'We were heartbroken, poor Lily suffered so much.'

Aunt Lizzie reaches across to take Lily's hand.

'Lily, come and sit by me. Sit here.'

Aunt Lizzie pats the softly upholstered sofa and Lily moves across next to her, giving me my picture of contrast but not conflict. They both sit straight backed, their knees together, their shoulders relaxed. Aunt Lizzie, a softly muted palette of greys and pale blues, Lily a vibrant declaration of red and aquamarine.

'I have to tell you something Lily. Something to help you cling on. Losing a child, even a child you have hardly known, is a tragedy. The loss is a terrible thing, no one can explain it to you. We love our children from the day we know they are to be ours, cling to them with spidery fine threads. It is a yearning so deep it replaces all other longings.'

'Well, the good news is...'

'Raymond, don't interrupt.'

I grimace at Lily but sit contrite, sipping at the tiny glass, afraid I might crush it in my bear like grip.

'Sometimes your children repay you handsomely. They grow into fine specimens, eager to please, industrious, intelligent and brave. You look on them from a deep pool of love that never diminishes. Sometimes your children disappoint you.' She pauses for a moment giving me time to remember Lawrence, her dead weight of a son.

'When Raymond left I was distraught.'

My eyes widen and I gulp back the teaspoonful of sherry.

'I wandered the rooms of the house, trying to understand why he would leave. He had a lovely home here. If my son had not been in the house at the time, I could probably have stopped him, or at least had a chance to hear an explanation. I waited for news from his family but none came. No one wrote to tell me he had gone home. I became quite frightened. Should I call the police, was he in danger?'

I would like another sherry as I'm fairly sure this one evaporated before it reached my stomach.

'I wrote to his family at the last address I had, but I heard nothing. I was too frightened to mention it to Edna, but in the end, it was she who put me out of my misery.'

'I can explain, Aunt Lizzie.'

'Raymond's grandma found me sat in the garden, the pruning shears forgotten in my lap, tears streaming down my face. He had been such company for me, I didn't know how to rebuild my world. There was nowhere for me to go. I had no need to go to the school, I had no need to go to the shops, I was once again sitting alone.'

Lily strokes Aunt Lizzie's arm.

'Edna brought me news whenever she had any, but it wasn't the same. I was pleased to know he was happy back home, but selfishly, that made me even more lonely. And then Edna had to leave and all news ended.'

'You had your own son,' I say, not willing to take the entire blame for this unexpected outburst.

'Yes I did. But he was a grown man, already busy ruining his life, he didn't need me in the way you needed me. And he was jealous of you. He couldn't see why I should want you in the house, he thought you were wasting his inheritance.'

Aunt Lizzie falls quiet, her tiny hands agitating nervously at her neck; she appears unsure whether to continue.

'And then in January this year, I found your letter, inviting me to your Christmas party. I would have come, and he knows it, so he hid it from me.'

'You didn't get the invite?' I ask, rather stupidly.

'Lawrence undid the letter and thought you were up to something. He decided you and Lily were probably down on your luck, and that you would be after money.'

'The cheek of him.'

I remember his whining demands for cash.

'He hid the letter at the back of the bureau; I found it when Christmas was long over.'

Aunt Lizzie is close to tears, like a little girl who has been told she cannot go to a party, she is both angry and frustrated. Any minute now she will stamp her foot.

'Well, your story has a happy ending,' says Lily, bravely trying to create an opening for me, 'and you are united at last. There's no need for Raymond to stand on ceremony; he can call round whenever he has the opportunity, after all, you're his family.'

'And the good news is,' I stop, expecting to be told to wait my turn. Aunt Lizzie's watery eyes look up.

'The good news is, Lily is pregnant again.'

A gong sounds in the hall, as if to reinforce my news.

Aunt Lizzie rises, excitedly, dabbing carefully at the corners of her eyes.

'Raymond, why did you let me carry on like this when you had such lovely news. I'm a silly old woman, making a fool of myself.'

'Nonsense,' I say, smiling broadly, 'I was doing as I was told.'

Alice appears at the door to herd us through to the dining room.

Lily links her arm through Aunt Lizzie's and frowns at me over the Aunt's head to do the same.

'You do know what this means though, don't you? Not only will you be seeing more of me, but Lily will be popping in to check that you are keeping warm, the baby will be placed on your rug, which he will stroke with his sticky fingers, and then there'll be his uncle, my brother Charlie, he won't want to be left out.'

'Gosh, so many Rileys all at once, how will I cope?' she laughs.

Alice waits until we are formed outside the dining room door before throwing it wide to create her own *Ta da.*

The dining table is a scene from a child's imagination. In a miraculously short space of time, Alice has created the perfect table. On a white damask cloth she has placed salvers and platters of delicately triangled sandwiches, tall spires of fruits, glazed confectionaries and fairy cakes. Now she is pouring a spicy smelling tea from an ornate silver teapot into cups so fine you can see the liquid through their shells.

'What a pretty room,' Lily says, looking towards the dappled evening lights of the garden. 'Wouldn't Charlie love to see that garden, Ray?'

I still have the irksome thought of Lawrence Delaney in my mind. 'Is Lawrence living here with you now, Aunt Lizzie? The garden's looking good, is he keeping it for you?'

'Goodness no, we would tear each other apart, with his interfering, grabbing ways. I couldn't abide it. Lawrence and I see each other when we have to, which for Lawrence is every Friday morning to collect his allowance, and that sometimes proves too much for us.' Aunt Lizzie giggles nervously at her disrespect for her son. 'Unlike Raymond,' she says, patting Lily's hand, 'my son

Lawrence did not take to work. He chose the life of the idle rich, but he isn't very good at it, the rich part, I mean.'

I like this. It is very pleasant to sit and hear my relatives abused, especially the ones I was hoping to abuse myself.

'But tell me everything, Raymond, starting with your wedding, your house, the Christmas party that I missed, your work, tell me about Charlie. How is he? Lily's note said he was living with you now?'

Lily and I between us tell Charlie's life, and I am pleased no one is telling this story about me; he sounds a right head case.

I listen as Lily talks, helping myself to slices of Battenberg and draughts of homemade lemonade. Naturally, I have read it wrong and Aunt Lizzie soaks Charlie up with all her leftover mothering love, drinking him in with thirsty reverence. The poor sweet lamb and the darling little mite are bandied about like he was some lost case, instead of already saved.

'Of course, he's much better now,' I say, trying to make him sound less like one of the walking wounded and more like one of the Riley survivors.

'Nevertheless, he's been through hard times, Raymond, and he'll need lots of loving care, something you might not be able to give him, when the new baby arrives. What he really needs is a job.'

'Well, you probably know as much about that as a possibility as we do, Aunt Lizzie, jobs are few and far between these days.'

'It's gloomy,' she agrees. 'The papers talk of frauds and swindlers as if they were a new form of businessman earning an honest shilling. Bouverie is proving to be the most successful businessman these days, every gambling loser looks to his tips for a route out of debt.'

We fall silent as Alice returns to the dining room. Aunt Lizzie passes tiny egg and cress corners to Lily, who must be comparing them to the doorstep wedges her father produces. I smile to see how easy it is to cock ones little finger when receiving a morsel so small. Alice replenishes our teacups. As she leaves the room, Aunt Lizzie says quietly:

'I have a job for him.'

I glance at Lily. 'What sort of job?'

'I need a handyman.'

'You already have a capable housekeeper in Alice. How can you afford a handyman? And it sounds like Alice can do most things you need.'

'Alice stays extra time when I need her, but it's an imposition on her and her family. If I had a handyman, Alice could do the hours she wants and he could do the rest.'

'Charlie isn't at all forthcoming, Aunt Lizzie,' says Lily, 'you might find it difficult to communicate with him.'

'My dear, if I can communicate with a drunken Lawrence and a petulant Raymond, I can see no problem in communicating with a quiet Charlie. I need someone who can move furniture to clean behind it, mend things when they disintegrate, tend the garden, fix my hinges when they squeak, dig out the potatoes, plant the nursery bed, chop my wood, all things a female housekeeper would declare not her job, though Alice is too polite to say so.'

Lily and I stare at each other, not knowing what to say. What will Charlie think of it? He will have to take the omnibus, I don't even know if he has travelled on transport before. I could come with him on his first journey, settle him into the route. Would it work? Would he take to Aunt Lizzie?

'I've a study full of books waiting to be read. With my failing eyesight I would enjoy hearing them aloud. If he's not good at his letters, I can teach him; if he's half as good as you were Raymond, he would be quite companionable.'

Companionable.

Never in a monkey's swing could you describe Charlie as companionable.

'And I would pay him. He could put some money aside for the day when he finds a young lady, as he will, if he's a Riley.'

Now we really are stepping into the realms of fantasy. 'It's a lovely offer Aunt Lizzie. Thank you. We'll talk to him. See if he would like to come one evening next week.'

These days, neither I nor Charlie scuttle along with our heads bent low. The tall houses are no longer menacing and the horizon has moved a little closer; either the landscape has shrunk or we have expanded to fill it, I am not sure which.

When the world gets wobbly, Lily props me up; when I waver off course, Charlie scowls and I stand corrected; when they fall apart, I do what I do best, I tell them to pull themselves together and get on with it.

Did I beat the system? Between all of us, was I the one that came up smelling of roses? Things have not been easy, and I am still always on the lookout for readies, but if the fortune that I have come into is happiness, then indeed, I am living the life of Riley.

The Life of Riley was inspired by a short autobiography handwritten by Lily, Sharon Plant's grandmother; the landscape of north London has changed dramatically in the 100 years since. Ray runs across fields to escape from Great Aunt Lizzie on a route that is now the A10; Weir Hall is on the Great Cambridge Roundabout; lunatic asylums, lying-in hospitals and workhouses have been replaced by coffee shops and galleries. In Lily's lifetime, the area was a mix of fields, marsh and tenements, many of which were razed by the Blitz. Nichols Square survived the bombs to be razed in 1962, against local protest, by Shoreditch Council.

Sharon knows the area well. She was christened in St Peter and St Paul Church on The Mount, grew up in Tottenham, went to Tottenham County School off White Hart Lane, bought bread from the hot wall bakery, went every Saturday to Tottenham Royal, formerly the Palais Dance Hall, and on Sunday driving lessons – she drove from Tottenham up The Mount to visit Nanny Lily. She also did babysitting in the local chip shop, spent a summer working in the pencil factory at Tottenham Hale, by which time it was owned by *Berol's*, and another summer working in the Tottenham Employment Exchange. The dialogue in the novel is entirely imagined, although the locations and some of the events are factual.